Lords ░░░

Bache ░░░

Friends since school, brothers in arms, bachelors for life!

At least that's what *The Four Disgraces*—Alex Tempest, Grant Rivers, Cris de Feaux and Gabriel Stone—believe. But when they meet four feisty women who are more than a match for their wild ways these Lords are tempted to renounce bachelordom for good.

Don't miss this dazzling new quartet by

Louise Allen

Read Alex Tempest's story in
His Housekeeper's Christmas Wish

And Grant Rivers's story in
His Christmas Countess
Coming December 2015

Look out for Cris and Gabriel's stories, coming soon!

Author Note

Enter the world of four close friends: aristocrats known in their university days as *The Four Disgraces*, now very much grown up—and considerably more dangerous! This is the story of the first of them, Alex Tempest, Viscount Weybourn, a man hiding a wounded heart behind a cynical façade. Alex would never describe himself as a knight errant, but when he rescues Tess Ellery from her personal dragons he finds his self-sufficiency is no protection against a woman determined to heal those wounds—and even make him love Christmas in the process of turning his life upside down. As for his heart… Well, you'll have to read the book to find out!

Next month will bring *His Christmas Countess*, the story of the second friend, Grant Rivers, who acquires a title and a new family all in the course of one very dark Christmas. And still to come are the stories of the other two—cool, reserved Cris de Feaux, Marquess of Avenmore, a man who has no intention of allowing any woman anywhere near his broken heart, and rake, gambler and walking scandal Gabriel Stone, Earl of Edenbridge, who would deny he even has a heart to be broken.

I hope you enjoy discovering how my four heroes discover the loves of their lives as much as I enjoyed writing their stories.

HIS HOUSEKEEPER'S CHRISTMAS WISH

Louise Allen

MILLS & BOON

Published in Great Britain 2015
by Mills & Boon, an imprint of Harlequin (UK) Limited,
Eton House, 18-24 Paradise Road, Richmond, Surrey, TW9 1SR

© 2015 Melanie Hilton

ISBN: 978-0-263-24813-5

Harlequin (UK) Limited's policy is to use papers that are natural,
renewable and recyclable products and made from wood grown in
sustainable forests. The logging and manufacturing processes conform
to the legal environmental regulations of the country of origin.

Printed and bound in Spain
by CPI, Barcelona

Louise Allen loves immersing herself in history. She finds landscapes and places evoke the past powerfully. Venice, Burgundy and the Greek islands are favourite destinations. Louise lives on the Norfolk coast and spends her spare time gardening, researching family history or travelling in search of inspiration. Visit her at louiseallenregency.co.uk, @LouiseRegency and janeaustenslondon.com.

Visit the Author Profile page
at millsandboon.co.uk for more titles.

For the Hartland Quay-istas—
Linda, Jenny, Lesley, Catherine and Janet
—with love

Chapter One

Alex Tempest did not normally trample nuns underfoot, nor anyone else, come to that. Alexander James Vernon Tempest, Viscount Weybourn, prized control, elegance, grace and athleticism—under all normal circumstances.

Skidding round corners on the ice-slick cobblestones of Ghent, however, was not normal, not in the gloomy light of the late-November afternoon with his mind occupied by thoughts of warm fires, good friends and rum punch.

The convent wall was high and unyielding when he cannoned into it. Alex found himself rebounding off the wall and into a nun, dressed all in black and grey, and blending perfectly with the cobbles. *She* was certainly yielding as she gave a small shriek of alarm and went flying, her black portmanteau bouncing away to land on the threshold of the convent's closed gates.

Alex got his feet under control. *'Ma soeur,*

je suis désolé. Permettez-moi.' He held out his hand as she levered herself into a sitting position with one black mitten–covered hand. Her bonnet, plain dark grey with a black ribbon, had tipped forward over her nose, and she pushed it back to look up at him.

'I am not—'

'Hurt? Excellent.' He could only make out the oval of her face in the shadow of the bonnet's brim. She seemed to be young by her voice. 'But you are English?' He extended the other hand. Presumably there were English nuns.

'Yes. But—'

'Let's get you up off that cold ground, Sister.' Her cloak, which seemed none too thick given the weather, was black. Under it there was the hem of a dark grey robe and the toes of sensible black boots. 'Take my hands.' Probably nuns were not supposed to touch men, but he could hardly get excommunicated for adding that small sin to the far greater offence of flattening her to the ground.

With what sounded like a sigh of resignation she put her hands in his and allowed him to pull her upright. 'Ow!' She hopped on one foot, swayed dangerously and the next moment she was cradled in his arms. After all, one did not allow a lady to fall, even if she was a nun. 'Oh!'

Alex braced his feet well apart on the slippery cobbles and looked down at as much as he could see of his armful, which wasn't a great deal, what with her billowing cloak and ferocious hat brim. But even if he couldn't see any detail, there was plenty for his body to read. She *was* young. And slender. And curved. He dipped his head and inhaled the scent of her. Plain soap, wet wool and warm, rapidly chilling, woman. Rapidly chilling *nun. Pull yourself together, man. Nuns are most definitely on the forbidden list. Pity...*

'I'll ring the bell, shall I?' he offered with a jerk of his head towards the rusty iron chain hanging by the door. It looked like the sort of thing desperate criminals clung to when claiming sanctuary, although, judging by the small barred peephole set into the massive planks, the sanctuary on offer might be rather less welcoming than a prison cell. 'It seems as though you have twisted your ankle.'

Mentioning parts of the anatomy was probably another sin, but she made no attempt to smite him with a rosary, although the body that was already stiff in his arms became rigid. 'No. Absolutely not. Thank—'

'I really think I should get someone to come out.'

'—you. I am due down at the canal basin. Sister Clare is expecting me.' Crisp, polite and obviously furious with him, but constrained through charity or good manners from saying so, he concluded. An educated, refined voice masking some strain or perhaps sadness. He was used to listening to voices, hearing what was behind the actual words; anyone was who did much negotiating. *What are you hiding, little nun?*

But the polite irritation was what was on the surface. That was fair enough. He'd knocked her down; the least he could do was to take her where she wanted to go and not to where, from the way her body arched away from the door, she did not want to be. 'But you should see a doctor. What if there is a bone broken?' Alex bent, juggled his armful of cross woman as best he could, caught the handles of the portmanteau in his fingers and straightened up. 'Which canal, Sister?'

'I am going to Ostend early tomorrow morning. Sister Clare runs a small hostel for travellers down at the port here and I will spend the night with her. But I am not—'

'This way, then.' Alex began to walk downhill. 'It just so happens I can take you to a doctor on the way.'

'I do not wish to be any trouble, but—'

'You cannot walk and all the cabs have vanished as they always do when one most needs one. It is not out of my way.'

And they were not actually going to see a *doc-*

tor, although Grant had virtually completed his medical education at Edinburgh when he'd been forced to give it up.

'Yes, but I—'

'Have no money?' Nuns were supposed to be penniless, he seemed to recall. 'Don't concern yourself about that, it is my fault you were injured and he's a friend. What is your name? I'm Viscount Weybourn.' He didn't normally lead with his rank, but he supposed a title might reassure her.

Her body shifted in his arms as she gave the sort of sigh that needed a lungful of air. She was probably mortified at being carried by a man, but if she wouldn't go back into the convent then there wasn't much option. He made another valiant, and unfamiliar, effort not to notice the feminine curves pressed against his body. He wasn't used to getting this close to women unless they both intended to take things considerably further.

'Teresa—'

'Sister Teresa.' Of course, nuns were named for saints, weren't they? 'Excellent. Here we are.' The lights of Les Quatre Éléments glowed though the gathering dusk and he headed for them like a mariner spying a safe, familiar harbour.

'An *inn*? Lord Wey—'

'A very respectable inn,' Alex assured her as he shouldered through the front door into the light and heat and bustle of a well-run hostelry. 'Gaston!'

'Milord Weybourn.' The innkeeper came hurrying out of the back. 'How good to see you again, milord. The other gentlemen are in your usual private parlour.'

'Thank you, Gaston.' Alex headed for the door on the right. 'And some tea? Coffee? What would you like, Sister Teresa?'

'*Gentlemen? Private* parlour? Lord Weybourn, put me down this—'

'Tea,' he ordered for her. Tea was soothing, wasn't it? His little nun needed soothing; she was beginning to wriggle in agitation like a ruffled hen and, *hell*, if she didn't stop she wasn't the only one who'd need it. Soothing, that was, not tea. He really needed a woman. How long had it been? A month? That was far too long.

Alex kicked the door closed behind him and leaned back against it for a moment while he sought for his usual composure. Nuns apparently did not wear corsets. The discovery was seriously unsettling. The soft weight of a small breast against his forearm was *damnably* unsettling. He was reacting like a green youth and he didn't like the feeling.

'My dear Alex, why the drama?' Crispin de

Feaux lowered the document he was studying, stood up and regarded the scene in the doorway with cool detachment. Possibly if he had erupted into the room pursued by sword-wielding soldiery Cris might have revealed some emotion, but Alex rather doubted it. 'Have you taken to abducting nuns?'

'Nuns? Surely not?' Over by the fireplace Grant Rivers swung his boots down from the fender and stood, too, dragging one hand through his hair. Characteristically he looked responsible and concerned.

'What do you bet?' Gabriel Stone dropped a handful of dice with a clatter and lounged to his feet. 'Although it hardly seems Alex's style. High-fliers, now...'

Alex narrowed his eyes, daring him to continue stripping her with that insolent gaze. Gabe grinned and slumped back into his chair.

'I slipped on the ice and knocked Sister Teresa to the ground, injuring her ankle in the process.' Alex pushed away from the door and carried his burden over to the settle by the fire. 'I thought you should check it for her, Grant.'

'There you are, Sister Teresa, you're in safe hands now and tea is on the way.' The infuriating creature deposited Tess on the settee opposite the handsome brown-haired man and sketched a bow. 'This is Grantham Rivers, a very handy man with a sprained ankle.' She caught the grin Lord Weybourn sent the doctor and the doctor's eye roll in return as his friend turned on his heel and sauntered over to the other two men.

'I am not—'

'A nun. I know.' The doctor sat down. He was polite, but didn't seem too happy. 'Unlike Alex, I know that nuns wear wimples and do not trot around the streets alone.'

'Do none of you allow a woman to finish a sentence?' Tess demanded. She had gone beyond miserable since her interview with Mother Superior a week ago had knocked all her certainties into utter chaos. She'd forced herself into the same state of stoical, unhappy acceptance that had kept her sane, somehow, all those years ago when Mama and Papa had died. Now the shock of being hurled off her feet had sent her into an unfamiliar mood of irritation.

Or possibly this was the effect men had on women all the time. As her association with the creatures since the age of thirteen had been limited to the priest, an aged gardener and occasional encounters with tradesmen, this could well be the case. For the first time in her life celibacy began to sound appealing. But now she was alone with four of them, although they *seemed* safe enough, sober and respectful.

'Normally, yes, we have much better manners. Alex is doubtless disconcerted at his very unusual clumsiness in felling you to the ground, but I have no excuse. How should I address you, ma'am?'

'Miss Ellery. Tess Ellery, Doctor.'

'Not doctor. Plain Mr Grantham Rivers. But I almost completed my medical training at Edinburgh, so I am quite safe to be let loose on minor injuries, Miss Ellery.' He regarded her as she sat there looking, she had no doubt, like a somewhat battered crow. 'May I take your cloak and bonnet? I will need you to remove your shoe and stocking so I can examine your ankle. Shall I send for a maid to attend you?'

He looked serious and respectable. Considering that she had not shed so much as a glove in male company for years, Tess wondered why she was not more flustered. Perhaps being knocked to the ground and then carried by a tall, strong, over-masterful aristocrat might have reduced her capacity for flusterment. Was that a word? More likely the fact that her world was so out of kilter accounted for it.

'Miss Ellery?' Mr Rivers was waiting patiently. She searched for normal courtesy and some poise, found a smile and felt it freeze on her lips as she met his eyes. He had the saddest eyes she had ever seen. It was like gazing into the hell of someone's private grief, and staring felt as intrusive and unmannerly as gawping at mourners at a funeral.

'No, no maid. I can manage, thank you.' Tess made a business of her bonnet ribbon and cloak clasp and murmured her thanks. He laid the garments at the end of the settle, then went to stand with his back to her, shielding her from the room as she managed her laces and untied her garter to roll down her stocking. 'I cannot get my boot off.'

'The ankle is swelling.' Mr Rivers came and knelt down in front of her. 'Let me see if I can remove it without cutting the leather.'

'Please.' They were her only pair of boots.

'Have you any other injuries?' He bent over her foot, working the boot off with gentle wiggles. 'You didn't bang your head, or put out your hand and hurt your wrist?'

'No, only my ankle. It turned over as I fell.' Removing the boot hurt, despite his care, so Tess looked over his head at the other three men for distraction. Such a strange quartet. Mr Rivers with his tragic eyes, gentle hands and handsome profile. Her rescuer, Lord Weybourn, tall, elegant and relaxed. Deceptively relaxed, given the ease with which he had lifted and carried her. The blond icicle who looked like a cross between an archangel and a hanging judge and the lounging dice player who seemed more suited to a hedge tavern frequented by footpads than a respectable inn in the company of gentlemen.

Yes, an unlikely combination of friends and yet they were so easy together. Like brothers, she supposed. *Family.*

Lord Weybourn met her gaze and lifted one slanting eyebrow.

'Ah, that made you jump, sorry.' Mr Rivers's fingers were probing and flexing. 'Tell me where it hurts. Here? When I do this? Can you wriggle your toes? Excellent. And point your foot? No, stop if it is painful.'

He certainly seemed to know what he was doing. He would bind it up for her and Lord Weybourn must find her some conveyance, given that the collision was all his fault and she wouldn't be able to get her boot laced again over a bandage. None of these men were behaving in a way that made her uneasy. There were no leers or winks, no suggestive remarks. Tess relaxed a little more and decided she could trust her judgement that she was safe here.

His lordship was half sitting on the edge of the table, laughing at something the dice player had said. Now he had shed his hat and greatcoat she could see that the impression of elegance could be applied to his clothing as much as to his manner. Ten years in a nunnery did not do

much for her appreciation of male fashion, but
even she could see that what he wore had been
crafted from expensive fabrics by a master who
could sculpt fabric around broad shoulders and
long, muscular legs, and that whoever looked
after his linen was a perfectionist.

Unlike his friends, the viscount wasn't con-
ventionally good looking, Tess thought critically
as Mr Rivers rested her foot on a stool and stood
up, murmuring about cold compresses and bandages. Mr Rivers was the image of the perfect
English gentleman: strong bones, straight nose,
thick, glossy dark brown hair and those tragic,
beautiful green eyes. The blond icicle belonged
in a church's stained-glass window, giving im-
pressionable girls in the congregation palpita-
tions of mixed desire and terror at the thought
of his blue eyes turning on them or that sculpted
mouth opening on some killing rebuke. Even the
dice player with his shock of black hair, insolent
gypsy-dark eyes and broad shoulders had the at-
tractiveness of a male animal in its prime.

But Lord Weybourn was different. Very masculine, of course… Oh, yes. She gave a little
shiver as she recalled how easily he had lifted
and carried her. And he had a touch of something
dangerously other-worldly about him. His hair
was dark blond, his nose was thin, his cheek-

bones pronounced. His eyes, under winging dark brows, were, she guessed, hazel and his chin was firm.

It was his mouth, she decided, focusing on that feature. It was mobile and kept drifting upwards into a half smile as though his thoughts were pleasant, but mysterious and, in some way, dangerous. In fact, she decided, he looked like a particularly well-dressed supernatural creature, if such things ever reached a good six feet in height with shoulders in proportion—one who ruled over forests where the shadows were dark and wolves lurked…

He glanced across at her again and stood up, which snapped her out of musings that probably had something to do with Sister Moira's *frisson*-inducing tales of Gothic terror, told at recreation time when Mother Superior was not listening. Only Sister Moira's fantasy beings never provoked feelings of…

'Is Rivers hurting you?' Lord Weybourn came over and hitched himself onto the table opposite. His boots were beautiful, she thought, watching one swinging idly to and fro. It was safer than meeting his gaze. 'I haven't managed to break your ankle, have I?'

'No, you haven't, fortunately.' Mr Rivers came back and hunkered down by her feet. 'This will be cold,' he warned as he draped a dripping cloth over her ankle. 'I'll bandage it up after you've had your tea and a rest.'

'This seems a very pleasant inn,' she said for want of a neutral topic. Conversation with men was a novelty. 'Do you use this place frequently?'

'From a long way back,' Lord Weybourn said. 'Even when the war was on some of us would slip in and out in various guises. Very handy, Les Quatre Éléments.' He grinned. 'We called ourselves the Four Elementals as our names fit so well.'

'Elementals? I know the four elements—air, water, fire and earth. So which are you?'

'Alex Tempest—air.'

'So you are water, Mr Rivers? That works well with your soothing medical skills.'

He gave a half bow in acknowledgement. 'Cris is de Feaux, hence the French *feu* for fire.'

'Of course.' She could easily imagine the blond icicle as an archangel with a burning sword. 'And earth?'

'Gabriel Stone is nothing if not earthy.' Lord Weybourn titled his head towards the dice player, who was playing left hand against right hand, dark brows lowered in a scowl of concentration.

Mr Rivers changed the cold cloth on her ankle again. Tess smiled her thanks, then forgot both injury and elements as a maid deposited a laden tray on the settle beside her. Tea, she had expected, but not pastries dripping with honey, little cakes and dainty iced biscuits. Lord Weybourn stole a biscuit and went back to the others.

'I should—'

'Eat up. Sorry,' Grant Rivers said. 'Interrupting you again.'

'I fear I will not know when to stop.' Vegetable soup and wholemeal bread had made a warming midday meal, but they had tasted, as always, of practical, frugal worthiness and sat lumpily on a stomach fluttering with nerves. There was nothing worthy about the plate beside her. Mr Rivers simply nodded and strolled off to join his friends, leaving her to sip her tea—with sugar!—while she contemplated the temptation. Perhaps just one of each? To leave them untouched would be discourteous.

Half an hour later Tess licked her fingers, feeling slightly, deliciously queasy as she contemplated a plate empty of all but crumbs and a smear of cream.

Mr Rivers strolled back and shifted the tray without so much as a smirk or a frown for her greed. 'I'll strap up your ankle now. Let's put this blanket over your knees and you can take a nap when I'm done. You were chilled and a little bit shocked, I suspect. A rest will do no harm.'

He was almost a doctor, he knew what he was talking about and she supposed there was no great hurry, provided she was with Sister Clare for the evening meal. And this was…interesting. Watching men, relaxed and friendly together, was interesting. Being warm and full of delicious sweets was indulgent. A mild sensation of naughtiness, of playing truant, was definitely intriguing. She knew she shouldn't be here, but they all seemed so…harmless? Wrong word. Perhaps it was her innocence deceiving her…

Tess blinked, on the verge of a yawn. Last night had been cold and her head too full of churning thoughts, hopes and worries for her to sleep much. Mr Rivers was right—a little nap would set her up for an evening of doling out stew to humble travellers who would otherwise be huddled in their cloaks on benches for the night. Then she would have to try to sleep on a hard bed in a chilly cell alongside Sister Clare's notorious snores before an even chillier dawn start. Sister Moira always said those snores counted as a penance in themselves, so they would be enough to pay for the consumption of a plate of pastries, Tess decided, as she snugged down in the corner of the settle and let the men's voices and laughter wash over her. Just a little nap.

* * *

'Mmm?' *Citrus cologne, starched linen...* She was being lifted again by Lord Weybourn. It seemed natural to turn her head into his shoulder, inhale the interesting masculine scent of him.

'You will get a crick in your neck in that corner, little nun. And we're becoming noisy. There's a nice quiet room just here, you can rest.'

That sounded so good. 'Sister Clare...'

'I remember. Sister Clare, down at the canal dock. Boat to Ostend in the morning.'

What is all this nonsense the sisters tell us about men? Anyone would think they were all ravening beasts... These four are kind and reliable and safe. And the mattress was soft when he laid her down and the covers so warm and light. 'Thank you,' Tess murmured as she drifted off again.

'My pleasure, little nun.' Then the door closed and all was quiet.

Chapter Two

Tess swum up out of sleep, deliciously warm and with a definite need for the chamber pot. *Too much tea.* 'Ouch!' Her ankle gave a stab of pain as she hopped across to the screen in the corner, made herself comfortable and then hopped back. It was still light, so she could not have slept long. In fact, it was *very* light. She pulled aside the curtain and stared out at a corner of the inn yard with a maid bustling past with a basket of laundry and a stable boy lugging a bucket of water. It was unmistakably morning.

She hobbled to the door, flung it open. The four men were still around the table. The dice player and the blond icicle were playing cards with the air of gamblers who could continue for another twelve hours if necessary. Mr Rivers was pouring ale into a tankard with one hand while holding a bread roll bulging with ham in the other. And Lord Weybourn, who she now realised was the most unreliable, infuriating man—regardless of her pulse quickening simply at the sight of him—was fast asleep, his chair tipped on its back legs against a pillar, his booted feet on the table amidst a litter of playing cards.

The fact that he was managing to sleep without snoring, with his mouth mostly closed and his clothing unrumpled, only added fuel to the fire.

'Lord Weybourn!'

'Humph?' He jerked awake and Tess winced at the thump his head made against the pillar. 'Ouch.'

The other men stood up. 'Miss Ellery. Good morning. Did you sleep well?' Mr Rivers asked.

'I told him. I told him I had to be down at the canal port. I told him the boat left very early this morning.' She jerked her head towards Lord Weybourn, too cross to look at him.

'It *is* early morning.' He got to his feet and she could not help but notice that he did not look as though he had slept in his clothes. He was as sleek and self-possessed as a panther. What *she* looked like she shuddered to think.

Tess batted an errant lock of hair out of her eyes. 'What time is it?'

The blond icicle glanced at the mantelshelf clock. 'Just past nine.'

'That isn't *early*, that is almost half the morning gone.' Tess hopped to the nearest chair and sat down. 'I have missed the boat.'

'You can buy a ticket on the next one. They are frequent enough,' the viscount said, stealing Mr Rivers's unguarded tankard. The ale slid down in a long swallow, making his Adam's apple move. His neck was strapped with muscle.

'I do not have any money,' Tess said through gritted teeth, averting her eyes from so much blatant masculinity. If she knew any swear words this would be an excellent opportunity to use them. But she did not. Strange that she had never felt the lack before. 'I have a ticket for the boat that left at four o'clock. It arrives in Ostend with just enough time to catch the ship across the Channel. The ship that I have another ticket for. I have tickets, useless tickets. I have no money and I cannot go back to the convent and ask for more. I cannot afford to repay it,' she added bleakly.

'Ah. No money?' Lord Weybourn said with that faint, infuriating smile. 'I understand your agitation.'

'I am not *agitated*.' Agitation was not permitted in the convent. 'I am annoyed. *You* knocked me down, my lord. *You* brought me here and let me sleep. *You* promised to wake me in time for the boat. Therefore this is now your problem to resolve.' She folded her hands in her lap, straightened her back and gave him the look that Mother

Superior employed to extract the admission of sins, major and minor. Words were usually not necessary.

She should have known he would have an answer. 'Simple. Grant and I are going to Ostend by carriage later today. You come with us and I will buy you a boat ticket when we get there.'

This was what Sister Luke would describe as the Primrose Path leading directly to Temptation. With a capital *T*. And probably Sin. Capital *S*. No wonder they said it was a straight and easy road. Being carried by a strong and attractive man, eating delicious pastries, sleeping—next door to four men—on a blissfully soft bed. All undoubtedly wicked.

After that, how could travelling in a carriage with two gentlemen for a day make things any worse? She wasn't sure she trusted Lord Weybourn's slanting smile, but Mr Rivers seemed eminently reliable.

'Thank you, my lord. That will be very satisfactory.' It was certain to be a very comfortable carriage, for none of these men, even the rumpled dice player, looked as though they stinted on their personal comfort. She found she was smiling, then stopped when no one leaped to their feet and started to bustle around making preparations. 'When do we start and how long will it take us?'

'Seven and a half, eight hours.' *Finally*, Lord Weybourn got to his feet.

'But we will arrive after dark. I do not think the ships sail in the dark, do they?'

'We are not jolting over muddy roads all day and then getting straight on board, whether a ship is sailing or not.' The viscount strolled across to one of the other doors, opened it and shouted, 'Gaston!'

'They do sail at night and I am taking one to Leith at nine this evening,' Mr Rivers remarked. 'But I am in haste, you'll do better to take the opportunity to rest, Miss Ellery.'

'I am also in haste,' she stated.

Lord Weybourn turned from the door. 'Do nuns hurry?'

'Certainly. And you know perfectly well that I am not a nun, my lord.' The maddening creature refused to be chastened by her reproofs, which showed either arrogance, levity or the hide of an ox. Probably all three. 'I am expected at the London house of the Order.'

'The Channel crossing is notoriously uncertain for weather and timing. They will not be expecting you for a day or so either way. Unless someone is at death's door?' He raised an interrogative brow. Tess shook her head. 'There, then. Arrive rested and, hopefully, not hobbling. Always a good thing to be at one's best when making an entrance. Breakfast is on its way.'

He sauntered out, lean, elegant, assured. Tess's fingers itched with a sinful inclination to violence.

'You might as well contemplate swatting a fly, Miss Ellery,' the blond icicle remarked. Apparently her face betrayed her feelings graphically. He inclined his head in a graceful almost bow. 'Crispin de Feaux, Marquess of Avenmore, at your service. Rivers you know.' He gestured towards the third man. 'This, improbable as it might seem, is not the local highwayman, but Gabriel Stone, Earl of Edenbridge.'

Lord Edenbridge stood, swept her an extravagant courtesy, then collapsed back into his chair. 'Enchanted, Miss Ellery.' His cards appeared to enchant him more.

'I'll send for some hot water for you.' Mr Rivers held the bedchamber door open. 'You will feel much better after a wash and some breakfast, believe me, Miss Ellery.'

Tess thanked him, curtsied as best she could to all three men and sat down on the bed to await the water. It wasn't their fault. She knew just who to blame, but because she was a lady—or, rather, had been raised to have the manners of one—she would bite her tongue and do her best to act with grace. Somehow. As for breakfast at this hour—why, it was going to be almost noon by the time it was finished at this rate.

As she had suspected, the carriage proved to be very comfortable. 'I keep this and my own horses over here,' Lord Weybourn explained when Tess exclaimed in pleasure at the soft seats and the padded interior. 'Job horses and hired vehicles are unreliable.'

'You come to the Continent frequently, my lord?' Tess settled snugly into one corner and submitted to Mr Rivers arranging her legs along the seat and covering them with a rug. A hot brick wrapped in flannel was tucked in, too. Such luxury. She would enjoy what good things this journey had to offer, especially as the future seemed unlikely to hold much in the way of elegant coach travel.

'We all do.' Lord Weybourn folded his length into an opposite corner while Mr Rivers took the other. They had given her the best, forward-facing position, she noted. 'Cris—Lord Avenmore—is a diplomat and spends half his time at the Congress and half doing mysterious things about the place. Gabe enjoys both travelling and fleecing any gamester foolish enough to cut cards with him and Grant here buys horses.'

'I have a stud,' Mr Rivers explained. 'I import

some of the more unusual Continental breeds from time to time.'

'And you, my lord?'

'Alex.' He gave her that slanting, wicked smile. 'I will feel that you have not forgiven me if you *my lord* me from here to London.'

It seemed wrong, but perhaps that degree of informality was commonplace amongst aristocrats. 'Very well, although Alex Tempest sounds more like a pirate than a viscount.'

Mr Rivers snorted. 'That's what he is. He scours the Continent in search of loot and buried treasure.'

'Art and antiquities, my dear Grant.' Alex grinned. 'Certainly nothing buried. Can you imagine me with a shovel?'

Tess noted the flex of muscles under the form-fitting tailoring of his coat. Perhaps it was not achieved by digging holes, but the viscount was keeping exceptionally fit somehow. *No*, she thought, *not a shovel, but I can imagine you with a sword.*

'I am a connoisseur, a truffle hound through the wilderness of a Continent after a great war.'

'Poseur,' Mr Rivers said.

'Of course.' Alex's ready agreement was disarmingly frank. 'I do have my reputation to maintain.'

'But forgive me,' Tess ventured, 'is that not

business? I thought it was not acceptable for aristocrats to engage in trade.' And perhaps it was not acceptable to mention it at all.

'Social death,' Grant Rivers agreed. 'So those of us who cannot rely upon family money maintain a polite fiction. I keep a stud for my own amusement and profit and sell to acquaintances as a favour when they beg to share in a winning bloodline. Alex here is approached by those with more money than taste. Gentlemen are so very grateful when he puts them in the way of acquiring beautiful, rare objects from his collection to enhance their status or their newly grand houses. Naturally he cannot be out of pocket in these acts of mercy. Gabe is a gambler, which is perfectly *au fait*. It is strange that he rarely loses, which is the norm, but you can't hold that against a man unless you catch him cheating.'

'And does he?'

'He has the devil's own luck, the brain of a mathematician and the willpower to know when to fold. And he would kill anyone who suggested he fuzzes the cards,' Alex explained. 'And before you ask, Cris is the only one of us who has come into his title. The rest of us are merely heirs in waiting. He's a genuine marquess.

'And you, little nun? Given that we are being so frank between friends.'

He knew perfectly well that she was not a nun,

but perhaps if she ignored the teasing he would stop it. 'I, on the contrary, have not a guinea to my name, save what Mother Superior gave me for food and the stagecoach fare in England.' Tess managed a bright smile, as though this was merely amusing. It had been quite irrelevant until Mother Superior's *little discussion* a week ago.

Dear Teresa had been with them for ten years, five since the death of her aunt, Sister Boniface. She had steadfastly declined to convert from her childhood Anglicanism, so, naturally, she had no future with the convent as a nun. Equally obviously, she could not go to her, er...*connections* in England. And then Mother Superior had explained why.

Teresa was twenty-three now, so what did she intend to do with her life? she had asked while Tess's understanding of who and what she was tumbled around her ears.

I must have looked completely witless, Tess thought as she gazed out of the carriage window at the sodden countryside. She had been teaching the little ones, the orphans like herself, but that apparently had been merely a stop-gap until she was an adult. And, she suspected now she had a chance to think about it, until Mother Superior was convinced no conversion was likely.

But it was all right; even if there was no money left from the funds Papa had sent to her aunt, she would manage, somehow. The dream of a family in England, people who might forgive and forget what Mama and Papa had done, had evaporated. She would not repine and she would try not to think about it. She could work hard and, goodness knew, she wasn't used to luxury.

Heavy clouds rolled across the sky, making it dark enough outside for Tess to glimpse her own reflection in the glass. *What a dismal Dora! This bonnet doesn't help.* She sat up straighter, fixed a look of bright interest on her face and tried to think positive thoughts.

What was wrong with the little nun? Alex watched her from beneath half-closed lids. Beside him Grant had dropped off to sleep, and he was weary himself after a hard night of cards, brandy and talk, but something about the woman opposite kept him awake. If she was not a nun, what was she doing going to a convent, dressed like a wet Sunday morning in November? Her accent was well bred. Her manners—when she was not ripping up at him—were correct and she was obviously a lady.

A mystery, in fact. As a rule Alex enjoyed mysteries, especially mysterious ladies, but this one was not happy and that put a damper on enjoyable speculation. There was more to it than her sprained ankle and irritation over missed boats, he was certain. Tess was putting a brave face on things whenever she remembered to. No coward, his little nun.

Alex grinned at the thought of *his* nun. The *nunneries* he was acquainted with were very different establishments. She raised one slim, arching dark brow.

'Comfortable, Miss Ellery?'

'Exceedingly, thank you, my lord…Alex.' Yes, that smile was definitely brave, but assumed.

'Ankle hurting?'

'No, Mr Rivers has worked wonders and there is no pain unless I put weight on it. I am sure it is only a mild sprain.' She lapsed into silence again, apparently not finding that awkward. No doubt chatter was discouraged in a nunnery.

'So what will you be doing in London? Making your come-out?'

She had taken her bonnet off and he remembered how that soft, dark brown hair had felt against his cheek when he had lifted her to carry her to her bed. It was severely braided and pinned up now, just as it had been last night, and he wondered what it would look like down. The thought made him shift uncomfortably in his seat and he wrenched his mind away from long lashes against a pale cheek flushed with rose and the impact of a pair of dark blue eyes.

His… No, *Miss Ellery* laughed, the first sound of amusement he had heard from her, albeit with an edge to it. Her hand shot up to cover her mouth, which was a pity because it was a pretty mouth and it was prettier still when curved.

'My come-out? Hardly. No, I will stay at the London house until the Mother Superior there finds me position as a governess or a companion.'

'With a Roman Catholic family?' That might take a while, there were not that many, not of the class to be employing well-bred young females of her type. Rich merchants were a possibility, he supposed.

'No. Not only am I not a nun, I am also an Anglican.'

'Then, what the bl—? What on earth are you doing in a nunnery?'

'It is a long story.' She folded her hands neatly in her lap and seemed to feel that ended the discussion.

'It is a long journey,' he countered. 'Entertain me with your tale, please, Miss Ellery.'

'Very well.' She did not look enthusiastic. 'I will make it as concise as possible. My father's elder sister, Beatrice, converted to Catholicism against the violent disapproval of her parents and ran away to Belgium to join an order of nuns.

'But Papa, after he came of age, started writing to her. My parents enjoyed travelling, even though there was a war on, and besides, it was often cheaper to live on the Continent.' She bit her lip and her gaze slid away from his. *A prevarication?* 'So just after my thirteenth birthday we were in Belgium and Papa decided to visit my aunt.'

'And that was when?' *How old is she? Twenty?* Alex tried to recall what was happening seven years past.

'Ten years ago. I am twenty-three,' Tess admitted with a frankness no other unmarried lady of his acquaintance would have employed.

'1809.' Alex delved back in his memory. He had been seventeen, half tempted by the army, finally deciding against it for the very good reason his father would probably have had a stroke with the shock of his son and heir doing something his parent approved of for the first time in his life. 'Most of the action was towards the east at that time, I seem to recall.'

'I think so.' Tess bit her lower lip in thought and Alex crossed his legs again. Damn it, the girl—woman—was a drab little peahen for all the rainwater-washed complexion and the pretty eyes. What was the matter with him? 'Anyway, it was considered safe enough. We arrived in Ghent and Papa visited the convent and was allowed to see my aunt, who was Sister Boniface by then. But there was an epidemic of cholera in the city and both Mama and Papa… They both died.'

She became so still and silent Alex wondered if she had finished, but eventually, with a little movement, as though shaking raindrops off her shoulders, she gathered herself. 'When Papa realised how serious it was he sent me to my aunt with all the money he had. I have lived there ever since, but now I do not want to become a nun and the money has run out, paying for my keep, so I am ready to make my own way in the world.'

'But your grandparents, your aunts and uncles—surely you have living relatives? Cousins?'

'There is no one I could go to.'

There had to be, surely? Her gaze slid away from his again and Tess stared out of the window. There was some story here, something she wasn't telling him, and she was too honest to lie. Alex bit his tongue on the questions. It was no concern of his. 'And the convent was not for you?'

Tess shook her head. 'I always knew I was not cut out to be a nun.' She managed a very creditable smile.

There must be relatives somewhere, Alex thought, forcing back the query. Perhaps the runaway aunt had caused the rift, which was hard on Tess. He understood what it was like to be rejected, but he was a man with money and independence, and these days, power of his own. He knew how to hit back and he'd spent more than ten years doing just that. This was a sheltered, penniless young woman.

'Now I know you better I can tell that you're not suitable for the cloister,' he drawled, intent on teasing her out of introspection. 'Too much of a temper, for one thing.'

Tess blushed, but did not deny the accusation. 'It is something I try to overcome. You did provoke me excessively, you must admit, although I should not make excuses.'

'Go on, blame me, I have a broad enough back.' Alex smiled at her and noticed how that made her drop her gaze. *Not at all used to men. A total innocent with no idea how to flirt. Behave yourself, Tempest.* But she was a charming novelty.

'I will spend December and perhaps January at the London convent, I expect. I do not imagine anyone will be looking to employ a governess or a companion just now.' She fiddled with the fringe on the edge of the rug. 'A pity, because it would be wonderful to spend Christmas with a family. But still, it is always a happy season wherever one is.'

'Is it?' Alex tried to recall the last Christmas he had spent with his family. He had been almost eighteen. His parents had not been speaking to each other, his batty great-aunt had managed to set the breakfast room on fire, his younger siblings had argued incessantly and at dinner on Christmas Day his father had finally, unforgivably, lost his temper with Alex.

There are some things that a mature man might laugh off or shrug aside as the frustrated outpourings of a short-tempered parent. But they are usually not things that a sensitive seventeen-year-old can accept with any grace or humour. Or forgive. Not when they led to tragedy.

Alex had left the table, packed his bags, gone straight back to Oxford and stayed there, taking care to extract every penny of his allowance from the bank before his father thought to stop it. When the news had reached him of just what his father's outburst had unleashed he'd settled down, with care and much thought, to convince his father that he was exactly what he had accused him of being, while at the same time living his life the way he wanted to.

'You will be going home for Christmas, surely?' Tess asked.

Alex realised he must have been silent for quite some time. 'I am going back to my own home, certainly. But not to the family house and most certainly not for Christmas.'

'I am sorry,' she said with every sign of distress on his behalf.

Beside him Grant gave an inelegant snort and woke up. 'Christmas? Never say you're going back to Tempeston, Alex?'

'Lord, no.' Alex shuddered. 'I will do what I always do and hole up in great comfort with good wine, excellent food, brandy, a pile of books and a roaring fire until the rest of humanity finishes with its annual bout of plum pudding–fuelled sentimentality and returns to normal. What about you?'

'I promised to call on Whittaker. I was with his brother when he died in Salzburg, if you recall. He lives just outside Edinburgh and I said I'd go and see him as soon as I was back in Britain.' Grant shifted his long legs into a more comfortable position. 'Can't stay too long, though, I'll go straight from there to my grandfather in Northumberland.'

'How is he?' Grant was the old man's heir and he'd be a viscount in his own right when he went, given that his father had died years ago.

'He's frail.' Grant was curt. He was fond of his grandfather, Alex thought with an unwelcome twinge of envy.

'He will be helped by your company at Christmas,' Tess said warmly.

'He'd be glad to see Grant at any time.' Alex

managed not to snap the words. 'What is it about Christmas that produces this nonsense anyway?'

It was meant as a rhetorical question, but Tess stared at him as though he had declared that it rained upwards. 'You are funning, surely?' When he shook his head she announced, 'Then I will remind you, although I cannot truly believe you are really such a cynic.' She paused, as though to collect her thoughts, then opened her mouth. 'Well, first of all there is…'

Please, no, Alex thought despairingly. If there was anything as bad as Christmas it was someone who was an enthusiast about it.

'Evergreens…' the confounded chit began. 'Cutting them and…'

Alex glowered.

Chapter Three

'And it is so cold, but that is part of the fun, everyone wrapped up and the snow crunching underfoot, and that gorgeous smell of pines.' Tess closed her eyes, the better to recall it. Memories of those wonderful English Christmases from many years ago, before Papa had said they must go abroad. There hadn't been much money and it had been a different village each year.

She had never asked why they kept moving; she had simply taken it for granted, as children do. Now, from an adult perspective, she realised they had probably been keeping one step ahead of recognition and scandal and that was why they'd left the country—the Continent was cheaper and there would be less gossip.

But we were happy, she thought, recalling snowball fights at Christmas and unconditional love all the year round. When she opened her eyes again Alex Tempest's mouth was pursed as though he had bitten a wasp. *Grumpy man.*

She pressed on, ignoring him, all the precious memories bubbling up, unstoppable. 'And planning what presents you can give your friends and finding them or making them. That's almost better than receiving gifts. There's all the fun of hiding them away and wrapping them up and watching the other person's face when they try to guess what's in the parcel.'

Mr Rivers was smiling, even though his eyes were still sad. Tess smiled back. 'And all the food to prepare. And church on Christmas Eve and the bells ringing out and being too excited to sleep afterwards and yet, somehow, you do.'

Lord Weybourn, *Alex*, looked as though he was in pain now. What was the matter with the man?

'Have you done your Christmas shopping already, Miss Ellery?' Mr Rivers asked. 'You seem to be someone who would plan ahead.'

'I had to leave my gifts with the nuns to give out. I sewed most of them and my stitchery is not of the neatest.' She wished she believed the cliché about it being the thought that counts, but she could imagine Sister Monica's expression when she saw the lumpy seams on her pen wiper. There was never any danger of Tess being asked to join the group who embroidered fine linen for sale, or made vestments for Ghent's churches.

'But next year I will have wages and I will be able to send gifts I have purchased.' There, another positive thing about this frightening new life that lay ahead of her. She had been saving them up and had almost reached ten. *Living with a family. A family.* The word felt warm and round, like the taste of plum pudding or the scent of roses on an August afternoon.

Tess left the thought reluctantly and pressed on with her mental list. *A room of my own. Being able to wear colours. Interesting food. Warmth. London to explore on my afternoons off. Wages. Control of my own destiny.*

She suspected that the last of those might prove illusionary. How much freedom would a governess's or companion's wage buy her? She glanced at Alex, but his eyes were closed and he was doing a very creditable imitation of a man asleep. He really did not enjoy Christmas, it seemed. How strange.

Mr Rivers continued to make polite conversation and she responded as the light drew in and the wintery dusk fell. Finally, when her stomach was growling, the carriage clattered into an inn yard and, as the groom opened the door, she caught a salty tang on the cold breeze.

'Ostend. Wake up, Alex. You sleep like a cat,

you idle devil.' Grant Rivers prodded his friend in the ribs. 'May I take the carriage on down to the docks? You'll be staying here the night, I'm guessing, and I'll send it right back.'

Alex opened one eye. 'Yes, certainly have it. Higgs, unload my luggage and Miss Ellery's, then take Mr Rivers to find his ship.' He uncurled his long body from the seat and held out his hand to Tess. 'If you can shuffle along to the end of the seat, I will lift you down.'

She was in his arms before she thought to protest. 'But I must find a ship, my lord.'

'Tomorrow. We will both take a ship tomorrow. Now you need dinner, a hot bath and a comfortable room for the night. Now, don't wriggle or I'll drop you.'

'But—'

'Goodbye, Miss Ellery.' Grant Rivers was climbing back into the carriage and men were carrying a pile of beautiful leather luggage, topped with her scuffed black portmanteau, towards the open inn door. 'Safe voyage and I hope you soon find a congenial employer in London.' He pulled the door shut and leaned out of the window. 'Take care, Alex.'

'And you.' Alex freed one hand and clasped his friend's. 'Give Charlie a hug from me.'

'Who is Charlie?' Tess asked as he carried her into the inn. It was seductively pleasurable, being carried by a man. For a moment she indulged the fantasy that this was her lover, sweeping her away…

'His son.' Alex's terse answer jerked her out of the dream.

'Mr Rivers is married?' Somehow he had not looked married, whatever that looked like.

'Widowed.' Alex's tone gave no encouragement for further questions.

Perhaps that was why Grant Rivers's eyes were so sad. She closed her lips on questions that were sure to be intrusive as the landlord came out to greet them.

'LeGrice, I need an extra room.' Alex was obviously known and expected. 'A comfortable, quiet chamber for the lady, a maid to attend her, hot baths for both of us and then the best supper you can lay on in my private parlour.'

'Milord.' Known, expected and not to be denied, obviously. The innkeeper was bustling about as though the Prince Regent had descended on his establishment. Perhaps she would see the Prince Regent when she was in London. Tess was distracted enough by this interesting thought not to protest when she was carried upstairs and into a bedchamber.

The sight of the big bed was enough to jerk her out of fantasies of state coaches and bewigged royalty, let alone thoughts of romance. 'Please put me down.'

It must have come out more sharply than she intended. Alex stopped dead. 'That was my intention.'

'Here. Just inside the door. This is a bedchamber.'

'I know. The clue lies in the fact that there's a bed in it.' He was amused by her vapours, she could hear it in his voice, a deep rumble that held a laugh hidden inside it.

Her ear was pressed against his chest. Tess jerked her head upright. 'Then, please put me down. You should not be in my bedchamber.'

'I was last night when I put you to bed.'

'Two wrongs do not make a right,' she said and winced at how smug she sounded.

'Nanny used to say that, did she?' Alex walked across to the hearthside and deposited her on a chair.

'Sister Benedicta,' Tess confessed. 'I sounded just like her, how mortifying.'

'Why mortifying?' He leaned one shoulder against the high mantelshelf and lounged, as pleasing to the eye as a carefully placed piece of statuary, the lamplight teasing gilt highlights out of what she had thought was simply dark blond hair. She wondered how much of that lazy perfection was deliberately cultivated.

'Because it was a commonplace thing to say and I have no intention of being commonplace.'

That faint smile curled Alex's mouth again and Tess found herself staring at his lower lip and puzzling over why, when he smiled, which stretched his lips, the centre of the lower one seemed somehow fuller.

'That is an uncharitable insult to Sister Benedicta,' she said hastily. 'Only sometimes, when she managed to string an entire conversation together consisting of nothing but clichés, I had to bite my lip to stop myself screaming in sheer boredom.' *Biting lips...why on earth should that image...? Stop it!*

'I will remove my dangerous male presence from your bedchamber and leave you to bathe in comfort.' He straightened up and strolled to the door. 'Supper in an hour, do you think?'

'Yes. Perfect. This is lovely, thank you. A fire and a hot bath and a maid,' Tess gabbled, as a pretty girl, all apple cheeks and blond braids, ducked under Alex's arm as he held the door open. He simply grinned at her and went out.

This was indeed the Primrose Path to Perdition. Luxury, warmth, leisure, being waited on. And all because she hadn't had the willpower to stay awake last night and insist she be taken down to Sister Clare to do her duty. It was not fair, she had thought she had conquered all those silly yearnings and *what-ifs* and *if-onlys*. Now she was having a taste of things she had dreamed about, all served up by an attractive man, and it would make her new life that much harder to adjust to. *My dangerous male presence. Oh, yes, indeed.*

It's a hair shirt, that's what it is, she thought wildly as a serving man lugged in a tin bath, set it in front of the fire and another brought buckets of steaming water to fill it. She was being given a hint of the life she might have had if Mama and Papa had not died, if she'd had a few pounds to her name. If she'd had a family.

If...if. If wishes were horses, beggars would ride. And there's another cliché. The maid said something and Tess grabbed her handkerchief, blew her nose inelegantly and made herself concentrate. *'Dank u,'* she said and submitted to having her cloak unfastened and her gown unlaced. *'Wat is uw naam?'*

Damnation. Tess was crying, or on the edge of it, he could hear it in her voice. He was not used to feminine tears unless they were accompanied by a tantrum and demands for expensive trinkets. Alex pushed himself away from the wall outside her door and negotiated the ill-lit landing towards his own room. Her ankle probably hurt, she was tired, she was cross, cold and hungry and she wasn't used to men. He shouldn't tease her. In fact, he should probably find some respectable Flemish maid of at least forty summers and employ her to travel with Tess to London while he took another ship.

On the other hand, *he* knew he wouldn't do anything out of line, she would probably feel fine in the morning once she was rested and he was enjoying her company. She was refreshingly different, was Tess. He was used to simpering young ladies who had been schooled in the arts of husband catching until they all appeared to have been pressed from the same gingerbread mould, or to experienced women of the world who would flirt and employ their charms on him, just as he amused himself in return.

Tess was as straightforward as a schoolroom chit, but with maturity and intelligence to go with it. Perhaps she was what all those little butterflies flitting around Almack's in their pastel gowns would have been like if they hadn't been spoiled. Anyway, he enjoyed her company, when she wasn't prosing on about Christmas and families, so he would award himself the gift of escorting her. After all, she would be safer with him than just a maidservant if there were men up to mischief on the way. He knew all about men up to mischief, none better.

And the indulgence of observing innocence at

close quarters was made safe by the fact of who she was. No one was going to descend like the wrath of God announcing that he'd compromised the chit and must now marry her. Marriage was not in his plans, and wouldn't have been, even if he had every intention of infuriating his family. A wife, he had long ago decided, would mean a loss of freedom for no discernible gain, given that mistresses combined sexual expertise with no limitations whatsoever on his lifestyle. One day, perhaps…but not yet, not for a long while.

He grinned at himself for finding virtue in doing what he wanted, sobered at the memory of her wide eyes and almost trembling lip and peered at the next door in search of his chamber. The room numbers were hard to make out in the gloom. Where the devil was his? *Ah, next one.* His foot made contact with something soft, there was a muffled sound somewhere between a mew and a squeak and a weight attached itself to the toe of his right boot.

Alex lifted his foot, hopped to the door, opened it and in the light from several branches of candles examined the small ball of orange fluff attached to the immaculate leather of his Hessian. 'Let go.' No effect. The dratted creature obviously only spoke Flemish. Ignoring the hastily muffled laughter of the maid who was laying out towels on the bed, he hopped to the chair, bent down and attempted to prise off the kitten without leaving scratches that would give his valet hysterics.

'You, I suppose, are a punishment for sending Byfleet on ahead with the heavy luggage.' He held it up by its scruff while it stared cross-eyed at him and mewed pitifully. 'He doubtless has a particular tool for removing kittens from footwear.' He turned to hand the kitten to the maid, but she had gone, the sound of her giggles fading down the corridor. Alex put the animal on the floor and it gazed up at him, tail tip twitching, its pink tongue protruding a fraction beneath its whiskers.

'I suppose you think you are endearing?'

The kitten mewed, then made a leap for the dangling tassel of his Hessian.

'No!' Alex caught it in midair. 'You are a menace. On the other hand, females like cats and they dote on babies of all varieties. I suppose she might take to you. You'll make her smile at any rate.' The maid had left the basket she had brought the towels in. Alex upended it over the kitten, which squeaked piteously. 'Humbug. You are obviously a loss to the acting profession. Here.' He screwed up a scrap of paper, pushed it under the basket and then began to undress to the sounds of shredding and fierce miniature growls.

* * *

Tess straightened her back and lifted her chin with the vague feeling that perfect deportment might compensate for wallowing in wicked luxury. A hot bath instead of a chilly sponge-down, soft towels, fine-milled soap, a fire. Bliss. Even having to put on her drab grey gown again could not entirely suppress the fantasy that she was now a glamorous woman, perfumed, exquisitely gowned and coiffed, an exotic creature that any man would put on a pedestal and worship from afar.

At least *afar* would be safe. Tess knew perfectly well from observation and whispered gossip what men got up to in close quarters given any encouragement, and her fantasy did not quite dare explore that. Although when she contemplated a certain gentleman's shoulders—

The door opened and Alex walked in, carrying, for some reason, a small wicker basket. 'You are very pink,' he remarked after one glance at her face. 'Bath too hot?'

'Er, no, I am sitting too close to the fire, I expect.' *And blushing like a rose, fool that I am.* Apparently it would take more than one luxurious bath to turn her into a lady capable of stealing a man's breath. 'What is in the basket?'

'A very early Christmas present for you.' He

placed it on her lap. 'I thought you needed cheering up.'

He had bought her a hat! Or perhaps a muff, or a pretty shawl. A lady could not accept articles of apparel from a man, she knew that. Tess used to sneak into the back of the room when Mrs Bond had given the lectures in deportment that were intended to prepare the young ladies who had been sent to the convent to finish their education. Tess should not have been there because, obviously, she was not going to be launched into society or have a Season, so she had no need to know all about attracting eligible gentlemen in a ladylike manner. But it had been a pleasant daydream.

Those rules did not apply to her, she decided as her fingers curled around the sharp corners of the basket. *I am not a lady. I am an impoverished...orphan. A bonnet is not going to compromise me.*

The basket seemed to move as she opened it, and then a small ginger ball of fluff scrambled out and latched on to her wrist. Needle claws dug into her skin. 'Ouch! You have given me a *cat*?' Not a hat. Was he drunk?

'A kitten.' Alex came to his knees in front of her, tossed aside the basket and tried to prise the ferocious little beast from her arm. 'Ow! Now she has bitten me.'

Good. '*He* has bitten you. Marmalade cats are usually male.'

'Really?' All she could see of Alex was the top of his head as he bent over her and wrestled with the kitten. The top of his head and those broad shoulders... What was it about that part of a man? Or was it only his? Tess had not reached the age of three and twenty without having admired some good-looking men from afar, and being closeted in a convent did nothing to suppress perfectly natural yearnings, however sinful those might be.

His big hands were gentle, both on her wrist and with the kitten, who was becoming more and more entangled in Tess's cuffs. 'Little wretch,' Alex was muttering. 'Infernal imp. If you were a bit bigger, I'd skin you for glove linings, I swear.' But she could hear the laughter in his voice as he did battle with his minuscule opponent. 'I wonder if tickling will work.'

Abruptly the needles were withdrawn from her wrist, there was a scuffle under her elbow and the marmalade kitten shot out, skidded across the polished boards and perched on the cross-rail of the table.

Alex lost his balance, pitched forward and for an intense, endless, moment her arms were full of his solid torso, his mouth was pressed into the angle of her shoulder and her face was buried in his hair.

He smelt of soap and clean linen, the now familiar citrus cologne and something…simply male? Or simply Alex? His hair was thick and tickled her nose, and when she shifted to support his weight her fingertips found the nape of his neck, bare and curiously vulnerable. His lips moved against her skin, she felt his hot breath and the tension in his body, then he was pushing back, rocking on to his heels, his eyes dark and his expression unreadable.

'Hell's teeth—' Alex huffed out a breath and smiled. It seemed a trifle strained. 'Sorry, I do not mean to swear at you and I certainly did not mean to flatten you. I seem to be making a habit of it.' Whatever he had felt in her arms it was not excitement, delight or any of the other things her fantasies had conjured up with a dream lover. *Naturally.*

'Why did you give me a kitten?' Tess asked, more tartly than she intended.

Alex shrugged and stood up. He had the sense not to carry on apologising, she noted. 'You are miserable. I thought it would cheer you up. Ladies seem to like small baby creatures to coo over.'

'I cannot speak for the *ladies* in your life, my

lord, but I do not *coo*. And do they not prefer diamonds?'

'I am surprised at you, Miss Ellery. What do you know about ladies who prefer diamonds?'

'Why, nothing.' Tess widened her eyes at him innocently. 'But surely your mother or sisters— or your wife, of course—would prefer a gift of jewellery to kittens?' She knew all about kept women from the whispered conversations when she joined the boarders after lights out. They all had brothers or cousins who were sowing their wild oats in London and they exchanged confidences about who were considered the worst rakes, the most exciting but dangerous young men.

'Hmm.' Alex shot her a quizzical look, but she dropped her gaze to her scratched wrist and began to wrap her handkerchief around it. 'I do not buy my sisters or my mother presents, and I am not married.'

'No, I suppose I should have deduced that you were not.' Tess tied a neat knot in the handkerchief and looked up.

'Indeed?' His eyes narrowed and she discovered that relaxed, amiable Lord Weybourn could look very formidable indeed. 'And how did you arrive at that conclusion?'

Chapter Four

'How did I deduce that you were not married?' Tess swallowed. She had strayed into dangerous personal territory and she could only hope he did not think she had been fishing…that she had any ulterior motive. She fought the blush and managed a bright smile. 'It was easy from what you said about Christmas. If you were married, your wife would not allow you to spend it cosily beside the fire with your brandy and books. You would be out visiting your in-laws.'

'So you imagine that if I were to be married I would live under the cat's foot, do you?' The relaxed, rather quizzical smile was back again.

'Not at all. But visits to relatives are what happens in families.'

'I wouldn't know. I am out of practice with them.'

'That is a shame.' She dreamed about being part of a family, a real family, even if there would

be bickering about whose turn it was to entertain the awkward relatives for the holiday season.
It was a long time since she had experienced a
Christmas like the ones she had enthused about
in the carriage. A long time since she had known
a family, and this man had that gift and was apparently happy to throw it away.

'A shame? Not at all.' Alex moved away as the
landlord, followed by a maid, started to bring in
their dinner. 'It is freedom.'

They said no more until they were alone
again. Tess ladled soup into bowls while Alex
shredded roast chicken into a saucer and put it
down for the kitten. 'There you are. Now leave
my boots alone. What are you going to call him?'

*So I'm going to have to keep him, am I? Trust
Alex to give me a kitten, not a bonnet.* 'Noel,'
she decided, adding a saucer of milk beside the
chicken. 'Because he is a Christmas present.'

'You really are an exceedingly sentimental
young woman.' Alex passed her the bread rolls.
'Butter?'

'Thank you. And I am not sentimental, it is
you who are cynical.'

'Why, yes, I cry guilty to that. But what is
wrong with a little healthy cynicism?'

'Isn't it lonely?' Tess ventured. It was ridiculous, this instinct to hug a large, confident male.
Perhaps that was how lust seized you, creeping

up, pretending to be some sort of misguided, and unwanted, compassion.

'What, forgoing gloomy evergreen swags, tuneless carol singers, bickering relatives and enforced jollity? I will enjoy a period of quiet tranquillity and then my friends return to town eager for company.'

Tess set her empty soup bowl to one side and waited in silence while Alex carved the capon. There was something very wrong within his family, obviously, if he did not give his mother and sisters presents and he preferred solitude in London to a festive reunion. She bit her lip and told herself not to probe. The atmosphere of plain speaking between the nuns that prevailed in the convent was not, she suspected, good training for polite conversation in society.

Alex passed her a plate of meat and she reciprocated with the vegetables, racking her brains for what might be suitable small talk. 'I do not remember London at all well.' *Or at all.* 'Is your house in Mayfair?' That was the most fashionable area, she knew.

'Yes, in Half Moon Street, off Piccadilly. Just a small place because I travel so much.'

That appeared to have exhausted that topic. 'Your valet does not travel with you?'

'I sent him on ahead, along with my secretary

and several carriages full of artworks. It was a most successful trip this time.'

Tess thought she detected a modest air of self-congratulation. Was that simply the pleasure at a successful chase or was Alex reliant on the income from his dealing? It seemed a precarious existence for a viscount. Maybe he could not afford lavish celebrations and entertainment at Christmas, she pondered, in which case she had been unforgivably tactless to have pressed him about it. Although he certainly seemed to spend money on his comforts without sign of stinting. Perhaps that was an essential facade, or he ran up large debts.

'Have I dropped gravy on my neckcloth?' he enquired, making her jump. 'Only you have been staring at it for quite a while.'

'I was thinking that your linen is immaculately kept,' Tess admitted. 'Your neckcloths and your shirts.'

Alex choked on a mouthful of wine. 'Do you always say what you think?'

'Certainly not. Should I not have mentioned it?' *But it had been a compliment...*

'Perhaps not comments about gentleman's clothing?' Alex suggested.

'Goodness, yes, of course. The outside world is such a maze, full of pitfalls.'

'Are you nervous of what you will find in

London?' He put the question in such a straight-forward way, without any show of sympathy, yet she sensed he understood just how frightening this was. Mother Superior had certainly shown no such insight, only the expectation that Tess would obediently accept her lot in life despite the blow she had delivered.

'Terrified,' she admitted baldly. 'But there is no point in giving way to it—that will only make it worse. I will soon find my way around my new world. I did with convent life after all.'

Alex watched her over the rim of his goblet, his hazel eyes intelligent, and not, for a change, mocking. 'It must have been a shock to find yourself there. Wine? This is very good.' He re-filled his own glass from the decanter.

'Thank you, but, no. I've hardly ever had it before and I do not think I should start now.' Tess scrutinised her conscience and admitted, 'You are offering me too much temptation as it is.'

The air went still, as though someone had taken a deep breath and not let it out. 'Temptation?' Alex said with care, as he set down his knife and fork.

'Food, servants, luxury,' she explained.

'Ah. The temptations of comfort, you mean.' He picked up his glass again and turned it slowly between long fingers. The heavy signet ring on his left hand caught red highlights from the claret. 'This is not luxury, although it is very civilised. You are tempted by luxury?'

'I do not know. I obviously have no concept of it if this is merely *comfort*.'

'What are your expectations of your new employment then?'

'Simplicity, I have no doubt. After all, I will be somewhere between a poor relation and an upper servant in the scheme of things. Mother Superior explained that very clearly.' *Along with everything else.* 'But I will be in a home and that is the important thing.'

'It is? I would have thought that salary and security would be the highest priority for someone in, forgive me, your position.'

'No, not for me. Being able to earn my own living and to have some security is essential, obviously. But being within a family is what is most important. If I am caring for children that is assured, but an elderly lady or an invalid will have family, too, people who care for them.'

There was movement around her skirts and Noel climbed up, claws pricking her thigh, before he settled down into a small, warm ball on her lap. Tess cupped one hand over him, felt his little belly tight as a drum with chicken and milk. The vibration of his purrs was soothing. 'Warmth. I want warmth.'

The maid came in with an apple tart and

cleared the used dishes. Alex watched in silence while Tess served them both, then took the cream with a murmur of thanks. 'You will miss that from the convent, I suppose. The close community.'

She stared at him, almost confused that he could understand so little. How to explain? Impossible. 'No. I will not miss it.' *Ever. That cool, detached, ruthless honesty that seems not to care how it hurt. 'You are a bastard, Teresa. That is the fact of the matter and you must adjust your expectations accordingly.' Horrid old woman...*

Tess felt stupid with weariness and carefully suppressed worry. The tart was delicious, but it was an effort to eat now. She pushed back her chair and stood, the kitten nestled in one hand. 'I must take Noel out into the yard or we will be dealing with an accident.'

'Give him to me.' Alex stood as she did. 'You can hardly hop out there with your bad ankle and your hands full of kitten.'

'What are you going to do with him?' Tess asked, suspicious. Perhaps he was regretting his impulse to saddle them with a demanding baby animal. She steadied herself with her free hand on the table.

'I will take him out to investigate a nice patch of earth, then I will put down yesterday's news-sheets near the hearth, add a saucer of milk and upend the basket over the top. Will that do?'

'Very well. I hope he will not miss his mother.' She worried as she tipped the kitten into Alex's waiting palm where it snuggled down, obviously feeling safe in the cage of his fingers. *Who could blame it?*

'If he cries I will take him into my bed, give him one of my best silk stockings to play with and ring down to the kitchen for some lightly poached salmon,' Alex assured her, his expression serious.

'I wouldn't want to put you to so much trouble. Perhaps I should have him in my room—' Then she saw the crease at the corner of his mouth and the wicked look in his eyes. Tess drew herself up to her full five feet five inches. 'You, my lord, are unkind to make a jest of me. Thank you for a delightful supper.'

She took a step to sweep past him in a dignified manner, forgot her sore ankle and twisted sideways with a yelp of pain.

'Definitely best not to drink the wine. You are quite unsteady enough as it is.' Alex caught her one-handed.

Her hip was against the table, her nose was buried in the V of his waistcoat and her hands, she discovered, were clenched around his upper arms. All she had to do was let go and straighten up, use the table as a support to make her way to the door. *Let go.* He felt so good, so warm and solid and…expensive. Fine broadcloth coat against her cheek, silk waistcoat against her chin, fine linen under her nose. Tess wanted to burrow into the luxurious softness with all that masculine hardness beneath it. His chest, those biceps, that big hand pressed against her back, the tantalisingly faint edge of musk.

'Tess?' His mouth was close to her ear—he must have bent down. His breath tickled, his lips were so near.

'Yes.' *Whatever the question is—yes.*

From the region of her diaphragm there was an outraged yowl, a wriggle and a small paw reached up and fastened onto the front of Alex's waistcoat.

'You little devil, that's Jermyn Street's best.' He stepped back, the kitten hooked to the fabric.

'I will leave you to deal with your kind present, my lord.' It was not easy to exit with dignity, not hobbling, pink in the face and with ginger hairs clinging to her drab grey skirts, but at least Alex had the more difficult task of extricating tiny claws from intricate, hideously expensive embroidery. 'Goodnight.'

Tess closed the door behind her, then cracked it open again at the sound of muttered curses. She'd wished she knew some swear words: now she did.

* * *

'Did you sleep well?' Alex enquired. His little nun was decidedly wan as they stood at the foot of the gangplank of the *Ramsgate Rose*. Come to think of it, he was feeling a trifle wan himself, what with kitten herding and a night spent fighting inappropriate arousal and an unfamiliar guilty conscience. Although quite what he was feeling guilty about he was not certain. He might be feeling an unexpected physical attraction to an innocent young lady, but he was perfectly well able to resist it. He'd come across enough of them in the past and simply diverted any physical needs to the mistress of the moment. It was just that he had never spent so much time with one of the innocents before.

'Thank you, yes.' Tess was tight-lipped, her knuckles showing white on the handle of the wicker basket. They had eaten in their own rooms that morning and this was the first good look that he'd had of her in broad daylight.

'Nervous?' Alex ventured. A sharp shake of the head. 'Do you get seasick?' *Oh, well done, Tempest, now she's gone green.* If not green, then certainly an unhealthy shade of mushroom.

'I was when we came over to the Continent, but that was years ago. I am sure I will be fine. It is simply a matter of willpower, is it not?'

Not in Alex's experience, not after seeing

any number of strong-willed friends casting up their accounts over a ship's rail. 'Not so much strength of will, more a question of tactics,' he offered, taking her elbow to guide her up the steep planks. 'We stay on deck as much as possible, eat dry bread, drink plenty of mild ale.

'And don't try to read,' he added. Even with his own cast-iron stomach the recollection of trying to study the *Racing Chronicle* in a crowded, overheated cabin brought back unpleasant memories. Grant's appropriately named filly Stormy Waters—by Millpond out of Gale Force—had romped home by a head without any of Alex's guineas on it that week at Newmarket.

Most of the passengers were making for the companionway down to the first- and second-class saloons. Alex steered Tess to a slatted bench under the mainmast and settled her on it with the cat basket, her portmanteau and his boat cloak. 'I'll go and see to my luggage, you set the kitten on anyone who tries to take my seat.'

At least that produced a smile, he thought, intercepting an icy glare from a beak-nosed matron as he made his way to the rail to watch his luggage being swung on board. Obviously she didn't like the look of his face. He shrugged mentally. He hadn't liked hers much, either.

At first it was easy to keep Tess's mind off her stomach. The harbour was full of things to look at, the kitten needed tending to and, even when they cast off, the view was entertaining enough, the water sufficiently sheltered. Alex was rewarded with smiles and the colour in her cheeks and found himself experiencing a warm glow of satisfaction.

The chit would have him as sentimental as she was, he thought with an inward grimace, but if thinking avuncular thoughts was sufficient to stop him recalling that she was a grown woman only a few years younger than he was, then so be it. Tess Ellery was an innocent and he was not, which left him back exactly where he started— as an escort to a respectable lady.

She had fallen silent while he brooded. Alex glanced sideways and saw that the greenish tinge was back, the roses had gone and, from the set of her mouth, the smiles with them. 'It is quite rough, isn't it?' Tess ventured.

Not as rough as it is going to get was the honest answer. 'A little lively, yes,' Alex agreed. 'Tell me about your ideal employment. A cosy old lady or a pair of charming children?' Some must be charming, not that he had ever encountered any for any length of time, other than his own younger siblings. He and Matthew had scrapped and bickered, and his sisters had been, by definition, girls, which meant they were as irritating and mystifying to a youth as females could be. He supposed he'd felt affection for them, he just didn't feel he knew them.

'I do not mind.' Tess showed some signs of animation. 'Just so long as it is a family.'

'Otherwise you will miss the convent life too much?' he suggested as he shook out his boat cloak and put it around her shoulders. Spray was beginning to blow back from the prow. It might be unusual to find himself acting responsibly, but at least he wasn't being treated to the kind of spoiled tantrums his most recent mistress would have thrown under these circumstances. Which, come to think of it, was why she was no longer in his keeping.

'Thank you.' Tess snuggled into the heavy wool with a wriggle that reminded him of that dratted kitten making itself comfortable. 'Miss the convent? Oh, no. It is worse being lonely in a crowd than by yourself, don't you think?'

Alex tried to remember when, if, he had ever felt lonely. Alone, yes, but he was comfortable in his own company and always had been. When he wanted human contact he had a wide social circle; when he needed close friends he had them, the other three members of what the dean of his Oxford college had referred to bitterly as the Four Disgraces.

'I suppose so,' he agreed. 'But in the convent,

all those Sisters must have been like sisters, as it were.'

Tess gave a little shrug as though the cloak had developed uncomfortable creases. 'Friendships are not encouraged. The sisters treat everyone the same and the boarders go home for holidays and they make friends within their own group. They all come from very good families.'

'And you do not?'

'I am an…orphan with no connections. But everyone was very kind,' she added brightly.

Alex was conscious of a sudden and startling urge to box the ears of the unknown Mother Superior. He had no trouble translating *very kind* into *impersonal, remote, efficient, cool*. Tess had been fed, clothed, educated, kept healthy and respectable. Her body and her morals had been cared for; her heart and her happiness, it seemed, could look after themselves if she did not choose to become a nun. Although that was not so very different from a child's upbringing in any aristocratic family. He was sure his mother had loved him, but it had never occurred to her to play with him, let alone talk to him outside the hour before she changed for dinner.

'I'm sure they were kind.' And now she was heading for a life of respectable drudgery, neither a member of a family nor an upper servant. But she seemed to realise already what her position was, even if she had rose-coloured ideas about the joys of family life. It would be no kindness to tell her that and, he supposed, a miracle might happen and she would find herself in the household of her dreams. He looked at the cloudy sky, then fished out his watch. 'Have some bread and ale, best to eat a little, often.'

'Thank you. In a minute.' Tess got up and folded his cloak one-handed, clutching at the mast with the other. 'I need…I mean, I assume that the…'

'Ladies' retiring room?' Alex suggested. 'Yes, that will be down below.' He stood and gave her his arm as far as the entrance to the companionway. 'Can you manage the stairs with your ankle? Sure? Hold on tight as you go.'

The smell hit Tess halfway down the steps. Hot, crowded humanity, food, alcohol, an unpleasantness that she guessed was the ship's bilges and a clear intimation that several people had already been unwell.

Only urgent personal need made her fight her way through the crowded first-class cabin and whisper in the ear of an amiable-looking lady.

'Over there, my dear. Wait a moment.' She dug in her reticule and handed a small object to Tess. 'Take my smelling salts.'

Five minutes later Tess hobbled back, returning the bottle with sincere thanks and a mental resolution to hang on, however long the rest of the voyage proved to be.

She picked her way back to the stairs and encountered a frigid stare from a middle-aged matron in a large bonnet. She looked vaguely familiar. *She probably thinks I am an intruder from second class*, Tess thought, avoiding her eyes. She certainly would have been if it were not for Alex's insistence.

How easily things can change, she thought as she stumbled with the motion and caught hold of a handrail. *If Alex hadn't been in a hurry on icy cobbles I would have caught a boat yesterday, I wouldn't have a sore ankle, I'd have been packed into the second-class cabin feeling ill, I wouldn't own a ginger kitten and my life wouldn't be complicated by proximity to a large, infuriating—and devastatingly attractive—male.*

On the whole, even with the ankle, she rather thought she preferred things this way, an adventure before life became worthy and serious again.

Chapter Five

The infuriating male in question was waiting for her when she emerged into the fresh air on deck. 'Hellish down there, isn't it? Come on back to our roost and be thankful it isn't raining.' Alex sounded quite unconcerned about the effect of salt spray on his expensive greatcoat or the disorder of his wind-ruffled hair now he had abandoned the fight to keep his hat on his head.

'What is it?' he asked once he had her settled again. 'I'm delighted to see that green tinge has gone, but I did not expect to see a smile.'

'You dress so elegantly, but look at you now.' She cocked her head to one side to study him in the waning light. It would be dusk soon. 'You are not the slightest bit concerned about your clothes or your hair. I believe you are a fraud, my lord.'

'I think not. I take my appearance very seriously. One has a reputation to uphold,' Alex drawled, but there was an edge to his voice as he said it and the mischievous tilt to his lips had been replaced by a thin smile.

You are not what you seem, Lord Weybourn, Tess thought as she snuggled back into the embrace of the boat cloak. The problem was, he did not seem to be the same person from one hour to the next. He appeared the indolent man of fashion, yet was close friends with a trio of gentlemen who looked as though they could hold their own in a back-alley fight, and his body was hard as nails under that expensive tailoring. He sneered at her enthusiasm for Christmas, called her sentimental, threatened Noel with a future as glove linings—and yet he was kind to her, had given her a kitten and was infinitely patient with the creature's attacks on his person.

He was also very—sinfully—attractive. She had no business acknowledging that, she knew perfectly well. She was a convent-reared young woman about to begin earning her living. Her antecedents were handicap enough, but any smudge on her reputation would mean an end to her prospects for decent employment, and the sooner she resigned herself to frugal, upright spinsterhood, the better.

'What was that great sigh for?' Alex enquired. 'Hungry?'

'No, I'm just…' *Wishing for the moon. Wishing I had never set eyes on you so my foolish*

*imagination had nothing to work with. The angle
of your jaw, the scent of your skin, the way your
hair curls at the ends with the damp wind... The
impossibility of a man like you in my life.* 'Cold.'

'Me, too.' He began to unbutton his greatcoat.
'Let's get rid of that coal scuttle of a bonnet and
do something about it.' Before she could protest
the thing was off her head and jammed behind
her portmanteau and she was on Alex's knee,
the flaps of his coat around her, the hood of the
cloak over her head.

'Alex! My lord, this is—'

'Outrageous, I know. Stop squeaking, you
sound like Noel.' His voice by her ear was definitely amused. 'This is shocking, but practical.
The choices are go below and be warm but nau-
seous, sit up here in chilly isolation or share body
heat.' She felt his legs move, a most disconcert-
ing effect. 'There, the kitten's basket is under
the cloak, too. Happy?'

'Ecstatic,' she muttered. Alex's snort of amusement was warm on her neck. 'I suppose the sea
crossing isn't this bad in the summer.' She did
her best not to think about the grey sea under
the darkening, slate sky, the tossing white wave
crests, the icy water.

'It can be delightful in the summer,' Alex confirmed. 'Go to sleep.'

'Huh.' It was her turn to snort. She might as
well try to fly.

* * *

Tess woke cramped, warm and confused in a snug cave, huddled against something that moved in a steady rhythm. It took her a while to sort through the sensations. Someone else's skin, a fresh cologne, salt, a seat that shifted slightly beneath her, a world that rocked and heaved. *A ship. A ship and Alex.*

She sat still for a moment, inhaling the essence of warm, sleepy man. Somehow she had got between the flaps of his coat as well as his greatcoat and her cheek rested on skin-warm linen. *Dangerous.* Tess struggled upright on his knees, batting the edges of his greatcoat apart so she could see out.

'Good morning.' Alex pushed her to her feet, keeping one hand on her arm as she staggered. 'There's the English coast ahead.'

'Thank heavens.' She felt sticky and thirsty, but there was land, the sun was struggling out of the clouds low on the horizon and the long night was over.

'Have some ale.' Alex was on his knees beside the luggage. He passed her an open bottle and then scooped a protesting kitten out of its basket. 'Yes, I know. We are cruel and horrible and you want your breakfast. You can share mine.' He poured a little milk into his cupped palm from a stoppered jar and Noel lapped, purring furiously while Alex extracted cold bacon one-handed.

'Do you want to eat or shall we wait until we can find a decent inn?'

'Wait,' Tess said with decision. She felt all right now, but there was no point in tempting fate, especially when she had to venture below decks again. That couldn't wait, but she lingered a moment, hand braced against the mast, looking down on Alex's tousled head as he bent over the kitten. Such a kind man.

'I'll just…' She waved a hand towards the companionway. 'I won't be long.'

It was much worse below decks now after a rough, crowded night. Even the smartest passengers looked haggard and unkempt. The first-class saloon was crowded and difficult to negotiate and, when Tess emerged from the room assigned to ladies, she turned to see if she could make her way forward and up through a different hatch.

She skirted the second-class cabin, an even more unpleasant sight than the first class, and tried a narrow passageway with a glimmer of what looked like daylight at its end. It opened out into a small area at the foot of another set of stairs so she gathered her skirts in one hand, took the handrail with the other and started to climb, one step at a time.

'What we got 'ere, then? You're trespassing into the crews' quarters, sweetheart. Lost, are you? Or looking for some company?'

A sailor, big and burly, was descending the steps towards her. Tess retreated backwards, away from the smell of tar and unwashed man, the big hands, the snaggle-toothed smirk.

'I want to get back on deck. Kindly let me pass.'

'Kindly let me pass.' He mimicked her accent and kept coming. 'I don't take orders from passengers.' His eyes, bright blue in his weather-beaten face, ran over her from head to foot and a sneer appeared on his face as he took in her plain, cheap gown. 'I can show you a good time.' He put out a hand and gave her a push towards a door that was hooked open. Inside she could glimpse a bunk bed.

Tess turned, clumsy with her painful ankle, and he caught her by the shoulder. 'Not so fast, you stuck-up little madam. What the—?'

He broke off as one elegantly gloved hand gripped his shoulder. 'You're in the way, *friend*,' Alex drawled, his tone suggesting they were anything but friends. His gaze swept over Tess and she stopped struggling.

'And something tells me this lady does not welcome your attentions.' His voice was low, almost conversational, his half smile amiable.

'I suggest you remove your hand from the lady.'
Alex was as tall as the sailor, but looked about
half his weight. The man shifted his stance to
face him, his posture becoming subtly more
threatening as he dropped his hand from Tess's
shoulder.

Tess looked at the great meaty hands and the
knife in his belt and swallowed. Then she began
to pull off her gloves. If he attacked Alex, her
only weapons were her nails and her feet. 'This
brute—'

'This little *lady* came looking for some company.' He leered at Tess. 'Then the silly mort got
all uppity on me.'

'And you are?' Alex sounded almost comatose
with boredom as he drew off his right glove and
tossed it to Tess.

'I'm the second mate of this 'ere ship and I
don't take any nonsense, not from bits of skirt
what don't know their place and not from passengers, neither.'

'Hmm. I wasn't intending nonsense,' Alex
remarked, the last word almost a growl. He
bunched his fist and hit the man square on the
jaw. The sailor went down like a felled tree, hit-
ting his head on the handrail as he went.

'Damn.' Alex shook his hand. 'I hope I haven't
killed him. It means such a fuss with the magis-
trates.' He sounded like himself again.

He gave the unconscious man a nudge in the ribs with one booted foot. 'No. He's breathing.' Alex stepped over the sprawled figure and frowned down at Tess. 'Are you all right? Did he do more than touch your shoulder? Because if he did he's going to wake up minus his wedding tackle.'

'No.' She blinked at him, trying to square the carefree figure in front of her with the dangerous-sounding man who had delivered that sledgehammer of a blow. 'You hit him very hard.'

Alex shrugged. 'He deserved it and if you give a lout like that a tap, all you do is make him angry and more dangerous. Now, where can we stow him?'

'In there.' She pointed at the open door.

Alex dragged the unconscious man inside, then hunkered down, felt the sailor's head, rolled back an eyelid and pushed him onto his side. 'He'll do.'

Tess sat down on the bottom step. It felt safer down there, less as though the deck was going to come up and hit her. She wasn't used to violence, and facing that leering creature had made her stomach heave, but Alex…Alex had been wonderful.

She should have been appalled and frightened by the violence, but it had been thrilling, that explosive, focused power. Tess looked at Alex.

Most of the time he was so kind and carefree, but she now knew he was capable of behaving like a storybook hero. She had forgotten those muscles.

'Let that be a lesson to you,' said her hero flatly as he pulled on his glove and shut the cabin door. 'Do not go wandering off, do not speak to strange men.'

Tess felt her warm storybook glow vanishing. 'I didn't *wander off.* And I did not speak to him. He accosted me.'

'You are far too trusting—as bad as that blasted kitten. You let yourself be carried about Ghent by a strange man, you spend the night with four of them…'

'That is totally unfair! You knocked me down, you assured me I'd be safe!'

'Not so much trusting as gullible,' Alex snapped. The image of Sir Galahad wavered and vanished altogether. There were shouts on deck; the motion of the ship changed. 'We're coming into harbour.' Alex climbed up the companionway and looked round. 'We'd better get on deck before someone removes our baggage.'

Tess stalked after him with as much dignity as she could manage with a limp. As they made their way past sailors hauling down sails and securing ropes she saw that the harbour was getting closer by the second. *England. Home? It will be in time*, she reassured herself, trying not to glare resentfully at Alex's back.

He reached their place under the mast and turned, flexing his hand as though reliving that blow. 'I'm sorry, I should not have snapped at you. I was concerned when you did not come back.' When she did not speak, he shrugged. 'Look, I wanted to tear his head off and I couldn't, not once he was unconscious. I was... frustrated.'

'That's a very primitive reaction.' *And an exciting one, I fear.* When Alex simply grunted Tess smothered her smile and picked up Noel's basket. 'There's a good boy. Did you miss your uncle Alex, then?' There was a yowl and a ginger paw shot out of a gap in the weave and fastened on Tess's sleeve. 'Poor little chap, you want to get on dry land, don't you?'

'I have not made any promises about that hellcat,' Alex said. 'Any more nauseating baby talk and *Uncle Alex* will start thinking about glove linings again.'

Tess slanted a look at him that said she knew perfectly well he was bluffing. *Minx.* She seemed to be all right after that unpleasant scene. No vapours, no wilting into his arms at the most inconvenient moment. In fact, he had a strong suspicion that she would have had a go at the man herself, given half a chance. He managed to suppress a grin and checked their bags. 'Don't try to carry the cat basket. Wait there and I'll get someone to fetch the lot.'

He walked to the rail and waited while the ship bumped against the quayside and the gangplank was let down, then he hailed a porter and made his way back across the now-crowded deck to Tess. She was sitting patiently where he had left her, looking around with intelligent interest. Drab, neat, brave little nun, he thought. She looked serious, a little anxious. Then she saw him and her face lit up in a smile that held nothing but pleasure at his return and something inside him went *thud*.

To have a woman smile at him was no novelty. The respectable ones were always glad to welcome him to their homes and their social events; the unrespectable ones greeted his interest with attention that flattered his title and his pocketbook, if nothing else. But Tess's warmth, her lack of artifice, were like an embrace. He was going to miss the chit when he handed her over, and he never thought he'd feel that about a respectable female. Or a lightskirt, come to that.

'Those bags there.' He pointed them out to the porter, who reached for the cat's basket, as well.

'Oh, be careful!' Tess caught it by the handle.

'I'll carry it.' Alex picked it up, gave Tess his

other arm and offered up a silent prayer of thanks that no one he knew was likely to be around to view one of the *ton*'s most stylish gentlemen in a travel-stained condition and escorting a nun and a ginger kitten off a cross-Channel ferry.

'Thank you.' She was still limping a little and he tucked his arm close, trapping her hand against his side to make sure she was safely supported. She was just the right height for him. 'You *are* kind, Alex.'

'No, I am not.' He steadied her down the gangplank, then directed the porter to follow them to the Red Lion. 'I'm too selfish to be kind.'

'Nonsense.' She gave his arm a little shake.

'I am. And too indolent to make the effort to be unkind,' he added.

'I don't believe that, either. Perhaps you don't care enough,' Tess murmured, just loud enough for him to hear.

'Care? Of course I care.'

'What about?' She tipped her head to one side to look up at him. 'Other than your *comfort*?'

'My friends.' He'd die for them if he had to, not that he'd ever say so. A man didn't need to; friends just knew. 'Hunting down art and antiquities.' *My honour.* That was something else you didn't talk about, but it was why he lived as he did now.

'Your family?'

Damn it, she was as persistent as that little cat once she had her claws into something. 'No.' Tess gave a little gasp and it stuck him that he might have been tactless. She had lost her own family and she probably did not need telling about someone who would mourn his mother and his sisters if anything happened to them, but who would be quite happy never to set eyes on his father and brother again.

'Here we are.' The open door of the Red Lion was a welcome sight and a distraction from uncomfortable thoughts. Alex dealt with the landlord, checked that the chaise was waiting, ordered hot water and a meal and paid the porter.

'There's your chamber over there.' He gestured towards the door out of the private parlour as they found themselves alone. 'They'll bring some hot water in a moment.'

Tess ignored the gesture and suggestion. 'I'm so sorry.' She stood in front of him, her face a picture of concern.

'Why? What for?'

'I'm sorry that you are estranged from your family and that I raised the subject. It must be so difficult.'

'Don't be sorry.' He shrugged. 'Certainly it isn't difficult. I just ignore them, they ignore me. They say you choose your friends but not your family, but you can choose how much you see of any of them.' Had home ever really felt like a good place to be? It must have done once, before his father had decided that he was so utterly unsuitable to be his heir, such a disappointment to him.

'But what if something happens to them?'

'It won't.' He took her by the shoulders, turned her around and walked her to her chamber door. 'My father's like an ox.' *Certainly has the sensitivity of one.* 'Now freshen up, then we'll eat and be on our way.'

Chapter Six

'Goodbye and thank you so much for your assistance, my lord. For looking after me and for Noel.' Tess stood outside the gates of the convent, her bag and the cat's basket at her feet. Would a curtsy be appropriate? He was an earl... On the other hand she would probably fall flat on her face, and what she wanted to do was certainly not to make a formal gesture. Not at all. She wanted to wrap her arms around his neck and kiss him on that wicked, mobile, mocking mouth.

She managed her best smile instead. *Chin up, back straight. Fairy-tale adventure over.*

'You'll be all right now?' Alex frowned at the metal-studded black oak of the door. 'This doesn't look like the most hospitable of places.'

'Convents don't, from the outside.' *Or the inside, in my experience.* 'And I will be perfectly fine. Thank you again.' She put out her hand, brisk and impersonal, and when he took it and gave it a quick squeeze she tried not to think about how his arms had felt around her.

Alex pulled the iron chain beside the door. Somewhere far away a bell clanged. 'I'll wait in the carriage until you are safe inside. Goodbye, little nun.' He stooped, dropped a quick kiss on her cheek and strode back to the chaise.

'Yes?' enquired a disembodied voice from behind the darkened grille while Tess was still fighting with a blush.

If she had only moved her head a fraction that brief kiss would have fallen on her lips. It would have been her first kiss. 'Teresa Ellery. Mother Superior is expecting me.'

The door swung open and she stepped inside. It banged closed behind her and she heard the sound of hooves on the cobbles as the chaise moved off. *The prison gates slammed behind the doomed woman... Stop it!* The effect on the imagination of reading Minerva Press novels, smuggled in by the boarders, was exceedingly unwelcome just at the moment.

She limped after the silent nun down a dark, tiled passageway to a door. The sister knocked and opened it, urged Tess in with a gesture, then closed it behind her.

Offices in convents must be all created from the same pattern book. Dark walls, small fireplace, solid, plain desk placed uncompromisingly in the centre of the room with the chair turned with its back to the window and any possibility of a distracting view. It was all safely, depressingly, familiar.

'Miss Ellery. I confess I am most surprised to see you.' From behind the desk Mother Superior studied her, unsmiling. She was thin and pale and Tess thought she looked unwell.

'Good evening, Mother.' She bobbed an awkward curtsy, hampered by her sore ankle. 'I was delayed on my journey—'

'So I understand.' The nun glanced to one side and Tess realised they were not alone. Seated against the wall was a middle-aged woman who looked vaguely familiar. '*Delayed* hardly seems adequate to cover your...activities. Mrs Wolsey was on the same boat as you from Ostend.'

Of course, this is the disapproving matron who glared at me.

'Mrs Wolsey has a niece boarding at the convent. She recognised the clothing of the Ghent house orphans and then she recalled seeing you there.'

It began to dawn on Tess that all was far from well. 'I missed the canal boat. I had a fall and hurt my ankle and—'

'And took up with some rake. Yes, that much is obvious. Your disgraceful behaviour was observed. Embracing in public, sleeping in his arms, going into an inn with him. I am both deeply shocked and exceedingly disappointed, as will be my Sister in Ghent when I write to inform her of this.'

'I can explain, Mother—' Tess began, only to be cut off by a slicing hand gesture from the nun.

'Enough. I have no wish to hear you make things worse by lying to me. I most certainly cannot have a woman of your character in this house. Your antecedents are bad enough, but this behaviour is the limit. You will leave at once.'

'My character? But I have not done anything wrong. I can explain everything that occurred. It was all perfectly innocent. And what about my employment?' The room swam with shifting shadows, flickering candlelight, waves of disapproval. It was unreal; she was bone-weary. Tess wondered vaguely if she was going to faint. Perhaps they would put her to bed if she did and she would wake up in the morning and this would all be a dream.

'You think that I could recommend you to any decent household? There is only one kind of employment for fallen women, my girl, and I suggest you go and seek it forthwith.'

Not a dream. Fight back. 'I did not *do* anything. I am not Lord Weybourn's lover.' Tess tried to stand up straight, find some authority in her voice. 'I had an accident, hurt my ankle. He helped me, just as I said.' *And I do not want to be here, with you, you judgemental old witch*, she thought as a spark of anger burned through the confused fog of misery. *My antecedents, you horrible woman? Two parents who loved each other, who loved me? I am illegitimate—how is that my fault?*

'Lord Weybourn? Hah!' Mrs Wolsey said. 'One knows all about the likes of him. A society rakehell, I have no doubt.'

'How does *one* know this?' Tess enquired. How dare this woman judge Alex? 'I hardly think you would move in the same circles as he does, ma'am.' The tail end of her temper was almost out of her grasp now.

'You insolent girl,' Mother Superior snapped. 'You will leave at once.'

'To cast a sinner out into the night is hardly a very Christian act.' Tess abandoned the effort to be civil, hobbled to the door and, with her hands full of the portmanteau and cat basket, somehow got it open. 'But I would not stay here now if you begged me. Good evening to you both.'

Behind her she heard a small bell ringing violently and the sound of Mrs Wolsey's voice. She seemed to be gibbering with anger. Tess reached the front door before Sister Porteress caught up with her, flung back the bolts, stepped over the threshold and left the door swinging on its hinges. Moments later it slammed behind her with emphatic finality.

'And I hope your righteous indignation keeps you warm at night,' Tess muttered. In front of her was Golden Square, a white-stone statue at its centre glimmering faintly in the light from the lamps set outside the houses. Men muffled up against the dank mist hurried past, a cab rattled over the cobbles on the far side. A clock, quite close, struck nine.

Tess put down her luggage to pull her cuffs over her knuckles. Her mittens felt as though they had been knitted out of thin cotton, not wool, and her toes were already numb.

A woman walked slowly down the side of the square, so Tess picked up her things again and limped across to her. 'Excuse me, can you tell me if there is anywhere near here where I can get lodgings? Only—'

'Get off my patch,' the woman hissed, thrusting her face close to Tess's. She smelt of spirits and strong perfume. 'Unless you want your pretty face marked.'

'No, no, I don't.' Tess backed away and the woman stalked past with a swish of petticoats, only to slow to a hip-swinging saunter before she reached the corner.

'Evening, my dear.' A male voice behind her made her jump. 'Feeling friendly, are you?'

'No, I am not.' Tess whirled round. 'Go away or I'll…set my cat on you.' There was a feline shriek of indignation from the swaying basket and the man stepped aside and walked off hastily.

'Sorry, Noel,' she murmured. 'We can't stay here, it isn't safe.'

Perhaps if she found a hackney carriage the cab driver would take her to a respectable lodging house. There didn't seem to be much alternative. If she stayed on the streets she would either be assaulted, taken by some brothel keeper or she would freeze to death.

Tess slipped her hand though the slit in the side of her skirt seam and touched the reassurance of her purse. Thanks to Alex she still had the stagecoach fare from Margate to London in her pocket and some guilders that she could probably change at a bank in the morning. They were all that stood between her and penury, so she just had to pray that lodgings were cheap.

'What do we have here?' A man's voice, so close behind her, had her spinning round. There were two of them.

'Good evening.' She tried for a confident tone. 'Could you direct me to a cab rank, please?'

'We can direct you, missy, that's for sure.'

There was a chuckle as one of them moved round behind her. 'Right down our street.'

On a cold, dank evening there was nothing quite like the simple pleasure of one's own chair, by one's own fireside with a bottle of best cognac to hand. Alex stretched out stockinged feet to the blaze and swirled the glass under his nose. He had the rest of the evening before him to digest a good meal, catch up on his correspondence, read a book…*worry about Tess in that bleak convent.*

No wide hearth with unlimited coals for her. Certainly no brandy to keep her warm after a plain dinner. He shifted, searching for a comfortable position in a chair that had always been perfect before. She was used to convent life. Just because he'd hate it didn't mean that she wouldn't be feeling as though she was home again.

And surely they'd find her a good position soon, one where she wouldn't be run ragged by some acid-tongued old woman or harassed by her charges' older brothers. Who did he know who might be able to employ her? The problem was, he didn't know any respectable matrons well enough to ask them to employ an unknown young woman without them leaping to conclusions based on his reputation, not Tess's. One look at that oval face with the expressive blue eyes, that soft, vulnerable mouth…

She was none of his business. Alex gave himself a mental shake, sat up and reached for the pile of letters his secretary, William Bland, had produced when he'd gotten home.

'The financial matters are all docketed and on your desk, my lord. There is nothing of pressing importance. There are a few invitations despite the fact that your return date was uncertain.' He'd handed over a stack of gilt-edged cards. 'And these items appear to be of a personal nature and have not been opened.'

By *personal*, William meant he had separated out all those with fancy-coloured wafer seals and any that had a whiff of perfume about them. They could wait, too, Alex decided, dropping them back on to the table beside his glass and picking up the invitations again. *No, no, possibly, definitely, no...*

There was the sound of the knocker. Curious. No one, surely, knew he was home yet? Alex squared off the pile of pasteboard rectangles and listened to the murmur of voices from the hall. Because he was away from home so often he did not trouble to employ a butler, and MacDonald, the younger of the two footmen, was on duty tonight.

The caller was still talking. Alex swung his feet down off the fender and pushed them into his shoes. Damn it, MacDonald was inexperienced, but even he should be able to get rid of unwanted visitors in less time than this. Alex stood up as the door of the study opened.

'A Miss Ellery has called, my lord.' MacDonald, who had a fine set of freckles to go with his red hair, was blushing painfully. 'I have told her that you are not at home, my lord, but she says she will sit on the front step until you are. So I have seated her in the front room because she does seem to be a lady, my lord. Only—'

Hell, what had gone wrong with the confounded female now? Alex told himself he was exasperated, not pleased. Not anxious. Certainly *not* pleased. 'Show her in, MacDonald.'

'Miss Ellery, my lord.' MacDonald opened the door.

There wasn't a female member of staff living in, either, Alex recalled. The scullery maid and Hannah Semple, his cook/housekeeper, came in by the day. Damn, this got stickier the more he thought about—

'Hell's teeth, Tess, what's happened to you?'

She stood there on the threshold swaying slightly, the basket in one hand, her bag clutched in the other. Her hair was half-down and a great bruise was coming up on her left cheek. Tess set down her luggage as he started towards her. 'I'm so sorry to disturb you at this hour, my lord. Only…'

Her eyes rolled up and her legs gave way as he reached her. Alex caught her now-familiar weight in his arms, laid her down on the chaise longue against the wall and bit down hard on the stream of oaths that fought for escape. 'MacDonald, send Byfleet down with the medical kit, tell Phipps to go for Dr Holt and you get round to Mrs Semple's lodgings and tell her I need her back here to spend the night. *Go!*'

Then he sat back on his heels and took a deep breath. His hands, he was shocked to see, were clenched, ready for violence, and he glared at them until they relaxed. She had been walking unsupported, he told himself; she had been able to argue with MacDonald. She couldn't be seriously hurt. He still wanted to punch whoever had done this to her.

'My lord?' Byfleet came in and set down a tray of gauze pads, small bottles and jars on a side table, the familiar kit for when Alex had overdone things in the sparring ring.

'This is Miss Ellery, a young lady I escorted over from Ghent. She should be in a convent in Golden Square, which is where I left her. I have no idea how she got here, nor what happened, but you can see her face.'

The valet, who specialised in never being flustered, bent over the couch. 'A nasty bruise. I would hazard the guess that she has come into violent contact with a brick wall. I suggest we remove her outer clothing, my lord, and that I clean the area before she wakes, in case the skin is broken.'

Between them they got Tess out of her bonnet and cloak, took off her boots, one of them unlaced already over the bandaged ankle.

'No gloves, my lord,' Byfleet observed, and held out Tess's right hand for Alex to see. There was a dark red stain under the nails. 'One concludes that she scratched her assailant.'

'Excellent,' Alex muttered and held the bowl for Byfleet as he began to clean her cheek. 'Is that going to scar?' Bad enough that they'd hurt her, worse if she had to look in the mirror at the results for the rest of her life.

'I doubt it, my lord.' Byfleet took a fresh piece of gauze, covered it in ointment and laid it over the bruise. 'She is young and seems healthy, and the skin is not broken.' He probed with his fingertips. 'Nor is the cheekbone.'

Tess regained consciousness suddenly and woke fighting. One moment she was limp under Byfleet's hands, the next she had lashed out for his face. Alex caught her wrists before she could make contact. 'Hush. Lie still, you are safe with me. This is Byfleet, my valet. He is helping you.'

'Alex.' She let him push her back against the

cushions. 'I'm sorry.' She began to smile at By-fleet, then stopped with a hiss of pain.

'The doctor and my housekeeper are on their way. Are you hurt anywhere other than your face?'

She lay still, obviously thinking about it. 'My ankle—I had to run. And my shoulder. They grabbed me and I swung round and hit a wall.'

There had been more than one of them, and she's a slip of a girl, defenceless. The instinct to punch something became a desire to get his hands around throats and not let go.

Byfleet moved to the foot of the chaise and began to unbandage her ankle. 'The doctor will need to look at this, my lord. It is very swollen.'

'Who was it?' Alex asked, trying to keep the fury out of his voice.

Tess shrugged, winced. 'Goodness knows, just two men who thought they'd found easy prey in the dark.'

'How did you get away?'

'I kneed one of them in the groin and then hit the other round the ear with my bag. Then I ran and there was a hackney. He'd just put down a fare, so I scrambled in.'

'Yes. Of course you did,' Alex said faintly. *A defenceless slip of a girl? Perhaps not.* 'After you had hit one bully, emasculated another and run on a sprained ankle. Why the blazes aren't you tucked up in bed at the convent?' he demanded.

Tess grimaced at his tone. 'Because I am a fallen woman, undoubtedly your mistress and unfit for decent company.'

'What?'

'Someone who knows Mother Superior was on the boat, she recognised me, saw us together on deck. I was asleep on your lap, if you recall.' Tess closed her eyes.

Weariness, pain—or shame? How dare they make her ashamed. She was innocent. He was the one who had been fighting lascivious thoughts for two days and nights...

'Mother Superior threw me out and I was looking for lodgings when this happened. I'm sorry to have bothered you, but afterwards, I didn't think I could manage to find anywhere to stay...' Her voice trailed away. Alex closed his right hand around her wrist and she rallied, opened her eyes. 'I'm sorry to be a nuisance. Tomorrow, when it's light, I'll find somewhere.'

A bustle in the hallway announced the arrival of Dr Holt and Hannah Semple. Alex stayed where he was beside Tess and explained the situation to both of them. It was an effort to keep the fury out of his voice as he described what had happened.

His housekeeper cast her bonnet and cloak

into MacDonald's hands. 'Poor young lady! I'll stay with the doctor.' She flapped her hands at Alex and Byfleet as though they were a couple of stray small boys underfoot.

Alex made himself get up and walk away, out into the hall. It was ridiculous to feel concerned. Tess was in good hands and he obviously couldn't stay in the room while the doctor checked her over. But still it felt wrong to be doing nothing and the only things that occurred to him—descending on the convent and giving the Mother Superior a piece of his mind and then scouring the Soho area for a couple of men with scratched faces—were obviously equally unlikely to prove effective.

Besides, she was not his responsibility. He had delivered her safe and sound. *Oh, for heaven's sake! Of course she's my responsibility. If I hadn't decided it would be amusing to have the company of an innocent for a while, she'd never have been in this fix.*

'I will rouse the kitchen staff to produce some soup, my lord.' Byfleet vanished through the service door. Trust his valet to come up with a helpful suggestion when all he could do was contemplate violence. Alex resisted the urge to kick the hall hatstand and went into the drawing room to wait with what patience he could muster.

Chapter Seven

To Alex's relief Dr Holt emerged after only ten minutes. He accepted a glass of brandy and the offer of a chair by the fire. 'An alarming assault on the young lady, but she is more shaken than hurt. There was no…er…interference with her person, if you understand me.

'The bruised area will heal without a mark, although it will be temporarily painful and disfiguring, I have no doubt. Miss Ellery's ankle appears to have been healing well after a slight sprain, from what she tells me, but the sudden strain has wrenched it again. She must put no weight on it for several days until the swelling subsides. I have left instructions with your housekeeper.'

Alex made a conscious effort and pulled himself together. 'That's a relief. Poor Cousin Teresa.'

'A cousin, is she?' The doctor rolled the brandy glass between his palms, then inhaled the vapours and leaned back with a sigh. 'Excellent cognac, this. I didn't like to encourage her to speak. It will be painful.'

And thank heavens for small mercies. 'She came up to London to visit an old friend on an impulse, I gather, hoping for an introduction as a governess,' Alex improvised. 'Found her away from home, became confused, ended up in the wrong place at definitely the wrong time. I'm a distant connection, but this was the only address she could recall in her distress.' He leaned across to top up the other man's drink. 'I'll send her home in my carriage as soon as she's up to it.'

'Awkward that, you being a bachelor and so on,' Dr Holt remarked. 'Still, who's to know, eh? And you've an excellent housekeeper in Mrs Semple.'

Did he believe that piece of invention about Tess being a cousin? Not that it made much difference whether he did or not, considering that the presence of even a first cousin in the house would be considered shocking when there were only servants to chaperon her.

'Damned awkward,' Alex agreed. He made himself lean back casually, crossed his legs to appear relaxed. 'Still, not much to be done about it at this time of night. Glad I could find you at home and didn't have to call out someone upon whose discretion I cannot rely.' The hint was as much of a threat as he needed to make. No society doctor was going to risk the wrath of a titled patient, especially when the young lady in question was some drably clad poor relation and not a source of fascinating speculation.

There was a tap on the door and Hannah Semple came in and bobbed a curtsy. 'I've made up a bed in the Blue Chamber, my lord. Shall I get MacDonald to carry the young lady up?'

'I'll be with you in a moment, Mrs Semple.' Alex shook hands with the doctor and saw him out, then went back to the study. Tess was lying back against the chaise longue cushions, her face pale, the bruise on her swollen cheek coming out in red-and-purple patches already. 'I'll take you to your room. You'll feel more yourself in the morning.'

'I'm sorry to be such a nuisance,' Tess murmured again.

'Stop talking and stop apologising.' Alex bent and gathered her up. She was too thin, he thought as he went up the stairs, careful not to knock her foot against the wall. Didn't they feed them in those blasted nunneries? No more than a wisp of a thing, for all her height and those distracting curves. He'd knocked her for six in Ghent, injured her, then two louts had set about her, and in between she'd had a tiring sea voyage with another attempted assault and a nasty shock when she reached what should have been a safe haven. Any other female of his acquaintance would be distraught by now.

What the devil am I going to do with you, little nun? he thought, looking down at the tangled mass of hair that obscured her face from him. Tess was safe for tonight, but by this time tomorrow he had to have a plan—and her out of the house.

'Here we are.' The door to the Blue Chamber was ajar and he shouldered his way in to find that a fire was burning cheerfully in the grate and the covers were turned back. Hannah Semple had even thought to provide a stool to go over Tess's ankle to keep off the weight of the blankets.

'What about Noel?' Tess tipped her face up so she could look at him. 'Poor thing, he was so upset with all the banging about.'

'I'll look after Noel,' Alex promised, staring into the deep blue eyes fixed so earnestly on his. For some reason his breathing was all over the place. *Must be out of condition. I'd better get along to Jackson's for some exercise.*

'Oh, thank you.' Her arm tightened around his neck and, before he could react, Tess's soft mouth was pressed to his.

Heaven. Hell. Alex struggled against temptation and felt it slip under his guard like an opponent's rapier entering his side. The smell of Tess was familiar, but the taste of her was like a new drug, a draught of best champagne, a mouthful of summer berries. He ran his tongue along the join of her lips and felt her surprise, swallowed the little gasp as she opened to him. There was innocence in that reaction, but this was no girl, this was a grown woman in his arms, a sensual woman, who was exploring her natural instincts, and the effect, after so many assured and experienced women, was deeply erotic.

His hands tightened on the soft, slender body as he took one long stride towards the bed, his mouth still on hers. Her tumbled hair brushed over the knuckles of his right hand, the one around her shoulders, and it was every bit as soft and tactile as he had imagined. When it was all down it would reach her waist, would brush over his naked chest—

His foot hit the bedpost and jarred him back to the reality of what he was doing, with whom he was doing it. Alex snapped back his head, laid Tess against the pillows and stepped away as though a chain had jerked him.

'I'm sorry. I did not mean to do that.' As an apology that was wrong in so many different ways he couldn't begin to count them. What the devil was the matter with him? He wasn't usually this clumsy.

'It was my fault.' Tess was trembling, her face

flushed, her eyes wide. On her cheek the ugly bruise was deepening. 'I meant to say thank you and I didn't think… I meant to kiss your cheek.'

Of course she had. After the day she'd had now he had taken her innocent gesture and turned it into another assault and she was blaming herself. 'Tess—'

'Thank you, my lord.' Hannah came in, brisk and efficient and smiling, her words a clear dismissal. She had known him since they had both been children and, it was quite clear, she was going to take no nonsense from him now. 'You can leave Miss Ellery to my care.'

'Goodnight, Miss Ellery,' Alex said formally. 'Mrs Semple will look after you excellently, you may be sure.'

'I'll be sleeping in the dressing room, my lord.' Hannah nodded towards the corner of the room. 'With the door open. Then if Miss Ellery becomes alarmed in the night I am close at hand.'

With a poker at the ready for randy males was the unspoken part of that declaration. Alex managed a smile for her and took himself off. He needed brandy. No, he needed to strip off and stand under the stable yard pump, but he was going to have to settle for brandy.

Back in the study he flung himself into his chair and reached for his glass, raised it to his lips as an indignant voice began to yowl from inside the wicker basket by the fireside.

'You took the words right out of my mouth, Noel,' Alex said as he set down his glass untouched and went to open the basket. Somehow, in a matter of moments, he had acquired a cat, a nun, and his well-ordered, pleasantly selfish life was upside down.

Had the housekeeper seen them? Tess fought against the instinct to simply close her eyes and pretend that kiss had never happened. But that would be rude. She met the other woman's gaze and read nothing but concern there.

'I've got a nightgown for you,' Mrs Semple said. 'MacDonald had the sense to tell me why I was being called for, so I thought I had best bring some things, just in case. Let's get you undressed and into bed, shall we, Miss Ellery?'

The other woman was not much older than she was, Tess thought as she did her best to help with the undressing. It seemed young to be a housekeeper. 'Is Mr Semple the butler here?' she asked with a vague notion of making polite conversation under extraordinary circumstances.

'I'm a widow, Miss Ellery. I don't live in as a rule, not with an all-male household, you understand.'

'But you're so young. Oh, I'm sorry, that was tactless, I'm not thinking very straight.'

'And no wonder. My husband was killed at Waterloo. He was one of his old lordship's grooms, but he was set on the army.' She tucked Tess in with a brisk pat at the sheets, then stepped back to survey the room. From her nod she was satisfied with what she saw. 'Now, what can I fetch you to eat, Miss Ellery? A nice little omelette with some bread and butter and a cup of tea?'

'That sounds perfect, thank you.' Tess closed her eyes and leaned back into the comfort of piled pillows. She wondered vaguely if she would be able to stay awake to eat it and drifted off to sleep.

'She's asleep.' Hannah Semple closed the study door behind her and came to take the chair opposite Alex. 'And what have you got there?'

Alex stroked his palm over the kitten's body and smiled as the rumbling purr vibrated through his hand. 'This is Noel. I set out to cross the Channel and come home alone with a pile of artworks, yet ended up with one kitten and a nun who isn't.'

Hannah kicked off her shoes and curled up in the armchair. 'And what, Alex my lad, are you going to do with them?'

'I was hoping you'd be some help with that,

Hannah.' He looked at her with affection, his childhood playmate, the daughter of their estate manager at Tempeston. He'd watched her march off to follow Willie Semple to war when both he and Hannah were just seventeen, and she'd written to him five years later when she returned to England, a widow in search of a place. In front of the other staff she was meticulously formal; alone with him they were simply old friends.

'The kitten goes with Tess—but what the blazes am I to do with her?'

'Take her to bed by the looks of things,' Hannah observed.

Alex winced. 'You saw that? She meant to kiss me goodnight on the cheek. Things slipped. She's an innocent, Hannah, not the kind of girl to take to bed.'

'And you'd know. But I'd agree with that. She's as green as spring grass, you've only to look at her.' That was definitely a verbal cuff round the ear, he thought. 'What's she doing in London?'

Alex recounted the tale. 'I need to find her decent employment,' he concluded. There was no way he could wash his hands of her now.

'You need to get her out of this house,' Hannah countered. 'She can come back with me tomorrow, if she's up to it. I've a spare room in my apartment, nothing fancy, but she'll be safe, comfortable and respectable. *Then* we can find her employment.'

The relief of it caught him by surprise, but not as much as the pang of regret that Tess would be leaving. 'I'll pay for her lodging, of course, and whatever you need to furnish her room. And she'll need kitting out with some respectable clothes. I don't know what that nunnery thought it was doing, sending her out at this time of year in those thin things.'

'I'll see to it. You're used to setting up birds of paradise in bijou little houses, not respectable young women in decent lodgings.' Hannah sorted through the items on the end of her chatelaine and came up with a set of tablets and a pencil. 'Now, what are your plans? Where are you going for Christmas?'

'I'm staying here, as well you know. Will you join me for Christmas dinner, Hannah?'

'I will not, but thank you. I'll be off to my in-laws like every year.' She sighed. 'I wish you'd go home, you stubborn man.'

'I *am* home, and in the absence of a warm invitation to the ancestral mansion, this is exactly where I am staying.' And there'd be the sound of trotters on the roof tiles as the flying pigs landed before that particular invitation arrived.

'It is ten years past, Alex.' Hannah looked

into the fire, not meeting his eyes. 'Surely it is time to forgive?'

'When I forget, then I'll forgive.' Surely she knew it was not just for him? A young man had died that bitter Christmas because of his father's blind prejudice and need to hit out at his elder son.

'You'll have to go back one day. You are the heir.'

'Over his dead body or mine. If it's the latter, then I suppose they'll let me have my shelf in the ancestral vault.' He smiled at her to show that this was something he did not care about, that it no longer hurt.

Hannah simply shook her head. 'You're as pig-headed as the earl is—you know that, don't you?' She cocked her head on one side and regarded him beadily. 'Why not take a wife and produce an heir? That's a revenge for you, Lord Moreland knowing that his precious lump of a younger son won't inherit.'

'And shatter all his fondly held beliefs about me? How unkind that would be. And what if I turn out to be as bad at marriage and fatherhood as he has?'

'Impossible.' Hannah grinned at him, suddenly finding her humour again. 'No one could be that bad. I'm off to bed. I just hope that nice lass doesn't have nightmares, bless her.'

When the door closed behind her with a soft click Alex sat on, stroking the kitten, his unfocused gaze on the sinking embers. Tess would doubtless tell him that Christmas, on top of everything else, was the perfect time for reconciliation and forgiveness. It was a good thing she was leaving. Just for a moment he believed that she might even convince him it was true.

'I ought to say goodbye to Lord Weybourn,' Tess said as Mrs Semple fastened the strap on Noel's basket. 'I must say thank you.'

'You can send him a note.' The housekeeper nodded to MacDonald, who opened the door and carried Tess's bag down to the waiting hackney. 'We need to get you to your new lodgings and work out what shopping you require.'

'I haven't much money,' Tess ventured. She had very definitely been removed from the house, she thought, finding herself wedged into her seat with the cat basket deposited on her lap. *Mrs Semple doesn't approve of me. She saw that kiss and she thinks...*

'His lordship's paying.'

She thinks I've slept with him, that now he's paying me off. 'It will be a loan. Just as soon as I have employment and a wage, I'll repay him.'

Mrs Semple made a noise that might have been agreement, might have been disbelief. She was looking out of the window with a frown that wrinkled her brow.

'Mrs Semple, I am not his mistress. What you saw last night—'

'Was quite innocent on your side. Yes, I know.' The housekeeper turned and smiled.

'On both sides.'

'He's a man, and I doubt he's been an innocent for many years, Miss Ellery. No, don't bristle up, he's no predator on decent girls, he won't be after seducing you. Or worse. But, like I say, he's a man, you are a woman, and a pretty one under all that drab clothing and bandages. If he didn't take an interest I'd be worried about his health.'

A half delighted, half shocked snort of laughter escaped Tess. 'You know Lord Weybourn very well?'

'Since we were both six years old. My father was the Earl of Moreland's estate manager. Alex is a good man. Stubborn as his sire, though.' The frown was back.

'You worry about him, don't you? What has gone so wrong with his family?'

Mrs Semple's mouth twisted into a wry smile. 'That's his story to tell you. But I will tell you something. He is flagellating himself for leaving you somewhere that wasn't safe for you. You'll hurt his pride, if nothing else, if you make a fuss about paying him back for a few bits and pieces and a decent wardrobe of clothes.'

'He wasn't to know there would be any problem,' Tess protested. 'And he certainly wasn't to blame.'

'If he had taken you to the canal boat in time, then none of this would have happened, and I know you should have insisted and so on and so forth, but Alex Tempest has an over-developed sense of responsibility for all that care-nothing air he pretends to have. So are you going to make him miserable or are you going to swallow your pride and enjoy some decent clothes?'

'I'll swallow it,' Tess conceded. *I'm so far down that Primrose Path I may as well face the fact that I'm ruined and have a man buy me clothes. It was a pity I couldn't be ruined properly while I was at it though...* The thought caught her unawares and she scrabbled in her purse for a handkerchief to turn her gasp into a cough. 'But nice clothes aren't suitable for someone looking for a post as a governess.'

'We'll see. I suspect when Lord Weybourn puts his mind to it he'll be able to steer you in the direction of something rather more elevated than your convent might have done.' Mrs Semple's gaze rested on her speculatively. 'Hmm. Yes, I can see all sorts of possibilities.' The frown vanished to be replaced with a mischievous smile. 'Now let's get this kitten settled and make a list of what you need. And call me Hannah, please.'

Chapter Eight

'Where the blazes is my coffee?' Alex enquired of thin air. The dining room was bereft of footmen, his coffee jug had been empty for ten minutes, there was no sign of his toast and the fire needed making up. He should have known it was too good to last, the peace and quiet and order that had reigned for almost a week since the departure of Tess and the kitten.

He wasn't helpless and it wasn't above his dignity to grapple with the coal tongs, but even so… With a sigh he got up, mended the fire and then gave the bell pull a prolonged tug. Silence. The hall, when he looked out, was deserted, the front door still bolted.

It was not unheard of for housebreakers to raid London houses, tie up the staff and make off with the silver with the owners none the wiser for hours. Breakfast time was a strange time to attempt it, though. Feeling slightly melodramatic, Alex retrieved his cane from the hall stand and walked softly to the service door under the stairs.

He was halfway down, wincing as a tread creaked, when he heard a thump and a clatter and took the remaining stairs in three strides. In the kitchen, her back to him, was a strange woman in a green gown. He could see the large bow of the voluminous apron that was wrapped round her, her glossy dark hair was topped by a large white cap; she had a badly bent toasting fork in one hand and the remains of half a dozen slices of bread around her feet.

'You useless male *object*, you!' she announced in tones of loathing.

One glance around the kitchen was enough to show Alex that he was the only male in sight. 'Madam? If you care to tell me who you are I will endeavour to be of rather more utility.'

She whirled round, trampling the bread in the process. 'Oh, no,' Tess said flatly. 'You.'

'Me,' Alex agreed and propped the cane unobtrusively in a corner. So not burglars, but an invasion that was far less easy to deal with. He told himself that the feeling in his chest was the after-effects of stalking burglars. Or dread. 'What are you doing here—other than pulverising bread and breaking the kitchen equipment—and where is Mrs Semple?'

Tess moved into the light. *Oh, my God, her face.* The bruise was now multicoloured and she had the fading remains of a black eye. 'And you are supposed to be resting that ankle.' Alex trampled on the urge to scoop her up and make her lie down. She wouldn't thank him for mentioning the way she looked, and thinking about it would probably only make it hurt more. *And once I have my hands on her I may not be able to let go.*

'Hannah is very much under the weather and in bed with a headache, so I am attempting to make your breakfast. Everything was going well, wasn't it?' She tossed the toasting fork on to the table and frowned at him. 'The ham and eggs? The sausage? The hot rolls? They were all perfect, I thought. Only there is no more coffee and Noel knocked the bread off the table the moment I had sliced it and I bent the toasting fork when I made a dive for it.'

'Where are MacDonald and Phipps? Or Byfleet, come to that?' One end of the table was laid for four breakfasts with plates at various stages from egg smeared to laden but scarcely touched.

'MacDonald has run out for coffee and bread. I sent Phipps to the lodging house with some medicine that Hannah asked for. Byfleet has gone to Jermyn Street, I think. Buying shirts.'

That was delivered in a rapid mutter from a crouched position on the floor where Tess was retrieving broken slices of bread.

'Dare I ask why he needs to buy shirts at this time in the morning?' The nape of her neck was exposed, soft and pale and vulnerable, begging for his lips. Alex took the toasting fork, braced the wrought iron handle against the tabletop and leaned on it. It was more or less straight when he squinted down the length. His brain was more or less in control of his animal instincts, too.

Tess stood up with her hands full of bread, flinched when she found herself facing the prongs and looked round for somewhere to deposit her load.

'On the fire,' Alex suggested.

'Throw food on the fire? I can't do that. Sister Peter says it goes straight to the devil if you do that.'

'And you believe her?'

'Of course not.' Tess found the slop bucket and tossed in the broken slices. 'But it's like not walking under ladders and tossing salt over your shoulder—one just gets into the habit.'

'And I suppose nuns get into more habits than anyone,' Alex observed, as he hitched one hip on to the table. He found a crust and buttered it lavishly. He should be both irritated and worried to find Tess back in the house; instead he felt oddly cheerful. Uncomfortably aroused, but happy.

Tess's harassed expression transformed into a grin. 'That is a terrible pun!' She picked up the toasting fork and studied it. 'My goodness, you are strong.'

'It is all the exercise I get tossing nuns about. Shirts?' Alex prompted, resisting the instinctive grin in return. It would be dangerous to let things get too cosy.

'All your clean ones were in the ironing basket in the scullery this morning, apparently. Then Noel found them.'

'Ah.'

'More *urgh*, actually, although Mr Byfleet expressed himself rather freely on the subject.' She eyed him warily. 'I can make you some tea and bring it up if you like.'

'No, I would not like. I will sit down here and wait to find out why my infallibly efficient housekeeper has run out of coffee, why when she has never, in all the years I've known her, succumbed to a headache, she has taken to her bed with one and why, when she has, she sent you to make my breakfast.'

'Hannah has been spending a lot of time with me, I'm afraid, buying clothes and settling me in. I expect she's been distracted and forgot to check the store cupboard. And she was very quiet yesterday evening. I thought she was simply deep in thought, but perhaps it was the headache.'

'Have you had your breakfast?' Alex found the honey and spread it on another crust.

'I had mine first.' Tess began to gather up the dirty crockery and took it through to the scullery. He noticed her limp had completely vanished. 'Hannah says a scullery maid will come in later.'

'So I believe. Tess, come back here and sit down.' He waited until she returned and sat, neat and composed in her new dress and clean white apron. She folded her hands in her lap and regarded him, head on one side, like an inquisitive bird or a child waiting for an eccentric adult to do something entertaining. Very meek, very attentive. Why did he have the suspicion that she was laughing at him? 'You shouldn't be here.' All he had to do was put his foot down; it should be a simple enough matter.

'I am a perfectly good plain cook.' Now she was managing to look wounded, blast her. 'You would never have known I was here if it wasn't for the problem with the coffee and the toast. Your staff are highly respectable.' Alex opened his mouth, but she sailed on. 'And who is to know?'

'I know.' *And I am finding it decidedly unsettling.* 'You are not a servant.'

'I am acting as your housekeeper. That is at least as respectable as being a governess in many households.'

'Not for an unmarried lady, it isn't.' Alex dusted crumbs off his fingers and stood up. 'I'll call a hackney to take you back to the lodging house.'

The door to the area opened and Phipps came in, gawped when he saw Alex and whipped off his hat. 'Good morning, my lord.'

'Good morning. And how is Mrs Semple's headache?'

'Not good, my lord. I didn't see her, only Mrs Green, the lodging house keeper. She says it's the influenza and two more of her lady lodgers have it.'

'I must go and nurse Hannah.' Tess was on her feet, pulling off cap and apron.

'No, miss. Mrs Green said that she and her girl will look after the ladies and that Mrs Semple said you weren't to go back and risk catching it. She's had your bags packed and I've brought them here with me.'

'Absolutely not. You cannot stay here,' Alex began as the door opened and a thin woman came in.

'Morning, all. I'll get the copper on the boil and— Oh!' She stopped dead at the sight of Alex and Tess. 'Where's Mrs Semple? I'm Nelly 'Odgkins, come to do the weekly wash.'

'She's sick,' Tess said before Alex could intervene. 'Can you carry on as usual, please, Mrs Hodgkins?'

'Right you are, mum.'

'Miss Ellery—'

'I've got the coffee and three loaves, Miss Ellery... My lord?' MacDonald grounded the shopping baskets and stared at Alex as a scrap of a girl slid into the room through the door behind him.

'Mornin', Mr MacDonald, Mr Phipps. Ooh...' She stopped and stared, wide-eyed.

'You must be Annie. Off you go to the scullery and start on the breakfast dishes,' Tess said firmly.

Alex strode round to shut the door in the hope of stemming the flood of incomers and, hopefully, the evil draught of cold December air.

His shove met with resistance against a brawny shoulder and a head covered with a battered low-crowned hat appeared round the door. 'Morning, all. I've got some fine mutton cuts here, Mrs Semple. Er?'

'Good morning.' Tess waved the butcher inside, then turned to Alex. 'You need a housekeeper, my lord,' she said, low voiced, then clapped her hands for attention. 'Annie, come out here for a moment, please. Mrs Semple is down with the influenza, I'm afraid, and I am Mi—*Mrs*

Ellery, the housekeeper in her absence. Phipps, please get a kettle boiling for his lordship's coffee. MacDonald, pass me the loaf, then you can start making the toast. I'll be with you directly, Mr—?'

'Burford, mum. Don't you worry yourself, I'll be fine over here till you're all sorted.' He took himself over to a bench in the corner, grounded his basket with a grunt and sat down, hands on knees, with every appearance of settling down to watch a play, much to Alex's irritation.

'I'll see you in the study after breakfast, *Mrs Ellery*,' Alex said. Any trace of pleasure at being alone with Tess had vanished. Who, he thought bitterly, was going to appear next? The parish constable? He scooped up the kitten, who had bounced out in pursuit of the butcher's trailing bootlaces, and retreated upstairs with as much dignity as he could muster.

'Routed from my own kitchen, Noel. Now what am I going to do with her?'

Noel yowled and bit Alex's thumb.

A fresh pot of coffee, hot toast and the last pot of what Phipps assured her was Mrs Semple's best strawberry conserve would surely soothe a troubled male breast at breakfast time, Tess thought. Halfway up the back stairs she remembered her apron and went down again to take it off and straighten her cap, which showed a tendency to slide on her tightly coiled hair.

'You look the part, Miss…er…Mrs Ellery,' MacDonald said with an encouraging smile that only confirmed that what she *looked* was in need of encouragement.

At Alex's door she knocked. *I must stop calling him that, even in my head.*

'Come.' It was hardly welcoming. Perhaps the jam had been a mistake, too obvious a peace offering.

Tess walked in, wishing this was rather less like being summoned to Mother Superior's study and that she could manage a confident smile. But that still made her cheek ache. 'My lord.' She bobbed a curtsy, folded her hands and waited.

'For goodness' sake, Tess, sit down and stop play-acting.' He was using the point of a paperknife to flip over a pile of gilt-edged cards on his desk.

'I am not. I am endeavouring to behave like a proper housekeeper in front of your staff and any visitors.'

'You cannot be my housekeeper. You cannot stay here.' Alex jammed the paperknife into a jar of pens. 'You are most certainly not going to come into contact with any visitors.'

'I am perfectly competent and they taught us

housekeeping and plain cookery at the convent. This is a small house. I can manage very well.'

'That is not what I mean.' His gaze, those hazel eyes shadowed, was on her mouth, his own lips were set in a hard line.

They had felt firm, yet soft on hers. Strong, yet questioning. They had asked questions she… Tess closed her eyes and Alex made a sound, a sudden sharp inhalation of breath. She blinked and he was still staring at her.

'It's about that kiss, isn't it? You think I was throwing myself at you.' The words were out before she could censor them. She had been so certain he knew it had been a mistake, so certain that he had disregarded it with an ease she could only dream of managing herself.

'No. Yes. Partly.' Alex had his elbows on the arms of his chair. Now he clasped his hands together as though in prayer and rested his mouth against his knuckles, apparently finding something interesting on the surface of the desk. When he dropped his hands and looked up she could see neither amusement nor desire in his expression. 'You should not be in a bachelor household, it is as simple as that. I am not in the habit of pouncing on my female staff and, although I can find explanations for what happened the other night, they are not excuses, not acceptable ones.'

He frowned. 'I can't imagine what Hannah was thinking of, sending you here. She was as set on moving you out as I was.'

'She is ill and perhaps she'd had long enough to think about it and know I was perfectly safe here.' Tess stopped herself pleating the fine wool of her skirt between her fingers. 'I think she was more worried about you than about me, at first.'

'About me?' That at least wiped the brooding expression off his face. Alex sat up and stared at her.

'I suspect she thought I was attempting to seduce and entrap you,' Tess said primly. It was ludicrous, of course.

Alex threw his head back and laughed, a crack of sheer amusement. 'You?'

'I know. Ridiculous, isn't it?' *Of course it is.* So why did his laughter twist inside her with a stab of what was perilously close to shame? She managed a little cackle of her own, just to show how funny it was.

'She was obviously sickening for the influenza even then,' Alex said, with a shake of his head for the preposterousness of it.

Yes, *preposterous* was the word. Teresa Ellery, as ignorant as Noel was about the big wide world, battered and bruised, dressed as a convent orphan, might arouse Lord Weybourn's chivalrous instincts, but not his amorous ones.

That kiss, the one she'd built all those castles in the air about in her dreams and daydreams, was nothing more than the instinctive reaction of any man to a woman in his arms foolishly pressing her lips to his.

'Anyway, I cannot go back to the lodgings. As well as the risk of catching the influenza myself, the landlady is quite busy enough as it is with sick nursing,' Tess said. 'If I am not seen above stairs when you have visitors, who is to know?'

He scrubbed one hand across his face, an oddly clumsy gesture for such an elegant man. 'I suppose I can hardly send you off to an hotel. There's a bedchamber above mine you could use,' he said with evident reluctance. 'None of the male staff sleep on that floor and it has a door that locks. We must get a maid for you, one to sleep in the dressing room.' He reached out and pulled the bell, then fell silent until MacDonald came in. 'Take Mrs Ellery to our usual domestic agency and assist her in finding a suitable lady's maid.'

'A *lady's* maid?'

'You are a lady, aren't you?' One brow lifted.

'Well, yes.' *No, I'm not.* 'But a housemaid would do.'

'We have two housemaids. They come in three times a week to do the cleaning. We do not require any more.'

'Yes, my lord.' To wrangle in front of the staff was impossible. Tess stood up, dropped a neat curtsy and waited for the footman to open the door for her. 'We will go immediately, if you have finished your current tasks, MacDonald.'

'It's a very good agency,' MacDonald confided as they stood outside the door with its neat brass plate. 'His lordship gets all his staff here.'

Twinford and Musgrave Domestic Agency. Est. 1790. It certainly sounded established and efficient, Tess told herself. They would guide her, which was a good thing, because she had only the vaguest idea of the details of a lady's maid's duties.

MacDonald opened the door for her. 'Mrs Ellery from Lord Weybourn's establishment, requiring a lady's maid,' he informed the man at the desk, who rose after a rapid assessment of Tess's gown, pelisse and muff. She was grateful for Hannah's insistence on good-quality clothes or presumably she would have been directed to join the queue of applicants lined up on the far side of the hall herself.

'Certainly, madam. Would you care to step through to the office? My assistant will discuss your requirements and review the available—'

He was interrupted by a baby's wailing cry. The door opposite opened and a young woman backed out, clutching the child to her breast. 'But, Mr Twinford, I can turn my hand to anything. I'll wash, I can sew, scrub—'

She was of medium height, neatly and respectably dressed, although not warmly enough for the weather, Tess thought, casting an anxious look at the baby who was swathed in what seemed to be a cut-down pelisse.

'You've turned your *hand* to more than domestic duties, my girl.' The voice from the office sounded outraged. 'How can you have the gall to expect an agency with our reputation to recommend a fallen woman to a respectable household?'

'But, Mr Twinford, I never...' The woman was pale, thin and, to Tess's eyes, quite desperate.

'Out!' The door slammed in her face and she stumbled back.

'I do beg your pardon, Mrs Ellery. Shocking!' The clerk moved round the side of the desk. 'Now, look here, you—'

'Stop it. You are frightening the baby.' Tess stepped between them. 'What is your name?'

'Dorcas White, ma'am.' Her voice was quiet, genteel, exhausted. Close up, Tess could see how neatly her clothes had been mended, how carefully the baby's improvised coverings had been constructed.

'Are you a lady's maid, Dorcas?'

'I was, ma'am. Once.'

'Come with me.' She turned to the spluttering clerk, who was trying to get past her to take Dorcas's arm. 'Will you please stop pushing? We are leaving.' She guided the unresisting woman out to the street and into the waiting carriage. 'There, now at least we have some peace and we are out of the wind. You say you are a lady's maid and you are looking for a position?'

'I was, but I can't be one now, not with Daisy here. I'll do anything, work at anything, but I'll not give her up to the parish.'

'Certainly not.' All that was visible of the baby was a button nose and one waving fist. 'Where is her father?'

Dorcas went even whiter. 'He…he threw me out when I started to show.'

'What, you mean he was your employer?' A nod. 'Did he force you?' Another nod. 'And his wife said nothing?'

'He told her I'd… He said I had…'

She would get the full story later when the poor woman was less distressed. 'Well, we won't worry about that now. I need a lady's maid. You can come and work for me. Or for Lord Weybourn, rather.'

'You are Lady Weybourn?' Dorcas was staring at her as though she could not believe what she was hearing.

'Me?' Tess steadied her voice. 'No, I am his new housekeeper, but it is an all-male household and I need a maid for appearances, you understand.' She looked at the thin, careworn face, the chapped hands gently cradling the baby, the look of desperate courage in the dark eyes. 'It would be more like a companion's post, really. Would you like the position?'

'Oh, yes, ma'am. Oh, yes, please.' And Dorcas burst into tears.

Chapter Nine

'Where is Miss...*Mrs* Ellery?' After the chaos of the morning, the previous day had passed uneventfully. Alex had dealt with his paperwork, visited some art dealers and then gone to his club, where he had dined and spent the evening catching up with acquaintances and what gossip there was in London in early December. A good day in the end, he concluded, one mercifully free from emotion and women.

He'd had some vague thought of calling on Mrs Hobhouse, a particularly friendly young widow. When he had last been in London she had sought him out, had been insistent that only Lord Weybourn with his legendary good taste could advise her on the paintings she should hang in her newly decorated bedchamber. It was so important to get the right *mood* in a *bedchamber*, wasn't it? It had impressed Alex that she could get quite so much sensual innuendo into one word.

At the time he had considered assisting her with viewing some likely works of art from a variety of locations, including her bed, and yet somehow, when it came to the point of setting out for Bruton Street, he found he'd lost interest.

This morning's breakfast had been excellent. Alex folded his newspaper and listened. Everything was suspiciously calm. It was surely too much to hope that Hannah had made a miraculous recovery and was back at her post.

'Mrs Ellery is in the kitchen, my lord.' Phipps balanced the silver salver with its load of letters and dipped it so Alex could see how much post there was. 'Shall I put your correspondence in the study, my lord? Mr Bland said to tell you that he has gone to the stationer's shop and will be back directly.'

'Very well.' Alex waved a vague hand in the direction of the door. His secretary could make a start on it when he got back; he wasn't ready to concentrate on business yet.

So Tess had spent the night upstairs in the bedchamber above his own, had she? Alex picked up the paper, stared at the Parliamentary report for a while. Hot air, the lot of it. The foreign news didn't make much more sense.

Spain, West Indies, the Hamburg mails…

He hadn't heard so much as a footstep on the boards overhead, but then she'd doubtless been fast asleep when he'd arrived home and had risen at least an hour before he was awake. So far, so good. The heavens hadn't fallen and he had obviously been worrying about nothing.

Alex tossed down the *Times*. He was woolgathering, which was what came of having his peace and quiet interrupted. What he needed to do was turn his mind to the possibilities for offloading a collection of rather garish French ormolu furniture that he was regretting buying. He made his way down the hall towards the study, then stopped dead when an alien noise, a wail, wavered through the quiet.

A baby was crying. Alex turned back towards the front door. Surely no desperate mother had left her offspring on his blameless front step? Well, to be honest it was hardly blameless, but he had made damn sure he left no by-blows in his wake.

The noise grew softer. He walked back. Louder—and it was coming from the basement. Then it ceased, leaving an almost visible question mark hanging in the silence.

When he eased open the kitchen door it was on to a domestic scene that would have gladdened the palette of some fashionable, if sentimental, genre painter. Tess was sitting at the table with a pile of account books in front of her. Byfleet was standing by the fireside, polishing Alex's newest pair of boots, while Annie sat at the far end of the table, peeling potatoes.

And in a rocking chair opposite Byfleet was a woman nursing a baby while Noel chased a ball of paper around her feet. The stranger was crooning a lullaby and Alex was instantly back to the nursery, his breath tight in his chest as though arms were holding him tightly.

A family. They look like a family sitting there. Alex let out his breath and all the heads turned in his direction except for the baby, who was latched firmly on to its mother's breast. The woman whipped her shawl around it and stared at him with such alarm on her face that he might as well have been brandishing a poker.

'My lord.' Tess sounded perfectly composed, which was more than he felt, damn it. 'Did you ring? I'm afraid we didn't hear.'

There was a pain in his chest from holding his breath and he rubbed at his breastbone. 'No. I did not ring. I crossed the hall and I heard a child crying.'

The stranger fumbled her bodice together, got to her feet and laid the baby on the chair. 'My lord.' She dropped a curtsy and he noticed how pin neat she was, how thin. 'I am very sorry you

were disturbed, my lord. It won't happen again.'
Her voice was soft and her eyes were terrified.

'Babies cry,' he said with a shrug. Admittedly,
they weren't normally to be found doing so in the
kitchen of a Mayfair bachelor household. Himself, he'd been brought up in a nursery so remote
from the floors his parents occupied that a full
military band could have played there without
being heard and he'd had his earliest lessons in
a schoolroom equally distant where no parent
would have thought of dropping by. 'I was not
disturbed, merely curious.'

'This is Dorcas White, my lord.' Tess moved
over to stand beside the woman. Did she think
she needed to protect her from him? 'She is my
new lady's maid.'

'And the baby?'

'Is mine, my lord.' Dorcas looked ready to
faint.

Alex looked down at her hands, clutched together in front of her. No ring. He met Tess's
blue gaze and read a steely defiance in it that
took him aback.

'The baby's name is Daisy, my lord.'

'Thank you, Mrs Ellery. I am aware that babies are people, too.' She coloured up. Annoyance, he supposed. That made two of them. 'So
we have acquired another stray, have we? I suppose I must be thankful that the baby is already

with us or I have no doubt I would be expected to house oxen and a donkey in my stables come Christmastide.'

Tess drew in a deep breath through her nose and narrowed her eyes at him. 'I suspect that verges on blasphemy, my lord. Dorcas is very well qualified as a lady's maid.'

'And comes with excellent references, no doubt?' It came out sharply and Tess's chin jutted. So she didn't like his tone? There was still an ache in his chest that he didn't understand, memories of childhood he thought he had locked away in his head. His tight, small, bachelor household had become full of women, virtually a crèche. He was entitled to snap—he was amazed he wasn't shouting.

'Might we have a word, my lord?' Tess enquired with a sweet, false smile. 'Upstairs?'

He held the door for her and followed her stiff back along to the study. Tess did not wait for him to get behind the barrier of his desk and sit down before she attacked. 'No, Dorcas White does not have references. A man who forces himself on a servant and then tells his wife that *the slut* flaunted herself at him when he'd had a few drinks, that she'd been *asking for it*, is not someone who writes a reference for his victim.'

'Are you certain?' Even as he said it he felt ashamed of himself. Those thin, desperate hands, those wounded eyes, the way she had held her child… No, that was not some little hussy who had taken advantage of Tess's good nature. 'Yes, of course you are, and I can see you are right,' he said before the angry rebuttal was out of her mouth. 'What does she need for the child? Buy it for her, whatever it is.'

If he had been looking for a reward, which he hadn't, he told himself, he would have got it in the smile that transformed Tess's face.

'Who is the father?' He suppressed his own answering smile. This was not a laughing matter.

'I have no idea. I didn't ask her. Why?'

'Because he needs dealing with,' Alex said, startling himself. What was he, some knight errant, dispensing justice for wronged damsels? 'Still, I suppose you'll never get the name out of her and I don't want her worried that the swine will find out where she is.'

'Oh, thank you,' Tess said and clutched his hand. 'Thank you for understanding. I knew you were Sir Lancelot really, however much you grumbled about Noel and things.'

Her hand was small and warm and strong in his and he closed his fingers around it, even as he said, in tones of loathing, '*Sir Lancelot?* Do I look like some confounded idiot clanking around in armour? And besides, he was a decidedly dubious type—making love to his king's wife like that.'

'I thought when you hit that sailor that you were a storybook knight and then you were grumpy with me so I changed my mind. But it is all a front, the grumpiness, isn't it?' Her eyes were dancing; it seemed she was as amused by her nonsense as he was.

His meek little nun was teasing him, he realised, and this time could not suppress the answering smile. Alarm bells were ringing even as he lifted her hand and pressed the back of it against his cheek, her pulse rioting under his fingers. *Charm and sweetness. You cannot let yourself enjoy them, not for your sake and definitely not for hers.*

'Yes,' Alex agreed. 'It is all a front, but behind it is not your *preux chevalier*, there's a real, live, flawed man with many masks and many, many faults.' He moved her hand so he could nip lightly at her fingertips in warning and felt, more than heard, her shuddering indrawn breath. 'A man who is hypocrite enough to despise the father of the child down there and yet who cannot forget the feel of your mouth under his, your body in his arms.'

Tess became still, her eyes wide and questioning. *She's an innocent*, he told himself. *Even if she can deal with illegitimate children and speak*

*frankly about what has happened to Dorcas. She
needs warning, scaring a little, even.*

He loosened his grip on her fingers and her
hand slid up to cup his cheek. She was not wary,
not at all alarmed by him. The touch was not
sexual, not even sensual. It was intended, he realised with something like shock, to comfort.
When was the last time anyone had touched him
like that?

'You are very hard on yourself, aren't you,
Alex?' Tess murmured. 'You aren't a saint, you
certainly aren't a monk, so why do you expect
it of yourself?'

'I am a gentleman,' he said, his voice harsher
than he'd intended. 'The least I can do is try to
behave like one around decent women.'

'You are trying. Very hard, I think.' She
cocked her head to one side with that questioning look he was learning to beware of. 'I may be
a virgin, and that may have been my first kiss,
but I am quite capable of recognising sensual
attraction when I experience it. There is something between us, isn't there?'

Alex found himself incapable of answering
her as she wrestled so honestly with things no
young lady was supposed to think about, let
alone articulate.

'I am quite capable of saying *no*, at least, I am
when I haven't been hit on the head and fright-

ened half out of my wits,' Tess said decisively. She lowered her hand and stepped away. 'We got carried away, we both did. But the onus should not be all on you to be prudent.'

'Prudent?' Alex found he had to move away from her. If it was a retreat, he didn't care, and the big desk was a reassuringly solid barrier. 'Naturally it is down to me to behave properly.'

'If I was the sort of young woman who has a hope of marrying, then of course it is,' she agreed. Tess perched on the arm of a chair and he wondered if, for all her calmness, her legs were a bit shaky. 'But I'm not, am I? So I need to make decisions based on different criteria, such as, do I want to be your mistress? What would make us happiest, while it lasted?'

'Tess, stop this! You cannot discuss being my mistress, and happiness is the last thing we should be considering.'

'Is it?' She frowned at him, her brow wrinkled. 'But what is the point of a…liaison if it doesn't make people happy? What is the point of life, come to that?'

'Frankly? I do not know about the meaning of life. I just get on with living it as best I can. But a liaison? It is about sex on one side and financial gain on the other,' Alex snapped. He drove his fingers through his hair and tried to get his feet back on solid ground. This was like finding oneself knee-deep in fast-flowing water when one thought all one was doing was having a stroll beside a stream. 'It is commerce. It is not something you should even think about.'

Her expression seemed to indicate that she was thinking about it, very carefully, very seriously.

Alex fought the urge to run his finger around a neckcloth that seemed far too tight. He coped with sophisticated ladies, wanton widows, expensive high-fliers, all without turning a hair. Why the devil was he finding it hard to deal with one outspoken innocent? 'Look, Tess, men and women find themselves physically attracted all the time. We have to deal with it like everyone else does. You just pretend it isn't happening.'

She nodded. 'I can see that is usually best. But this isn't making you happy, is it?'

'It is making me damnably confused, if you must know.' Did she think he expected sexual favours as a payment for giving her shelter? Did she think that in return for shelter she had a duty to make him *happy*, whatever she meant by that? She certainly wasn't casting out lures or flirting, although he doubted she knew how. 'But that is beside the point. You are a lovely young woman, Tess. I would have to be a plank of wood not to be attracted to you.'

That made her smile, at least. 'Thank you.

It wasn't that I had decided we should have an *affaire*, you understand. But I don't want you feeling guilty all the time if things happen. I expect I will learn not to notice when we touch by accident, or when I meet your eyes and I seem to read things in them.'

She could read him like a book, he was sure, even if she didn't understand some of the long words. 'It will do me no harm to feel guilty occasionally.' Alex made his tone lighter. 'We'll not speak of this again.' *Who do I think I am deceiving?* 'Now, about Dorcas—make certain she understand she's safe here. I'm not going to throw her out if the baby cries. I won't have her hiding it away for fear of that. A baby should be with its mother.'

'Yes, of course. Thank you, I will reassure her.' Tess stood up. 'Thank you for letting me stay. I know it is disrupting things, even if we leave aside…you know. But I work hard and I'll earn my keep, I promise.'

'You don't have to work at all.' Alex put as much bored languor into his tone as he could. 'You could stay in your room with Dorcas to chaperon you until Hannah is well again or we find you a post. As you are well aware, if I'd delivered you where you asked, on time, none of this would have occurred.'

'I have my pride, too, you know.' Tess bobbed

her infuriatingly proper curtsy and went out as though they had discussed nothing more momentous than a minor staffing problem.

Alex sat down took a deep breath and pulled his pile of correspondence towards him. Tess had been brought up to tackle issues head-on and without hypocrisy, it seemed. But hypocrisy was one of society's main safeguards, and without it she was vulnerable. So was he. The widow who wanted to buy pictures was looking increasingly tempting. It was too long since he had been with a woman; that was all it was, this need to hold Tess, to take the pins from her hair, the clothes from her body, to lie down with her and…

She had shocked Alex, Tess realised. Seeing the baby had upset him for some reason, and it wasn't the fact that little Daisy's crying had annoyed him. He was angry with Dorcas's employer, which was understandable, for any decent person would have been, but there was something else, something deeper in his reaction.

And that moment when she had taken his hand had been…startling. She'd had no intention of flirting and she had no idea how to. She certainly hadn't thought of trying to provoke him into kissing her again, but the energy that had flowed between their joined fingers still sparkled along her veins. It had seemed to her important to try to understand where they stood, to tell him how she felt. But that had been a mistake. He had not wanted that kind of honesty from her. And she couldn't simply take his protection, his money, and do nothing in return. She expected to work for her living, and she owed it to Hannah to keep her from worrying about the household while she was ill.

When Tess got to her feet and went into the kitchen it was empty except for Dorcas, who was hemming handkerchiefs with the baby fast asleep in a makeshift crib by her side. She looked up. 'Is he…is his lordship very angry?'

'Not at all, just startled. He says we are to buy whatever Daisy needs and you are not to be afraid that he will be annoyed if he hears her crying.' Tess sat down on the other side of the fireplace. 'Lord Weybourn is simply not used to having women about the house, that is all.'

Chapter Ten

'Are you sure you wouldn't rather come back to Half Moon Street? I could make up the room across the passage from mine, and now I have Dorcas with me we can nurse you easily.'

'That is thoughtful of you, Tess.' Hannah Semple groped for a handkerchief as she began to cough. 'Oh, drat and blast this! We sound like a colony of seals I once saw on the coast.' From the room opposite came the echo of the same sound. 'But I'm better here in my own home with my things around me. And no one is very sick now, just laid low with this wretched chesty cough, so Mrs Green and her girls are managing to look after us easily enough.'

She curled her fingers around the cup of tea that Tess handed to her and sipped, her nose glowing pinkly though the steam. 'Besides anything else, I'd drive Lord Weybourn mad with the coughing.'

'He doesn't seem to be disturbed by the baby.'
Tess poured herself a cup and settled back in the
fireside chair. 'And she cries a lot, bless her.'

'I find it hard to imagine, Alex taking in a
baby.'

'You thought he would send her away? He
wasn't pleased, not at first, but that just was the
surprise, I think.'

'Oh, I don't mean he would send them off into
the night. But I'd have expected him to find her
lodgings or something, not have them live in.'
Hannah sneezed, then sat regarding Tess over the
top of the handkerchief. 'You've turned his house
upside down with your strays by the sound of
it. I'm amazed he hasn't reacted more strongly.'
She sat up against the pillows. 'Has he had any
visitors?'

'No, he goes out a lot and there have been
endless invitations, but there've been no call-
ers. I don't think he's issuing invitations with
me there.'

'Perhaps that's why he's being so tolerant.
After all, kittens and babies underfoot wouldn't
do much for his carefully maintained image.'

'What image?'

'Elegant, imperturbable, languid and cultivated. A fastidious pink of the *ton* on the surface.
He's a serious sportsman on the quiet, but unless

you saw him after a hard round at Gentleman Jackson's you'd be forgiven for not noticing.'

Tess laughed. 'That's just a mask. Underneath he's funny and very kind. And the sparring explains the muscles.'

'Hmm. You've noticed them, have you?' Hannah gave her an old-fashioned look. 'He's thought about nothing but himself for ten years.' Despite the thickness of her voice she sounded remarkably tart.

'But he *is* kind.'

'I didn't say he wasn't. He's charming, he treats people well—and he organises his life so no one gets behind the mask or disturbs his well-ordered life.'

Tess kicked off her shoes and curled up in the chair. Outside the rain was threatening to turn into sleet and the wind howled in the chimney, making the flames dance and reminding them that December had most definitely arrived. Inside all was snug and comfortable, she had thought. Now Hannah was making her uneasy.

'His mistresses must,' she suggested with the sensation of jabbing her tongue against a sore tooth. 'Get close, I mean.'

'I very much doubt it. They can get inside those well-cut clothes, they can rumple his sheets—but lay bare the man underneath? No.'

'But...' *But I get to the real man sometimes.*

I can touch more than his skin. She almost said it, then realised how pathetic it would sound. *I'm different. He lets me in. He trusts me. And Hannah, who has known Alex for most of their lives, will smile and be kind about my illusions. She might even think I'm developing a* tendre *for him. How humiliating.*

'Why does he need a mask?' she said instead. 'What is he hiding?'

Hannah laughed and set off a coughing fit. She waved Tess back to her chair when she reached for the water glass. 'I'm all right. He isn't hiding, he is creating. He has remade himself from scratch these past ten years.'

'Ten? But he's twenty-seven now. What happened when he was seventeen?'

'He left home.' Hannah frowned at a harmless print hanging over the fireplace. 'For good, I mean. He'd been at university for one term. He came home for…he came home for a visit, and when he returned to Oxford he never went back to Tempeston again.'

'But seventeen is very young.' What had she been like at seventeen? Full of questions and uncertainties, her body no longer that of a girl, her emotions torn between a yearning to be back in the safety of childhood and an uneasy impatience to discover the world. What must it be like for a boy, out by himself in that big, dangerous world?

'Yes, it is young,' Hannah agreed. 'But he had friends and anger and intelligence to keep him going.'

Anger. 'What happened? What drove him away?'

Hannah shook her head. 'As I said, it is not my story to tell. If Alex ever does tell you about that Christmas, then you will know you really have got under the mask, under his skin. If he trusts you with that, then he has entrusted you with his soul and everything fragile within that tough carapace he has built around himself.'

They sat in silence. Hannah seemingly worn out after her outburst, Tess unable to find words. So it had been Christmas. Was that why he was so cynical about the festival? Eventually she said, 'But don't his parents want to be reconciled with him?'

'Have you ever wounded someone badly?'

Tess shook her head. 'I don't think so. I hope not.'

'If you had, then perhaps you would understand. If you injure a person close to you so cruelly that your own conscience is riven, then sometimes you become angry with them for making you feel so guilty. His father did something inexcusable, something that resulted in a death, something that slashed Alex to the heart. Lord Moreland is a man who never found himself at fault, who has never been known to own a wrong or to apologise. I expect nothing has changed.' She shrugged, a complicated heaving of blankets and shawls. 'Therefore, if he is not at fault, then Alex must be. If he had hurt Alex, then Alex must have been to blame. Do you understand?'

'I think so. How dreadful.' The words were inadequate, but she could find no others. Tess reached out a hand to the fire for some warmth. 'Could Alex not make the first move to reconcile?'

'You know those horse-drawn tramways? There are iron or wooden rails and the horse can draw a heavy load quite easily along them?' Hannah did not wait for an answer. 'To move from that exact track would need huge effort and would most certainly overturn the cart, injure the horse, possibly kill the driver. Should the driver try to leave the tracks, drive a new path, risk that injury, just on the off chance it might work?'

The silence stretched on. Tess looked up and found Hannah's eyes were closed, her breathing slow and deep. She had fallen asleep, worn out, perhaps by emotion.

Tess uncurled herself and put on her shoes, found her things and tiptoed out.

'I don't think Mrs Semple is well enough to come back to work, not this side of Christmas. I know it is almost three weeks away, but there is all the preparation to be thought of.' Tess folded back the notebook she was using to keep lists of things to be done. Now a fresh page was headed *Christmas??* and she had caught Alex just before William Bland, his secretary, arrived. She was determined to pin him down for some answers.

'I thought she was not seriously ill.' He stopped mending the end of his pen with a pocket knife and looked up. 'I must send the doctor round again.'

'She *is* getting better, but the infection seems to have settled on the lungs of all of the sufferers and they are worn out with coughing. She needs a holiday somewhere she can be looked after. What would she usually do at Christmas?'

'Go back to her husband's family in Kent. It's a big family and she's very fond of them.' Alex squinted at the pen nib, then stuck it in the standish. 'I could send her down early, in the coach with rugs and hot bricks and one of the men to escort her.'

'That sounds like a good idea. Shall I arrange it?'

'No. I'll go and talk to her, if that dragon of a landlady will let me, a dangerous man, into her female fortress. Anything else in that very efficient little notebook?'

'I need to know exactly what happens here at Christmas. What the arrangements for the rest of the staff are, whether you'll be entertaining, whether you'll be out much. I need to plan for meals, shop for provisions,' she added when he looked at her blankly. 'Phipps and MacDonald tell me they don't have family in the south and then there's the coachman and your grooms.'

'What happens is that I don't expect to see them from the morning of the twenty-fourth until the evening of the twenty-sixth. They fill the coal scuttles and leave the place tidy and I eat out at my clubs. I can cope with making my own bed once a year,' he added, presumably in response to her opening and closing her mouth like a landed carp. 'I told you—I spend Christmas by my own fireside with a pile of books and a bottle or so of good brandy. All of my friends of a sociable disposition will be out of town.'

'Then, you do not mind what happens below stairs so long as it does not disturb you?'

'Or burn the house down or bring in the parish constable. Exactly.'

'Right.' Tess closed her notebook with a snap. This house was going to have a proper Christmas regardless of what his lordship expected. 'And above stairs you just want appropriate preparation made?'

'Certainly. You can manage that?'

'Oh, yes, especially if you are out most of the time.'

'That would be helpful, would it?' Alex asked absently. He was already running one finger down a column of figures. 'I'll be at the club a lot of the time.' He flipped open his desk diary and made a note as there was a knock at the door. 'Come in!'

'My lord?' Mr Bland looked in, his arms full of papers. 'I have the auction catalogues from Christie's you wanted, but I can come back when it is convenient.'

'No, we've finished, haven't we, Mrs Ellery?'

'Indeed we have, my lord.'

When she went down the indoor staff were all below stairs. 'MacDonald? Please ask the stable staff to join us. All of them. Annie! Leave the scullery cleaning a moment and come in here.'

They crowded into the kitchen, Annie still clutching her scrubbing brush, Byfleet the flat-irons he'd been about to set on the grate. The grooms brought the rich, warm smell of horses to mingle with the aroma of baking bread as they stood awkwardly by the back door.

How long had she been here? Tess wondered

as she surveyed their faces. Scarcely a week? It was hardly much more since she had staggered in, battered and exhausted, and yet this was beginning to feel like home, and she was gaining a confidence she never expected to find. In the new year, when Hannah was well again, she could set out on her quest for employment feeling so much better equipped.

The staff were waiting patiently. Tess jerked her thoughts away from the prospect of employment agencies and smiled. 'I have been discussing Christmas with his lordship. Mrs Semple is much better, you'll be glad to hear, but she'll be going off to her in-laws in Kent very soon to recover. Now, how many of you will be spending Christmas at home with your families?'

Annie held up her hand, realised it was holding a dripping brush and gulped. 'Me. I'll be at me lodgings, I s'pose, Mrs Ellery, ma'am.'

'No one else?' Heads shook. 'And who's at the lodgings, Annie?'

She shrugged. 'The other lodgers, ma'am.'

Tess had a fairly good idea what home must be like for Annie. 'Do you think you would like to join us for Christmas, Annie?' The girl's jaw dropped, then she nodded energetically. 'You can have one of the upstairs rooms for a few nights. What do the rest of you usually do?'

'Make do,' Byfleet volunteered. 'We're all

men, so we get in some food from the cook shops, his lordship lets us have extra money and plenty of beer and a bottle or so from the wine cellar. We smoke, play cards, yarn a bit.'

'We'll be a mixed party this year,' Tess said briskly. 'I can cook a proper Christmas dinner if I have some help.' *I hope.* She glanced at the row of cookery books on the mantelshelf. 'Then we can go to church afterwards, for midnight service. Christmas morning we'll exchange presents and enjoy ourselves for the rest of the day.' She looked around the room. 'What do you say?'

'I say *yes*,' MacDonald said with a broad grin. 'I'll get out my fiddle and Will there has got his flute. And with the youngsters we'll have a proper Christmas.' He started counting heads. 'There's the three from the stables, me and Phipps, Mr Byfleet, Dorcas and little Daisy, Annie and you, ma'am.' He grinned. 'That's ten, a snug little party, Mrs Ellery.'

'It is indeed,' Tess said. *And if I can work a miracle there will be eleven of us. So far, so good. We have a party. Now we need presents.*

Alex tossed the sale catalogue aside. Nothing in it got his acquisitive juices flowing. He felt bored, he realised incredulously. No, not *bored* exactly. Stale? Tired of London, tired of routine. Unsettled. It was ridiculous. He was normally so involved with his work and with his social round that Christmas was a welcome opportunity to sit back and relax. He regarded his drawing room with disfavour. It was too damn tasteful, too blasted orderly.

It was Tess who was responsible for this mood, he suspected. She was turning the place upside down. Hannah had been efficient, but mostly invisible. She left him to himself except for the occasional evening when she would shed her housekeeper's cap and come and curl up in a chair in the drawing room and gossip over a glass of wine. She was an old friend, she had a busy life of her own beyond his front door and she left him alone to live his life as it suited him.

But Tess was there, in the house, day and night. And she expected things of him beyond the regular payment of housekeeping money and a list of meal times when he wanted to be fed at home. She expected him to *react*, to involve himself with the concerns of the other staff. And she was up to something with this Christmas obsession of hers. And that was leaving aside the nagging awareness of her physically, the effort it took not to think of the slim figure, the soft mouth, those wise, young, blue eyes.

There was a tap on the door, the modest yet definite knock he was learning to associate with his temporary housekeeper.

'Come in.' Yes, it was his little nun with her confounded notebook. He got up from the sofa where he'd been sprawled and waved her to the chair opposite.

Not such a little nun now, he thought as she settled her well-cut skirts into order. With good food and a warm house she had lost that pinched, cold look. Taking command suited her, put a sparkle in those blue eyes and a determined tilt to that pointed chin. And the food had done more than keep her warm, it had given her curves that were most definitely not nun-like.

My staff, my responsibility, he reminded himself, sat down and dumped the Christie's catalogue firmly onto his lap.

'Are you all right, my lord? I thought you winced just now.'

'Alex, for goodness' sake.' He smiled to counteract the snap. 'And it was just a touch of…er… rheumatism.'

'Rheumatism?'

He shrugged and the catalogues slid helpfully, painfully, into his throbbing groin. 'What can I do for you, Tess?'

'Christmas presents,' she said. She flipped open her notebook, produced a pencil and stared at him as though expecting dictation.

'Whose Christmas presents?'

'For the staff. The men, of course, Dorcas and

little Daisy. And Annie. I think Annie should stay for a few nights, I don't like to think of her having to go back to that lonely lodging house.'

'Who the blazes is Annie? The scullery maid? No, don't answer that. Do what you want about staff meals, but why presents? I give them all money on St Stephen's Day.'

'Of course you do and I am sure it is very generous. But Christmas presents are special, don't you think? Personal.'

Alex considered a range of things he could say and decided it was probably safer not to utter any of them, not when faced with a woman armed with a notebook. 'I'll give you some money and you can buy them.'

'I think the staff would really appreciate it if you chose them yourself.' He could feel himself glowering and could only admire her courage as she continued to smile. 'It is more in the Christmas spirit, don't you think?'

'Tess, you know perfectly well what I think about Christmas spirit. Codswallop. Humbug. Ridiculous sentimentality.' Anyone else would have backed down in the face of that tone and his glare. All the men he knew certainly would have done. They obviously raised them with backbones of steel in convents.

'But I know you value your staff,' she said in a voice of sweet reason. 'We could go out this afternoon unless you are very busy.' By not so much as a flicker did her eyes move towards the pile of discarded journals, abandoned catalogues, crumpled newspapers and the other evidence of a lazy morning. 'It isn't raining. And I have a list.'

'I'll wager you have.' Alex got to his feet. 'I surrender. Wrap up warmly, I'll get the carriage sent around.'

Half an hour later when he met her in the hall she was wearing a smart mantle that matched a deep-blue bonnet and she had decent gloves on. *How pretty she is with the bruise gone and that bonnet framing her face.* 'Where is Dorcas?' he snapped.

'Daisy was fretful and Dorcas has a lot of work on her hands hemming petticoats for me and it would only distract Annie from her work if she has to watch the baby, as well. We don't really need Dorcas, do we?'

The innocent question, the questioning tilt of her head to one side, got to him every time. He just wanted to kiss her silly. *Which is not going to happen.* 'Not if you feel comfortable alone in a closed carriage with me.' Alex kept his voice neutral, but she still turned a delicate shade of pink.

'Of course I do. We discussed…that. I thought we had forgotten about it.'

Forgotten that kiss? Forgotten that you admitted that the attraction wasn't just one-sided? When you become prettier and happier with every day that passes? When hell freezes over. Alex wasn't going to lie to her. 'I think we are doing a very good job of pretending it doesn't exist,' he said drily. 'Best put that veil down in case anyone sees you. Now, where to?'

'A music publishers first, there's one in Albemarle Street. I want music for MacDonald and Phipps—good tunes, ballads, dances. MacDonald can play the violin and read music and Phipps plays the flute, but only by ear, so MacDonald's going to teach him to read music. They've only got one or two pieces now.'

Alex helped her out of the carriage and into the shop, his ears ringing, while Tess talked. He had learned more about his footmen in ten minutes than he'd known in five years, he realised as he stood back to let her go through the door into the shop in front of him.

Chapter Eleven

'That was easy,' Tess said fifteen minutes later as she gave a satisfied pat to the brown paper parcel on the carriage seat. 'Now then, tobacco jars for Perring and Hodge. John Coachman says he'll not be responsible for his actions if he has to deal with two grooms squabbling over which tobacco is whose much longer. And he takes snuff, so a new box for him, don't you think?'

Alex directed John to Robert Lewis's tobacconist shop in St James's Street and sat back to digest the discovery that he was actually enjoying himself. Part of it, of course, was Tess's company. Her enjoyment of the shops, her enthusiasm and cheerful goodwill was infectious, and he found he had no objection at all to the image he saw reflected in shop windows of the two of them arm in arm. But strangely, it was more than that.

'Do you know, I find this oddly satisfying, like working out the attribution of a painting,' he confessed as they emerged later from Gray's the jewellers with a coral-and-silver teething ring for little Daisy. 'Are we done now?'

'Not yet.' Tess looked back over her shoulder as she got into the carriage.

Alex closed the door behind him and then stayed on his feet to shift parcels on the seat. 'More?'

'Well, yes. There's—' Tess began as the carriage started off, then stopped with a lurch.

Alex twisted round, caught his balance and lost it again as the vehicle jerked forward, accompanied by a vigorous exchange of curses from on top of the box. He just missed the seat; Tess grabbed for him and he hit the floor with her on top, one sharp elbow planted firmly in his midriff. *'Ough.'*

'Alex? Oh, I am so sorry, I've hurt you.' She was sprawled down the length of him, the two of them wedged on the floor. He looked up, through eyes watering from the impact, into her face, so close. The tip of her nose was pink from the chill, her lips were parted, her eyes were wide with concern. *Adorable. She's adorable.* And outrageously arousing with every inch of her pressed to him.

'Winded…' he managed. 'That's all.' He closed

his eyes the better to enjoy the sensation of her curves, the erotic, impossibly innocent, scent of plain soap and a dab of lavender water.

'Alex! Alex, can you hear me?' She squirmed, trying to get to her feet without, he supposed, trampling all over him. 'Have you hit your head?'

Alex groaned, opened his eyes and found himself still nose to nose with Tess. *This is more than any man can be expected to withstand*, he told himself, gritting his teeth.

With a dolphin-like heave she got herself up at the expense of no more than an inch or two of skin scraped from his shin bones. 'I am so sorry I squashed you, Alex. Just lie still. I'll pull the cord and tell John Coachman to drive direct to your doctor.'

'No need.' He found his voice from somewhere and sat up before Tess observed the interesting effect her squirming had produced on his body. 'I'm fine. Just...' *Hanging on to my self-control by my fingernails.* Alex put both hands on the squabs and pushed himself up and onto the seat next to her. 'Winded, as I said. What were we talking about?' *Something, please God, dull and non-inflammatory.*

'A donkey!' For a moment he thought she meant him, which was nothing but the truth, given that he was an experienced man about town reduced to a quivering mass of sexual frustration by a chit from a nunnery.

'Oh, isn't it sweet?' Tess pointed out of the window to a costermonger's barrow pulled by an improbably fluffy little donkey.

'Yes,' Alex agreed cautiously. It was not the word he would have used. 'But we do not need a donkey.' The way she collected things he could expect to come home to find an ass and an ox in the stables, just for Christmas. He wouldn't put it past her to go to Pidcock's Menagerie and borrow a camel for atmosphere.

Tess smiled at him, apparently able to read his mind. 'Of course not.'

Alex was seized with a contrary urge to buy her one, just to see that smile again. He repressed the whim. 'Now where?'

'A toyshop. I want a doll for Daisy.'

The shop, whose owner had obviously stocked up well for the approaching season, was a treasure trove. Alex restrained himself from buying a full set of lead soldiers just to arrange on the study mantelshelf. The display of dolls was astounding, and he blinked at the array of miniature femininity. Tess was studying the far corner where the plainest examples were arrayed.

Alex made for the most magnificent, complete with real hair and elegant clothing. 'There's no need to stint, I don't expect Dorcas can afford to give the child many toys.'

'She's too young for one, really, but I think it is nice if she grows up with a doll who will become an old favourite. But a baby needs a simple, soft doll, like those.' Tess lifted down a medium-size rag doll, then turned back to the counter past a row of wooden dolls, their hair and features painted on. She stopped and touched one, just with the tip of her finger, and something in her smile sent a cold shiver down Alex's spine.

'What's wrong, Tess?'

'Nothing. Only memories.' Her hand hesitated for a moment over the brightly coloured skirt, then she gave herself a little shake and took the rag doll across to the counter. 'I had a doll like that once.' Tess was looking at the wooden dolls again. 'Mama gave it to me for Christmas when I was six.'

'What happened to it?'

'The nuns took it when I went to the convent.'

'But you were, what, twelve by then?'

'Thirteen, and far too old to play with dolls, of course. I didn't play with her, though, I talked to her. She was my friend,' Tess said simply.

When they were outside on the pavement she blinked as if she had been miles away. Or years, perhaps, Alex thought. 'Did you not have friends?'

'Not really.' Her expression went blank. 'We moved an awful lot. And not when we were travelling, of course. I was perfectly happy,' she said hastily when he opened his mouth. 'I had Mama and Papa. But you know what it is like when you are a child, you need an ear to whisper your secrets into, someone to tell your troubles to. Some children have imaginary friends, Patty was my confidant, that is all.'

Yes, I know. Peter was all of that to me, but he was real. Friend, confidant, someone to tell my troubles and my secrets to. Only he hadn't been able to tell me his biggest secret and because of that, he's been cold in the ground these ten years.

'Where do you want to go next?' Alex asked and fished out his clean handkerchief for Tess.

She blew her nose briskly, stuffed the linen square into her reticule and said, 'A bookshop. Dorcas enjoys novels.'

Alex left Tess browsing amidst the stacked tables in Hatchard's in Piccadilly. 'Will you be all right here for half an hour? I've just remembered something I need to do.'

By the time he came back she had accumulated a pile of six books, two new notebooks and some sheets of wrapping paper with gold stars stamped on it. 'The notebooks and two of the books are for me,' she explained as he carried them to the counter for her. 'You must take those out of my wages.'

'Don't be foolish.' Alex looked at the spines. 'Cookery books and notebooks are essential housekeeping equipment.' He waved aside the assistant waiting to carry the parcel out to the carriage. 'Now we are going to Bond Street and Madame Francine's.'

'Madame—a modiste?' Tess stopped dead on the pavement. 'I am not going to help you choose garments for your light of love, my lord!'

'Foolish,' he repeated, marching her firmly towards the carriage. 'Garments for you. Hannah gave me a list, said that she had not finished outfitting you.'

'She had. I have everything I need.' She was beholden to him enough.

'What do you know about it, little nun?' He waved a folded sheet of paper under her nose.

'But—'

'But nothing. Here we are.' He helped her down, swept her into the shop, deposited her firmly in a chair and proceeded to charm the pantalettes off Madame Francine, as Tess said bitterly to Dorcas later.

She was taken off to a fitting room, measured,

clucked over and finally allowed back to where Alex was waiting, perfectly at his ease on a spindly gilt chair, his nose in a copy of *La Belle Assemblée.*

'All will be ordered as you desire, my lord.' Madame Francine glanced at the list. 'We have taken foot tracings so the shoes will be delivered at the same time.'

Tess knew better than to make a scene in the shop, but she began to protest as soon as they reached the carriage. 'Alex—my lord—I cannot have you buying me more clothes. It is not at all proper, beside any consideration of the cost.'

'Do I appear to be poverty stricken? Unable to afford a modest wardrobe for a lady housekeeper?'

'No, but that is not the point.'

'Those old crows sent you out into the world dressed like a skivvy. Do you expect me to leave you like that?'

'You outfitted me as you would have a footman with his livery. That is understandable. And what you gave me was quite sufficient.'

'*Sufficient* is a mean, tight, word. You are a pretty young woman, Tess, not a footman. It gives me pleasure to see you dressed nicely. You bring colour to the house.'

She felt the blush burn upwards and with it the anger. 'Pretty. I see. You expect me to show my gratitude, I suppose? Madame Francine knows you very well, doesn't she? I suppose that is where you take all your mistresses.' As soon as she said it she knew she had misjudged him.

'Yes, I have taken mistresses there before. You think that is how I regard you? You think that of me?' Alex's face was an expressionless mask.

'No. No, I do not. I am sorry, I reacted without thinking. I hate the idea of some sort of financial transaction, but… You want me. I may be inexperienced, but when we fell on the floor of the carriage…' Her vocabulary failed her.

'You noticed I was aroused?'

It was possible that a thunderbolt might strike, or the carriage horses bolt or the king pass by in procession. No miracle occurred to save her. Tess jerked up her chin and made herself look Alex in the eye. 'Yes.' *Yes, I did notice that hard ridge of flesh pressed into my stomach. Yes, I do know what it means and, no, I was not shocked. I was excited. Shamefully, achingly, excited.*

'You may also have noticed that I did nothing about it.' Now his voice was as colourless as his expression. 'I would have to be…a completely different kind of man not to be aroused by you. I can ignore this, just as any gentleman can. We are not all the victims of our animal natures like Dorcas's previous employer.'

'I know.' She kept her chin up, even though

she wanted to bury her face in the carriage rug. 'It is on my mind because…' *Because I wish you were not such a gentleman.* Impossible to say it. Tess closed her eyes and swallowed. 'I wonder why you are not married.'

'I do not intend to marry,' Alex said, as calmly as if he was stating that he had no intention of visiting Germany.

That snapped her eyes open. 'You don't intend to marry? But that's ridiculous!'

'So is being quizzed on the subject by a convent-reared gentlewoman in my own carriage.' There was a definite edge to his voice now and colour up over his cheekbones. If he resembled any of the mythical creatures of Sister Moira's fairy tales, it was no longer a benevolent one. 'Why is it ridiculous that I do not intend to marry? Are you of the opinion that everyone should?'

'Of course not. In my case, for example, it should be obvious that I will not wed.' One dark brow lifted, but she pressed on. 'I am a penniless nobody with a living to earn. You are an aristocrat, heir to a title. Surely marriage is expected of you?'

'Exactly. I do not choose to do the expected.' There was an unfamiliar, bitter twist to his mouth now.

'Then, it is simply a self-indulgent whim?'

Alex turned those slanting hazel eyes on her. 'Throwing brickbats now I have made you uncomfortable, Tess? It is not a whim, it is a deliberate act by someone who is otherwise powerless to avenge a crime.'

His father. Hannah said someone died that Christmas ten years ago. 'You are depriving your father of the hope of the succession, aren't you? But you have a brother.'

His lips curved into a smile that sent cold chills down her spine. 'Indeed I have. Let us just say that if I were a stockbreeder I could not hope for a more willing stallion nor fear having one who has proved so unproductive so far. According to gossip Matthew has spent his wild oats over three counties without so much as one bastard to his name.'

'I do not think I like you very much in this mood, Alex Tempest.' Tess dragged the carriage rug close around her legs.

'Nor do I,' he said, the dangerous smile vanishing. 'I do not think I have ever come across a lady who is prepared to speak as frankly as you, Tess.'

'Perhaps I just see the future more clearly. I will not marry and I am unlikely ever to find myself in a situation where I can discuss such subjects so openly with a man. I will be gone soon after all. Hannah will return after Christmas and I will have to take myself off to the employment agencies.

'Are you not cutting off your nose to spite your face? After all, you are not a virgin, are you, my lord?' There was a woman in the carriage who looked like her, sounded like her. The Tess Ellery who was listening to what this other Tess was saying, who seemed to be able to see her through Alex's eyes, shrivelled inwardly with shock.

A sudden, surprised gasp of laughter escaped him. 'No.'

'I thought not, not after the mention of mistresses. Nor a monk, either, I imagine?'

'No, not a monk, either.'

'So you are not proposing a life of sacrificial celibacy. You will punish your father and wallow in sin at the same time.'

'Wallow in sin? Tess, what *have* you been reading?'

'No doubt I am very naive, but I do not think you are happy.'

'And marriage would make me happy? I very much doubt it. I haven't the models for doing it right, besides anything else. If I've inherited anything from my father, it is probably an ability to make an appalling husband and father. Don't look at me with those great innocent eyes, full of righteous indignation, Tess.' He studied her face for a moment, then smiled, a smile free from the bitterness and mockery. 'Are you by any chance attempting to seduce me into happiness by using sweet reason?'

She thought about it for a moment. 'Yes, I believe I am.'

'I have to tell you it is not very erotic.'

'It is not intended to be erotic!' *Infuriating man, to be able to make me blush even more deeply than I already am.* 'I am not talking about *that* kind of seduction.'

'Your arguments have their merits, but for other men, I think. And I have to tell you that successful seduction requires passion and recklessness and surprise.' His lips were twitching now. It was not laughter directed at her, she guessed. Hoped.

'I would need to catch you unawares?' Tess suggested. There was a flicker of something inside her, a warm, fidgety glow. 'Be more passionate with my arguments?'

'Indeed you would. And I am not easily caught with my guard down.'

Tess pondered on seduction over the next week in the intervals between ordering supplies, puzzling over whether one goose, one turkey and a ham would be enough for the Christmas meals and negotiating the use of the boiler in between wash days in order to dangle the cannonballs of plum pudding in the cavernous pot.

Alex had been amusing himself by teasing

her and, perhaps, flirting a little, she guessed, although she had no experience of such a thing. According to the nuns seduction applied to sin, to devils luring souls into doing wicked things. In Minerva Press novels seduction was all to do with love and lust. Between the pages wicked women dressed in trailing silks lured the hero into their toils and then…the chamber door closed with a resounding thud, even in the most daring tale. Tess very much doubted she'd know a toil if she fell over it; she possessed no trailing silks and Alex would probably laugh himself sick at the sight of her slinking about in her very sensible flannel wrapper.

I am thinking about seducing him into bed, not into happiness, she thought. But that *would* be sin, not because she truly believed that making love was wrong, but because his conscience would hurt him if he took her virginity.

But if he was convinced it would do no harm… It was a delicious daydream, one that brought back the heat and the tingling feelings and the ache to be held, very close, very tight.

How would one go about seducing Alex Tempest? It was safe enough to weave fantasies, surely? Laughter seemed to lower his guard. Laughter and being close enough to touch might work. Catching the man at home and alone, though, that would the first step, and Alex was very, very good at being elusive.

'What I want for Christmas is an earl,' she informed Noel, who was in her room helping her to wrap Christmas presents by tangling the ribbons and hiding in boxes. 'Just the once. I know I'd have to give him back. I only want to borrow him. I suppose I would be quite hopeless at making love, but all the gossip says that men enjoy being with virgins. Which seems strange. But then men are strange, I'm beginning to find.

'I suppose I shouldn't be telling you this. You are much too young for such wicked conversation.' Tess scooped up the kitten, who was trying to eat silver paper, and tickled him until he was a limp, purring handful of fur. 'But I wish I could make Alex happy. He isn't, you know, not deep down. He's angry and hurting. I wish I could give him his family for Christmas, then he might settle down and find a wife and have children of his own.'

Noel made an ambiguous noise somewhere between a mew and a yowl. Tess lifted him up so his pink nose was inches from hers and his eyes crossed as he looked at her. 'You think we need a fairy godmother? They are in short supply in London, I fear.'

'What is in short supply?' Alex's voice said from behind her.

Chapter Twelve

Tess spun round on her knees and ended up on her bottom in a tangle of ribbons. 'You made me jump.' How long had Alex been standing there, one shoulder against the door frame of her room, listening to her? 'If you have been eavesdropping, then you'll know.'

'I have just arrived, was about to knock and the door swung open onto you complaining about shortages. What do you need?'

Unless he was an actor good enough for Covent Garden Theatre then he had only heard those few words. Tess offered up several prayers of thanks, one in Latin. 'Fairy godmothers. They are scarce, you must agree.'

'Why do you need one of those?' Alex pushed the door right open with his foot, but stayed where he was, pleasingly framed in the space. 'Just ask and I'll sort out your Christmas wishes.'

He was flirting, she was almost certain. There was certainly a wicked gleam in his eyes.

Tess got to her feet with as much grace as was possible, given that she had a kitten clinging to her skirts, and assumed her best housekeeper's expression. 'You wanted me?' she enquired.

Alex's gaze seemed somehow heavier, warmer as his eyes rested on her. It must be the different angle she was seeing him from now she was on her feet.

It was a moment before he replied. 'Only to tell you that I am dining at Brooks's tonight and I will be out to dinner at Lord Hawthorne's tomorrow night.' He flashed her his rapid, wicked smile. 'My last fling of dissipation and sociability before Christmas descends like a pall on London.'

'It is still only the thirteenth.' *What is he going to say when he sees what I have planned for Christmas?*

'I know, but everyone will start leaving for the country by the fifteenth, if they have not already gone.' He turned to leave, then glanced back over his shoulder. 'I've got a carpenter to make a proper cradle for Daisy. He'll deliver it tomorrow.'

'Oh, thank you.' Tess started forward, to touch his hand, kiss his cheek, then stopped as the realisation of what she was doing hit her. *No, it isn't fair, don't make it harder for him to behave like a gentleman.* She turned the movement into a clap of her hands. 'That's wonderful—an old drawer isn't really deep enough to keep out the draughts.'

He smiled and turned to leave. 'Thank you,' Tess whispered again as the sound of his footsteps across the hall faded away. It had taken thoughtfulness to notice the makeshift crib and to do something about it. It had involved him making an effort, *personal* effort, when he could have easily ignored a servant's child as something that was not his concern. 'There's hope for you yet, Lord Weybourn.'

The sound of the key in the latch froze Tess on top of the ladder. Around her in the hall both footmen and Dorcas stopped dead, their arms full of evergreens.

'Oh, my God, it's only seven o'clock, he's not due back for hours.' Phipps clutched the foot of the ladder, making it sway and Tess yelp and clutch the hanging lantern with both hands. The bunch of mistletoe she had been attempting to fix fell on to MacDonald's head, Phipps burst into laughter and Dorcas gave a small shriek.

The front door swung open slowly to reveal Lord Weybourn standing on his own front step, fog swirling around him as he held his latch key in one hand and a large wreath tied with scarlet ribbons in the other. 'This just fell off,' he said. 'I caught it. It appears to consist entirely of holly. Exceedingly prickly holly.'

'I knew I should have used wire, not string, to hold it to the knocker. Sorry, my lord.' Mac-Donald tossed the mistletoe to Phipps and strode forward to take the wreath. 'Ow. Oh, bug—I mean, ouch.'

'Oh, bug—ouch, indeed.' Alex came in and closed the door behind him. 'Phipps, do you intend to kiss me under that mistletoe or to take my hat and coat?'

'Take your hat, my lord.' Phipps threw the mistletoe to Dorcas and reached for Alex's cane. From her perch Tess could see the tops of Phipps's ears were bright red.

'And what, exactly, is this?' Alex enquired as he shrugged out of his caped greatcoat.

'Christmas evergreens. It is the twentieth after all.' Tess looked down into Alex's upturned face and tried to read his mood. Obviously arms full of prickly holly and his hallway in chaos was not how he expected to be welcomed home, but was he annoyed beyond that? 'We were not expecting you to return yet.'

'That much is obvious. Why are you up a stepladder, Mrs Ellery, when there are two able-bodied males here and three more in the stables?'

Because Phipps is scared of heights and MacDonald is clumsy was the truth, but she couldn't betray the footmen. 'A woman's artistic touch?' she ventured.

'I see.' Alex retrieved the now somewhat battered bunch of mistletoe from Dorcas and held it up to her, took a firm hold on the ladder, waited until she had tied the angular fronds in place and then said, 'Now come down, please.'

'Yes, my lord.' Tess attempted her best meek and obedient voice.

'Did I order Christmas evergreens?' he enquired when she was standing in front of him.

'You didn't forbid them, my lord.'

'A major oversight. I did not forbid massed carol singers, handbell ringers and a full-size yule log in the front room either. Are those to be expected?'

'No, my lord. At least, there will be carols downstairs. But no handbells, I promise, and the fireplaces are too small for yule logs.'

'And are any other rooms infested with fir cones?' Were his lips twitching? Just a little, perhaps.

'No, my lord. Just the hallway and below stairs.'

'I think I could tolerate a sprig or two of holly in the study. And fix that wreath back on the front door, MacDonald. We don't want the neighbours to think we are lacking in Christmas spirit, now do we?' *Yes, there is a definite twitch. Almost a smile.* 'You, Mrs Ellery, are a very bad influence on my household.' His gaze flickered up to the mistletoe immediately over her head. 'And on me,' he added softly.

Tess took three very deliberate steps backwards. 'Shall I have tea brought up, my lord?'

'Tea? No, brandy to the study, MacDonald. Is my post there?'

'Yes, my lord.' The footman doubled away; Alex vanished into the study.

Tess looked round at her remaining helpers. 'We are almost done, I think. Phipps, just let me have that remaining holly, the pieces with lots of berries, and I'll arrange it in a vase for the study. Dorcas, if you could tidy up and, Phipps, you remove the stepladder—' From the study there was the clatter of something metallic falling, then rolling. Then silence. 'What was that?'

'Sounded like the silver salver, Mrs Ellery.' Phipps hesitated, his arms full of stepladder. 'Should I go and see?'

'No, it is all right, carry on tidying up, I'll go.'

One of the few advantages of the Christmas season was a definite reduction in the amount of correspondence, Alex mused as he hitched one hip on to the corner of the desk and spun the salver round to pick up the bundle of post that had arrived since Bland had left after lunch.

He began to shuffle though the pile. Invitation, bill, bill, circular, tickets from the Opera House, letter from Rivers, a journal… And a letter on thick cream paper with a heavy seal. He turned it in his hands, saw the impression in the blue wax, a jagged line of lightning against a stylised cloud. *Tempest.*

For a moment he was tempted to toss it onto the fire unopened. Alex looked down at it in his hand. His shaking hand. *Coward.* With an effort of will he stilled the tremor then broke the seal.

Weybourn. Alexander. I do not know whether this will find you in London or what to do if it does not. Or what will befall us if you will not come.

It was his mother's handwriting. He hadn't seen it since he was seventeen. Alex stood up and the salver went spinning off the desk, hit the polished boards, spun and fell with a clatter.

Your father is very ill. He will not admit how ill, or how weak he is. Dr Simmington tells me he will not recover, that it is only a matter of time.

The elegant handwriting faltered and became less controlled.

> Matthew is not capable or able to take control of everything that must be done here. Alexander, I need you to come home. Your family needs you to come home. Your father will never admit he cannot cope, that he needs you. But despite everything, despite what your father did and said and what you vowed, I beg you, if you have any affection left for your poor afflicted mother, return to Tempeston.

> Lavinia Tempest.

The letter slipped from his fingers, drifted down to the carpet like a great falling leaf. *Return to Tempeston. Come home.* He closed his eyes.

'My lord? Alex?' A whisper of movement, a scent of lavender water, a touch on his arm.

Alex opened his eyes. Tess stood before him, the letter in one hand, the other resting on his forearm. Her face, puzzled and anxious, was turned up to his. 'What is wrong?'

'My father. Read the letter if you want.' He didn't seem able to move away, to think. *Your family needs you.*

'Oh, Alex.' There was a rustle of paper and

then Tess's arms were around him, her hand pulling his head down to her shoulder, her breath warm against his neck. 'I am so sorry. What terrible news.'

She held him as though he needed comfort, as though he had broken down. What was wrong with her? Didn't she realise he didn't care? He hadn't seen them for ten years.

Tess was murmuring nonsense in his ear, rocking slightly back and forth as she held him. Alex found his arms would move, that he could hold her, too, soft and warm and fragrant. Feminine and sweet and, under it all, a backbone of steel. 'I do not need comforting,' he said. But he let his cheek rest on the soft mass of her hair while he got his balance back.

Tess leaned back against his arms and looked up at him. 'Of course you do, you stubborn man. You love them and they hurt you and now they need you and it hurts all over again.'

'Tess.' There were no words and no coherent thoughts either, just wanting. Alex bent his head and kissed her and the world righted on its axis. She opened to him with the generous innocence that was Tess, untutored, a little clumsy as their noses bumped. He remembered the taste of her, slightly tart under the sweetness, like new cherries.

Her hands cupped his head, her fingertips

stroked his nape and her curves nestled against him as though a tailor had cut her to fit him. Only him. She gave a little gasp as he touched her tongue with his own, then bravely stroked back, gave a little wriggle and pressed closer.

He was going to have to stop. Through the incoherence that were his thoughts that imperative took shape, became urgent. *Stop, stop now. This is Tess.* And that, he realised, was why he did not want this to end.

When he lifted his head she blinked up at him, deliciously tousled and pink.

'Tess, we must—'

'Plan, I know.' She released his head, stepped back out of his arms. For a moment he was shocked by how easily she could set aside what had just happened and then realised this was the only way she could cope with it: pretend it hadn't happened, at least for a while.

'I'll ring for tea. There is a great deal to be done if you are to leave early tomorrow.' She went to the bell and pulled the cord, then sat down on the far side of the desk and regarded him with, he thought, some anxiety.

At least he could put a decent distance between them. Alex sat down in his desk chair. 'Your mother is going to need help,' she went on. 'An invalid in the house makes extra work for the male staff, I imagine, so our two footmen will be useful. Do your sisters live at home?'

'Laura's married and lives in Edinburgh. Maria is not at all practical. At least, she never used to be. She is…was, sensitive.'

'You'll need John Coachman and the grooms.' She was thinking aloud, frowning as she reviewed the staff.

'I take them all away and leave you alone?'

'There's Dorcas to keep me company. And Annie. The poor child is living in some lodging house. I cannot abandon her at Christmas after I promised she could come here. Three of us will be quite safe together for a few days.'

He'd have to go, he knew that. He couldn't ignore his own mother in the face of a plea like that. 'Come with me.'

'Come… You think your mother will need help sick nursing? Dorcas and I could assist with that, I suppose. But your mother isn't going to want to have strangers descend on her.'

'Tempeston is a big country seat, and it has the room to absorb an entire house party and all the additional servants. It can certainly cope with this household.'

She bit her lip and he wondered whether she was nervous about the thought of the big house, or of being with him. Then she took a deep breath and smiled. 'If you think I can help, then of course I will come, and Annie and Dorcas, too. We'll all come. It's the least we can do.'

Brave Tess. 'At least we have not got far to go, only into Hertfordshire, and the weather is fine.'

'Hertfordshire?'

'Yes, the Hertfordshire-Buckinghamshire border.'

She went very still, then gave herself a shake. 'Tempeston is so close? That *is* good news, we will be able to do the journey in the day.' There was a tap on the door and MacDonald came in before he could query why the mention of Hertfordshire seemed to take her aback.

'Tea, please. And some of the cake, thank you.' Tess waited until the door closed behind the footman. 'We will have to think about how to explain me.'

'And a baby. That might well need some explanation, also.' Alex found the everyday lunacy that was now his household was helping him get a grip. He realised with a jolt that he intended to go...*home.* He had jested about the family vault to Hannah; now there seemed to be a very real possibility that he would be expected to lay his father to rest in it in the near future.

'We could try a version of the truth,' he said, forcing himself to think of strategy and practicalities and not of the morass of emotions and anger and misunderstandings. 'I escorted you to England from Ghent for you to stay with an elderly lady as her companion. The elderly lady has died, you are stuck in London with no friends or relations and only Mrs White, your companion. I put you up, all very shocking, but what is one to do right before Christmas? Dorcas is the widow of a man who died very shortly after Daisy was conceived, which is why she is out of mourning now. You'll have to work out the details between you. If anyone asks me about you I can look convincingly blank—after all, I'm only acting as a courier.'

'That is brilliant, Alex.' Tess poured tea and passed him a cup. Her blushes had subsided, but her smile when she looked at him was still shy. He tried not to look at her mouth, pink and slightly swollen from his kisses. 'You will organise the carriages? There are rather a lot of us, and the luggage and the Christmas presents and the food.'

'Food?'

'We can't leave a goose, a turkey and a ham to rot, let alone all the puddings and the cakes. It will be less of a burden on your mother's cook if we take it.'

'Then, that's both of my carriages and the wagon for the heavy luggage.' Alex put down his cup, demolished a jam tartlet in one mouthful and stood up. Tess and her entourage were like an anchor, tethering him to safety. There were practical things to do, things involving a baby and a fat goose, things to keep his feet rooted in reality and the nightmares at bay. 'Tess?'

'Mmm?' She looked up, blushed and dropped her gaze to her notebook, already open on her lap.

'Thank you. Thank you for the comfort and the practicality. Thank you for that kiss.'

Alex locked away the thought of how much more he wanted than her lips as he pushed open the kitchen door. 'We are going to Tempeston tomorrow, all of us,' he announced. 'We're taking our perishable food, the Christmas presents, everything. Mrs Ellery will be down in a moment to give you instructions.' He looked round at their expressions, confused, excited and, in Annie's case, awestruck. 'And when we leave this house you will kindly remember that I never had a housekeeper named Ellery and if I did, she has nothing to do with Miss Teresa Ellery. Is that clear?'

There was a moment while they all stared at him, taking in the enormity of what he was asking, then Dorcas said, 'Annie, you run home and pack your bags then be back here, sharpish. I'll pack for Mrs…*Miss* Ellery, then I'll come down to help out here.'

Alex did not stop to give any orders. They

were competent and Tess would take control. He went out to alert the grooms, then, as they hurried to check over harnesses and dust off the wagon they usually used for transporting the bigger pieces of statuary and furniture he dealt in, found himself alone in the stall with Trojan, his hunter.

The big chestnut, apparently delighted with the company, rested his shoulder against Alex's and leaned his weight on him. 'Daft fool.' Alex rubbed him under the chin in the sweet spot that always reduced the animal to jelly and put up with having his palm dribbled into. It was peaceful here, smelt of warm horse and straw and saddle soap. Horses were an indulgence that still gave him a lot of pleasure. His father, having decided that his willowy elder son would never make a horseman, had lavished the best mounts on Alex's brother, Matthew.

Strange that he had never felt jealous of his brother. His father's opinion that Alex was a disappointment had hurt, but then, he had never known anything else. As a child he was the undersize one, the dreamer, the reader. He'd retreated back into his own head, his own company when punished or lectured, which must, he could see now, have made him even more infuriating to his noisy, energetic, utterly nonintellectual father.

His mother had worried and fussed—which had only made his father more dissatisfied and irritable. But the man hadn't been a monster; he'd obviously wanted to be proud of his sons and yet he hadn't been able to cope with one of them not fitting his mental image of the perfect heir. Were all parents like that, wanting perfection, expecting too much? Would he be like that in his turn if he was ever rash enough to contemplate a family? It was one of the unpleasant night thoughts that weighed against marriage.

Now his parents needed him; even Matthew needed him, although he was unlikely to admit it. Alex suspected he was going to be a bit of a shock to all of them. 'That's an interesting thought,' he observed to Trojan, who merely snorted. 'The power balance has shifted. What do I want now? An apology, but not for me. To be loved? Ridiculous. To be approved of? Now, there's the rub. There's some part of me that's still seventeen and wants approval, that hasn't learned that the only approval worth having comes from people whose opinion you value.'

And that was quite enough introspection for one evening. He slipped Trojan a carrot and shut the stable door. He had his mother to worry about—she'd sounded at her wits' end— and Tess. Tess, who, for reasons he failed to understand, trusted him. Desire was one thing; he understood that. But what possessed the foolish chit to trust him? It was that quality of innocence about her, he suspected. She had decided that he was redeemable from his cynicism and his self-centred lifestyle. Seduce him into *happiness* of all the wild ideas. It was going to take more than a few wreaths of evergreens and a wassail bowl to do that.

Chapter Thirteen

'Tired?' Tess stifled her own yawn and smiled at Dorcas, who perched, heavy-eyed, on the seat beside her. Opposite them Annie was already asleep again, one hand on little Daisy lying securely swaddled on the carriage's plush upholstery.

'Retiring at two and up at six is not my favourite choice of bedtime, Miss Ellery.'

'Not following on from the evening we had, that is certain.' Tess held on tight to the strap as the carriage rounded the corner on to the Edgware Road and headed north.

'It feels like a dream, packing everything and everybody up and leaving in such a procession.' Dorcas stroked the upholstery with the reverence she would accord fine silk as she peered out of the window into the gradually lightening morning gloom. 'And his lordship looking so dashing.'

Now Dorcas had drawn her attention to their

outrider Tess allowed herself to stare. It was the first time she had seen Alex on horseback, and she was not at all certain she was glad she had seen him now. He was magnificent, so at home on the big chestnut that it would only add to her store of delicious, and thoroughly uncomfortable, images to be taken out for daydreaming and then severely closed away again. Ever since that kiss yesterday it had been even more difficult to close the mental door on those fantasies.

'I wonder why he chooses to ride. It is such a damp, chill day and I doubt it is going to get much more pleasant.' How easy was riding? It had never occurred to her before, but Alex was controlling the big animal with no apparent effort at all. *Those muscles again, that deceptive strength.*

'Perhaps he does not want to be sitting with us because of the baby,' Dorcas said, jerking Tess back from her reverie.

'He could always tell Annie to take her to the other carriage if she became fractious,' she pointed out.

'I am sure he would not do that. He is such a gentleman and patient with her.'

Impossible man. He is nice to babies and kind to kittens, he looks wonderful on a horse. And he kisses like every sort of temptation I could imagine and more.

'Do you think they'll believe it, about me being a widow? Daisy's so very young.' Dorcas nibbled a fingernail as she looked at her daughter, fast asleep and blowing bubbles.

'Of course they will. We worked it out that you'll just be out of mourning. But you do need a wedding ring.' Tess pulled the chain that hung around her neck out from her bodice and unfastened it. 'Here, borrow this, it was my mother's.'

'But I can't take something so precious.' Dorcas put out her hand and then snatched it back.

'Try it on.' It was loose on the thin finger, but the knuckle was enough to hold it securely. 'She would have been glad of you wearing it if it helped someone, and that is what we are doing, isn't it?' *After all, it has never been a real wedding ring.* 'We are preserving my reputation and at the same time helping Lord Weybourn.' That was what the thin gold band had represented, the appearance of respectability. The lie.

They reached the market town of Watford in the early afternoon and pressed on into rolling hills clad with the golden brown of beech trees that held their dead leaves into springtime. Finally, as the light hung at the edge of dusk, they halted outside an inn on a small village green.

Tess watched Alex dismount, hand his reins to

one of the grooms and then go inside, followed by Byfleet carrying a portmanteau.

'Strange,' Tess mused, but Dorcas was feeding Daisy, and Annie tidying up all the paraphernalia from changing the baby, and both seemed to welcome the stop.

When the two men emerged again Alex was transformed. Gone was the rider in the low-crowned hat, the many-caped overcoat, the breeches and the long boots. In his place was a London swell, as exotic in the little village as a peacock in a barnyard.

Alex climbed into the carriage while Tess managed to close her mouth and stop goggling like a yokel.

'Ladies.' He settled onto the seat next to Annie, chucked Daisy under her fat chins with one exquisitely gloved forefinger and crossed his legs. Cream pantaloons. Skin-tight pantaloons. Tess shifted her gaze to the Hessian boots with silver tassels, then up to a waistcoat of cream moiré silk embroidered with lavender flowers. His coat was dark blue and his intricate, pale lavender neckcloth was secured by an amethyst stickpin. There was a gold seal ring on his left little finger, a quizzing glass hung around his neck and the subtle smell of his cologne filled the carriage.

He has shaved again, Tess realised, feeling

travel-soiled and unkempt in contrast. 'Lord Weybourn. Did you have an enjoyable ride?'

'I did, thank you. Are you ladies comfortable?' Annie giggled and he lifted his quizzing glass, reducing her to blushing confusion. 'Miss Annie, chief nursemaid.'

No one would guess he was within miles of a reunion he was dreading and a meeting with a dying father, Tess thought. Although his manner was…strange. Almost artificial. The young ladies at the convent had once been allowed to attend the theatre to see an improving play. Tess, who had tagged on to the party, found her way backstage and watched from a corner, fascinated, as the actors transformed themselves from ordinary people into creatures of fiction.

And that was what Alex was doing, transforming himself. He was becoming more mannered; his accent carried a subtle affectation. He wore his beautiful clothes like a mask, she realised. Or armour.

She knew before he spoke when they were nearing their destination. Alex sat up straighter against the squabs and his eyes followed the line of the high wall to their left. The carriage turned between a pair of lodge cottages and began to follow a winding road through parkland. Tess watched Alex, saw the mildly bored expression on his face and saw, too, the way his hand tightened on the strap, the white knuckles.

'Have we arrived?' It was an inane question, but she could stand the silence no longer.

'Yes. Welcome to Tempeston.' Alex was looking through the misted glass with an intensity that was a kind of hunger.

She glanced at the other two women, engrossed with the baby. 'You love it.' It was not a question.

'The river and the streams are my blood, the soil is my flesh, the stones of the house are my bones as they have been for generations of Tempests.' He stopped. 'And you have just caught me out in ludicrous sentimentality expressed in the most purple of prose. Forget it.'

Tess bit her lip to keep herself silent and leaned forward to rub her cuff across the window. Before her was the sprawling bulk of a house that formed a rough arc around a paved forecourt. The central block was lit, but the flanking wings were two dark arms waiting to close on them. She shivered as their carriage pulled up at the foot of the double flight of steps.

'Yes, it takes me like that,' Alex said, then smiled at Annie, who was visibly overawed. 'Nothing to worry about, it is only a house.'

The stones are my bones... And what waits inside? His soul? Tess tied her bonnet ribbons and collected up her reticule. 'Come along, Annie, make sure Miss Daisy is well wrapped up and stay close behind Mrs White all the time.'

'Yes, Mrs…Miss Ellery.'

The baby, mercifully, seemed settled and not inclined to grizzle. Tess imagined Alex's reception if he arrived with not only a strange young woman but an entourage that included a wailing babe in arms.

Light spilled down the steps as the double doors opened and two footmen ran down and opened the carriage door. Alex stepped out. 'Lord Weybourn and party. My mother is expecting us.' The second carriage drew up. 'My people.' Alex waved one hand in the general direction. 'A wagon is also following. See to it that everything is unloaded.'

'My… Yes, my lord. At once.'

One footman stood by to hand down the other occupants of the coach; the other doubled away and up the steps. By the time Tess reached the top, her hand on Alex's arm, a butler and two other footmen had appeared. The butler, she noted, had his expression perfectly under control; the two footmen were having trouble keeping the avid interest off their faces.

'My lord, it is a pleasure to see you at Tempeston once more.' The butler bowed.

'Garnett, good to see you. Mrs Garnett well?'

Alex might have been away for a month, not ten years.

'Very well, my lord, thank you for asking. James, his lordship's coat. William, the ladies. John, see to his lordship's people.' Daisy woke up and produced a loud gurgle. 'I see we must have the nursery readied. I will—'

'*Weybourn.* Alexander, you came.' A tall woman, slender and grey haired, came down the stairs, her hands outstretched. 'My dear boy, I knew you would not fail me.'

Alex stepped forward and caught her as she almost stumbled on the bottom step. 'Mother, take care.' He steadied her, then withdrew his hand. 'Fortunately I was in the country.'

It seemed to Tess that Lady Moreland made a conscious effort to control all emotion. She was more than slender, she was thin—her wrists seemed too fragile to support the weight of the rings that sparkled on both hands. The older woman looked past her son. 'We have guests, how delightful.' Tess could only admire the implacable mask of courtesy that enabled her to sound genuinely welcoming in the face of unexpected strangers at such a time. 'Alexander, you did not tell me you were—'

'Escorting Miss Ellery. Yes, indeed. I assured her that she could rely on your hospitality. This is Miss Ellery and her companion, Mrs White.

I brought them from Ghent on behalf of a mutual friend. Unfortunately the arrangements in London fell through.'

If anyone was going to lie to Alex's mother it was going to be her, not him. Tess stepped forward, hand outstretched. *She thought I was his wife, or at the very least, his betrothed. That mask slipped a little just then.* 'I do beg your forgiveness for my intrusion at a difficult time, Lady Moreland, but I found myself quite abandoned in a strange city with no hope of resolving my problems until the New Year. I hope I may be of assistance to you, and my companion, Mrs White, also. I am experienced in sickroom nursing.'

Good breeding was obviously enough to prevent Lady Moreland demanding why Tess found herself in such a predicament. 'Not at all,' she murmured, darting a glance at Alex. 'I thought for a moment that you were… Oh, and a baby, too?' There was the briefest betraying flicker of pain and hope in the fine hazel eyes. *Alex's eyes.*

'Mrs White's child, ma'am.' The hope died, leaving only the pain. 'I trust she will not disturb anyone. We have her nursemaid with us.'

'I have ordered the nursery to be put in order and the fires lit, my lady,' Garnett murmured. 'Young woman, if you follow John he will show you the way. His lordship's rooms are readied as you ordered, my lady. I thought the Chinese Bedchamber and the adjoining Rose Chamber for the ladies?'

'Excellent. If you and Mrs…er…White would like to go with Garnett, Miss Ellery? Alexander, I must speak with you in my boudoir.' She turned back up the stairs with a distracted smile in Tess's direction.

Alex turned to Tess, a perfectly pleasant, perfectly judged expression on his face. 'Do ask Garnett for whatever you require, Miss Ellery. I will see you both before dinner.'

'Thank you, Lord Weybourn.' Tess dropped the ghost of a curtsy and turned to the butler rather than watch Alex's erect back as he climbed the stairs behind his mother. *He's a grown man, he can cope.* But at what cost?

'Alexander.' His mother sank down on a chaise and pressed a scrap of lace and lawn to her lips. 'I hardly dared hope you would come.' She looked as though only the boning of her stays and sheer willpower were keeping her upright. 'I missed you so much, my son. Your letters have been a godsend, but I so longed to write back.'

His mother was fifty years old, he knew that, but looking at her now he could believe she was ten, twenty, years older. Her hair was almost entirely grey, she looked fragile to the point of breaking and the skin around her eyes was papery with a strain that was caused by something deeper and longer-lived than her husband's recent illness. He had missed her with a deep ache he had learned to ignore as best he could, as he would an amputated limb. The realisation that she had been hurting, too, was a stab to his conscience.

He had written to her once a month, knowing his father would have forbidden her to correspond with him and that he could expect no answer to his letters. It was desperation that had made her disobey now.

'You look tired, Mother.'

'I look old, you mean.' Her chin came up. 'And you look well. More than well. How you have grown, matured. Who is that young woman? I thought, no, I hoped, you were going to introduce her as your wife or your betrothed.'

'Really? After what my father says about me?' She winced and he bit his lip. She was not the one who deserved to be punished.

'Your father can be a great fool,' his mother said. It was the first time he had ever heard her utter a word of criticism of her husband.

'And a stubborn one. But, no, Miss Ellery is just what I told you, a young lady adrift in London because the arrangements made for her reception went awry.' He shrugged. 'At any other time of the year I could have found half a dozen ladies of my acquaintance to look after her, but you know what London is like before Christmas. And I could hardly deposit her in a hotel. And before you ask, no, the baby is not hers and most certainly not mine. The child is Daisy White. Now tell me what is wrong with my father.'

His mother sagged a little, then straightened her spine. 'The doctors say your father has a disease of the blood, one they cannot cure. He is deteriorating steadily.'

'Has he asked for me?' He kept the hope out of his voice, ashamed of the weakness.

'No.' She did not seem to realise that she was shredding the fragile Honiton lace of her handkerchief.

'And Matthew?' His brother, the perfect Tempest. Big, strong, physical. A hard rider, a hard drinker, a hard gambler, a hearty philistine. A man's man and always the apple of their father's eye.

'Matthew drinks, gambles, whores,' his mother said, her lips stiff with distaste for the words. 'He was never an intellectual.' Her raised brow dared Alex to comment. 'Now it is obvious that he incapable of taking up the work of the earldom. The agents do their best, but your father was always a man who kept his hand and his eyes on every aspect of all the estates, the business interests, the finances. He thought that Matthew took after him.'

'And that—as he did not believe I would marry, let alone father an heir, then—Matthew, or his son, would one day inherit it all. When did he realise?'

'That Matthew was incapable of managing a great inheritance? Not until he became so ill and even now he will not admit he needs help.'

'Of course not. That would mean calling me back.' Alex settled back in the chair, took a deep breath, found some sort of control of his voice. 'And possibly apologising. I imagine he is a very angry man.'

'You must be angry yourself.' His mother met his eyes. 'You must be angry with me.'

'You were in an impossible position.' He had known that right from the beginning. His mother was of a generation that would support their husbands whatever kind of tyrant they were. It was simply how she had been raised. 'Do you believe I am what he says I am?' *Lord, the last thing to discuss with one's mother.*

'That you are…not interested in women? Of course not. I have eyes in my head, I knew you went sneaking out of the house at night down to see Mary at the White Swan.' For the first time something like a smile twitched at her thin lips.

'I imagine I could tell you the date you lost your virginity. And while your letters to me contain nothing that might shock a maiden aunt, I do have my old friends in London. I hear the gossip.'

Alex had thought himself beyond blushing like a youth, but it seemed he was wrong. 'Does he know you sent for me?'

His mother got to her feet, as elegant and feminine as he always remembered her. 'I told him I would, but he did not believe me. I have never disobeyed him before, you see.'

I never knew she had the courage. That I did not remember. 'When will you tell him I am here?' He got to his feet, went to take her arm.

The door banged open with no warning knock. 'Hell's teeth and damnation.' The man on the threshold stared at Alex and then laughed. 'It really is you, my popinjay big brother, all grown up. Come to see if the old man's dead yet?'

'No. And do not swear in our mother's presence. Do you not knock on her boudoir door, or are you perhaps no longer a gentleman?' Alex found himself toe to toe with Matthew without realising he had moved. 'I will see you at dinner, Mama. You come with me.' He took his brother's arm, twisted it and had him out of the door before he could get his balance. He closed it behind them and pushed Matthew down the corridor out of earshot before he let him wrench free.

'Get your hands off me.'

Alex held both of his up, palm out. 'I imagine my appearance is a shock to you. Mother asked me to come.'

'The hell she did! And Garnett says you've got women with you and a baby.'

'There are two *ladies*. Gentlewomen, and you'll do well to remember that,' Alex said, keeping his voice soft, his hands by his sides. 'The baby belongs to Mrs White, the widow who is the companion to Miss Ellery. They find themselves unfortunately stranded in London. Mother has kindly offered them hospitality for the Christmas season.'

'We'll see what Father has to say about this.' Matthew turned on his heel and strode off towards the East Wing.

'You do that, brother mine,' Alex murmured as a door slammed violently in the distance. 'I just hope your reflexes are good enough to duck whatever he hurls at your head.'

Chapter Fourteen

'I am petrified,' Dorcas whispered. 'I've never been anywhere this elegant. I've never been anywhere except as a servant,' she added with a tremble in her voice.

'You told me your father was a doctor, Dorcas. You speak nicely, your manners are correct, your gown is perfectly acceptable. Besides, I don't think companions are expected to do more than sit in the background under these circumstances.'

'Good,' Dorcas muttered, her eyes on the back of the liveried footman sent to collect them for dinner. 'I'm glad we have an escort, this place is huge.'

The footman stopped, opened a pair of double doors. 'The Green Salon, ma'am.'

Tess took in a breath down to her toes. *I can do this.*

'Ah, good evening, ladies.' Lady Moreland held out one hand, gloved to the elbow in lavender kid. 'Do come and meet my younger son. Matthew, Miss Ellery, Mrs White.'

'Mr Tempest.' Tess inclined her head to the man who stood on the other side of the fireplace. She could see the resemblance to Alex, although he was shorter and stockier, but he had none of Alex's elegance or air of sophistication. He looked, she thought, sulky.

'I will leave Matthew to keep you company for a few moments while I make sure my husband has all he requires. I know you will excuse him eating in his chamber.' Lady Moreland shared a brittle smile between them and left the room.

'Miss Ellery. Absolutely charmed to meet you.' Matthew Tempest's gaze flickered over her figure, lingered on the bare skin exposed by the neckline of her simple evening gown. Tess felt her own smile congeal. She was not used to wearing anything so revealing and she was certainly not used to being ogled. Occasionally she caught a gleam of masculine awareness in Alex's eyes when they rested on her—more than occasionally, if she were to be honest—but not this blatant assessment. 'A bore for you to be landed with my brother's company,' he added.

'You think so, Mr Tempest? Lord Weybourn has been all that is kind.'

'He is hardly a ladies' man.' Mr Tempest

appeared to find that an inordinately amusing remark.

'He is, however, a gentleman,' Tess said as sweetly as gritted teeth would allow.

The laugh this time was a trifle forced. Not such a fool, Matthew Tempest, that he could not recognise an insult when it was offered. 'No doubt you feel very *safe* with him.'

Tess stared at him, then noticed the knowing smirk. He didn't mean... He couldn't. Yes, he did. She resisted the urge to box his ears and lowered her lashes coyly instead. 'As safe as a lady wishes to feel with a handsome gentleman.'

His jaw dropped and she strolled away to where Dorcas had perched on one end of a sofa. 'That poisonous little toad,' Tess whispered as she sat down beside her. 'He is jealous of his brother.'

'Oh, hush, Miss Ellery, he is coming over.'

Matthew Tempest had, it seemed, recovered his temper, or at least his composure. *Or else he thinks we are whispering about him and wants to find out what we are saying*, Tess thought as he strolled over to their sofa.

'May I fetch you ladies a glass of Madeira? Or sherry, perhaps? Ratafia?'

'Nothing, thank you,' Tess said as the door opened and Alex came in.

'Miss Ellery, Mrs White, forgive my tardiness. Matthew, now I see you in good light, how you have changed.'

'Hardly surprising, given that I was fifteen when you walked out on the family.' Neither brother made any move towards shaking hands, let alone embracing, Tess noticed. 'I had expected quite the court card, if not a fop.' There was reluctant admiration in Matthew's expression, Tess realised. Or perhaps envy. 'Tell me, who is your tailor? Weston?'

'Of course.' Alex's smile became more natural, as though to take the edge off the words. His clothing was so plain as to be almost austere. He wore black and white, his shirtfront with barely a ruffle, his only ornament the gold of his watch chain, the dull gleam of the intaglio seal ring and the glow of the amethyst in his neckcloth. 'Do you get up to town much?'

'No.' Matthew's voice was sulky. 'I'm kept tied to this place, at Father's beck and call.'

'He is sick after all. I have no doubt you're a help to him.'

'Ha! He's got perfectly good stewards and agents, but nothing will satisfy him but that he has to have a finger in every pie, read every report, send me out to check on this and that, and then what I tell him is always wrong, or too short in some tiresome detail or I've missed the point. Again.'

Tess felt a twinge of reluctant sympathy for the young man. His father must be seething with impatience at his own limitations and nothing Matthew did was going to be good enough. 'What would you prefer to be doing, Mr Tempest?' she asked him.

He shrugged, then seemed to realise he was speaking to a guest and a lady and took the sullen look off his face. 'Breed hunters. Hunt.'

'Be a country squire, in effect,' Alex said.

'Nothing wrong with that. I'm the younger son after all.' The aggression was back in his voice and Tess cast around for a neutral topic of conversation.

'I am so looking forward to seeing something of the English countryside. I have lived in Ghent for years.' From the hallway came the sound of raised voices and she broke off as the door opened.

Lady Moreland came in, still speaking over her shoulder as she did so. 'John, James, do be careful. Moreland, I do think—'

'I am going to eat dinner at my own board and see what this nonsense about that popinjay Alexander coming back is about.' The earl entered, batting irritably at the two footmen who were attempting to steady him on either side. 'Get off, damn it, I'm not in my coffin yet.' He stopped dead and stared. 'My God, he really is here. I thought Matthew must have been drinking. *Alexander?*'

'Father.' Two syllables. Two perfectly civil drops of ice.

Tess, her gaze flickering between the men, wondered if Alex was as shocked as his father. He had made a barely discernible movement when the earl came in. Now he was stock-still.

It must be like staring into a looking glass, one that aged the viewer on one hand and stripped years away on the other. They were obviously father and son. Everything proclaimed it—their height, their bone structure with those high cheekbones and thin nose. Alex had his eyes from his mother, but that was all. Lord Moreland had once had the physique to match his son; now the broad shoulders seemed bony and, despite the careful tailoring, his evening clothes looked loose, as though he had lost a lot of weight recently. His hair was still thick, but faded into grey now, and the heavy eyebrows were almost white. How old was he? Fifty-five, sixty? He should be in his prime, and he certainly resented its loss as much as he suffered from his symptoms.

'What in the blazes are you doing here, Weybourn?' Lord Moreland wrenched his arm from the grip of the supporting footman, took two steps and sank down on to the nearest chair.

'I have come to celebrate Christmas in the bosom of my family.' A nerve jumped in the angle of Alex's jaw, but his tone was bland. 'And, naturally, to enquire after your health.'

'Measure me for my coffin, more like. How did you hear I've had my notice to quit?'

'A well-wisher wrote to me that you were unwell.'

The silence seemed to shimmer, or perhaps she was feeling faint with tension. Tess caught the involuntary movement of her hand towards Alex and willed herself to stillness.

'And you brought guests with you.' Hooded eyes turned in her direction.

Tess made herself step forward. Her curtsy, by some miracle, did not waver, nor her knees fail her. 'My lord. I am most grateful for your hospitality to myself and my companion Mrs White at a most awkward time for us.'

'Miss Ellery, Father. Miss Ellery, the Earl of Moreland.'

'You'll forgive me if I do not rise.' The dark eyes assessed her gown, her lack of ornament, her ringless hands, then lifted to her face. 'Ellery? One of the Buckinghamshire Ellerys, I presume, by the look of you.'

Now she really might faint. Tess clenched her hands until the nails bit into her palms and the sting steadied her. 'I am not acquainted with the family you speak of, Lord Moreland.' And they were most certainly not acquainted with her; they had made quite sure of that.

'Very wise,' the man in front of her said. 'A top-lofty crew.'

'They do have a duke in their ranks, which probably accounts for it, Papa.' A pale version of Lady Moreland wandered into the room and blinked short-sightedly at its occupants. 'They are most dreadfully proud. Is that really Alexander?'

'Of course it is Alexander,' the earl snapped. 'Why don't you wear your spectacles, you foolish chit?'

'I've misplaced them.' The young woman drifted closer and squinted. 'Alexander, you've changed. How lovely to see you.'

'I should hope I have changed after ten years. And so have you, Maria.' Alex stooped and kissed her on the cheek. 'You were eight when I left. When do you have your come-out?'

'Oh, this Season, I expect.' She smiled and Tess was suddenly aware that for all her vagueness and pallor the girl had intelligence and more than a share of Alex's charm.

'Unless I cock up my toes, which is more than likely, the way you crows all fuss and flap around me.' The earl appeared to take a perverse pleasure in the prospect of ruining his daughter's debut with a year of mourning.

Alex, ignoring the interjection, turned to Tess. 'Miss Ellery, may I introduce my sister, Lady Maria?'

'How do you do?' Close up the hazel eyes focused and the air of vagueness disappeared. What had Alex said? That his sister was sensitive. Tess had taken that as meaning foolish or hysterical, but she rather suspected he had meant she was attuned to other people. 'Mama told me what a fix you are in, Miss Ellery. Such a pity. Never mind, you'll be comfortable here. Shall we sit down?' She went over to the sofa and held out her hand to Dorcas, who shot to her feet and took it as though it was red hot.

Tess joined them, ready to deflect attention before Dorcas melted with nerves. Behind her she heard the earl growl some comment to Alex, but she was too grateful to be able to sit down to listen to his words.

'Sit down, Weybourn.'

Alex took the chair opposite his father and made a business of crossing his legs, smoothing a wrinkle from his thin silk evening breeches, tugging a cuff. It gave him something to do with his hands and, after all, one could not hit one's own father, not when the old devil was ill.

'Why have you come back? To apologise?'

'Certainly I owe my mother and sister an apology for my absence,' Alex conceded. 'I am not aware of any other apology owing. From me, that is.'

He had remembered his father's eyes as brown. Now they seemed black against his pale skin. 'You expect *me* to apologise?'

'It is normal, when a gentleman wrongs another.' Alex kept his tone mild and found to his surprise that it was easy. He was confronting the bogeyman of his memories and his nightmares and here was a sick, frustrated, angry man, old before his time. Someone to be pitied, if he could find it in himself. If he wanted to find the capacity to pity. There was Peter to remember and avenge. Peter, who was ten years in the cold ground thanks to the man in front of him.

'But this is not something to discuss now.' Alex glanced around him, saw his mother's eyes on him, felt the weight of Tess's anxiety behind him. She was upset and by more than tension over this scene or their deception. He tried to recall when he had first noticed it, then set the puzzle aside. He could not focus on it, not now, with his father's sardonic gaze on his face and the hostility coming off Matthew in palpable waves.

'Certainly not in front of the ladies,' his father

agreed with a bitter twist of his lips that negated the reasonable tone and words. 'In my study at ten tomorrow.'

'Naturally. The usual place and time.' That was always the summons at dinner time whenever one of his sons had done something wrong, and that was usually Alex, not Matthew. Ten the next day, a time carefully chosen to ensure a night of anxiety and a lack of appetite at breakfast.

'Dinner is served, my lady.'

Alex rose and offered his hand to his father to help him stand. The big hand with its rider's calluses still hard on the palm hesitated, then closed around his and gripped, shifting over the evidence of Alex's own hard riding, the strength that endless practice with the foils gave, the healed scars on the knuckles.

The older man allowed him to get him upright, then he shook off Alex's grip. 'Take your mother in.'

'Of course, sir. Mama?' Alex gave her his arm and saw his father turn to Tess, hesitating behind.

'Miss Ellery.'

She came forward and rested her fingertips on his forearm. Had she ever sat down to a formal dinner before, even a small family affair? He doubted it. But her chin was up and she seemed confident enough. The woman who could stand up to loutish sailors and fight off randy attackers could cope. *Not my little nun anymore*, he thought with a twist of something remarkably like regret.

With four ladies and three men the table was, of necessity, unbalanced. Alex took the seat on his mother's right and smiled encouragement at Dorcas, pale but determined, opposite him. Tess, diagonally across on his father's right, was looking composed and appeared to be discussing Brussels lace, of all things, with Matthew, but the table was too large to hear clearly. She was on her own.

What was it his father had asked her? Whether she was one of the Buckinghamshire Ellerys, that was it; that was what had discomposed her so. *Strange.*

The meal seemed endless, with the quality of a dream. It was as though ten years had passed in ten hours with the wave of some malevolent sorcerer's wand. The table was the same, the china service the familiar one, the decoration and pictures in the dining room unchanged and yet everyone in the room had aged and altered.

And then Tess turned her head, looked directly at him and smiled. If she had reached out and touched his hand, he could not have felt the gesture more directly. *This is the right thing*, the smile told him. *Take courage, you can do this.*

Somehow they all got through the meal, maintained a light, empty social chatter through every course. When his mother rose to lead the ladies out Matthew went to take his father's arm and supported him from the room. Alex did not make the mistake of offering his own assistance.

He went to present himself in the drawing room, but found only Maria. 'Miss Ellery and her companion have gone to bed and Mama is with Papa.'

'Not very entertaining for you.'

'I am used to it,' Maria said with a shrug and her faint smile. 'Matthew will be off to some local alehouse or another, I have no doubt, so at least we may be comfortable and I am all agog to hear about your life in London.'

It was almost eleven before Maria yawned her way off to bed, to dream, she assured him, of mantua makers, Almack's and strolling in Hyde Park with her brother, to the envy of every other young lady.

Alex found the decanters, poured himself a brandy and made his way to the library. It still had the old familiar look of neglect, despite having been polished and dusted. Alex trailed a finger along the edge of a shelf and it came away clean. No doubt his mother and sister had their own books in their boudoirs and bedchambers, not in this bastion of male importance with its leather bindings and gold tooling, massive furniture and imposing lecterns and atlas stands.

Did his father or Matthew ever set foot in here? When he had lived at Tempeston the library had been one of his refuges, a treasure trove of stories and facts, imagination and mind-stretching realities. No time for those now.

He found the massive volume bound in red leather and lifted it down, flipping through the pages. Eden, Eldridge…Ellery. James Augustus Finmore Ellery, third Marquess of Sethcombe, married…had issue… Four sons, five daughters. One son and two daughters died in infancy, the other three sons married with families of their own. Two of the surviving daughters also married. No familiar names amongst that host of hopeful youngsters. His finger reached the bottom of the list.

Jane Teresa Ellery, born 1775, died, unmarried, 1809.

1809. Died unmarried. This was Tess's mother, surely. He stood there, his fingernail scoring a line under the name. Why did that matter so much, to him? To Tess, obviously, the stigma of illegitimacy must be why she was so resigned to a life in service. But for him? He could pity her, admire her stoical determination to overcome her heredity and make a living for herself, but it was more than that—he felt winded as though he had received a blow in the diaphragm.

When the reason hit him it rocked him back on his heels. The heir of the Tempests did not marry anyone but a pure-bred aristocratic heiress. But *marriage*? Where had that come from? Surely he had not been thinking of Tess in those terms? The door handle rattled. Someone was coming.

Chapter Fifteen

The room was deserted, but there was a branch of candles on the table next to a untidy pile of journals that seemed out of place in the rigidly ordered space. Tess lifted them and flicked through. *Notes and Queries*, *The Gentleman's Magazine*, *Proceedings of the Royal Society*. She straightened them into a neater pile and set it next to the thick red book they had been balanced on, the *Peerage*.

'Drat the man. Where is he?' It seemed as she stood there that she had been mistaken and the silent room was not empty after all. Tess told herself firmly that there was nothing to be alarmed about. This was not a Gothic novel, there were no ghosts and her nerves were merely a trifle overset. She had disturbed a servant setting things to rights, or perhaps the earl employed a librarian or— 'Alex!'

'I'm sorry, did I alarm you?' He rose to his

feet and emerged from what must be an alcove behind a massive atlas stand, an open book in one hand. He seemed pale in the candlelight.

'Oh. Oh, Alex.' Tess was not conscious of moving, let alone running, but somehow she was in his arms, her own tight around him. And she was crying, with no idea why.

'Hey, what's this? Tess?' His fingers were under her chin, tipping her head back. She managed a comprehensive, unladylike sniff and blinked the tears away. 'Who has upset you?'

'No one. Everything. I'm so sorry, I should never have come here with you. Your mother doesn't need us—Dorcas and me, that is. Your father is…I had some stupid idea that you only had to walk in and he'd forget whatever had made him reject you and he would welcome you with open arms. But he is hard and angry and bitter.' She stared fixedly at the amethyst in the folds of his neckcloth. 'You were quite right. I am sentimental and foolish. There isn't some Christmas magic that will make this all right. It is hard enough for you without having me and all your staff here.'

'Tess.' Alex pulled her in closer, apparently careless of the effect of her wet cheeks on his crisp linen. 'If it wasn't for you this would be a hundred times more difficult. I want to rant and hector and lay down conditions. My instinct is to give my father an ultimatum, to force him to surrender all the business of the earldom into my hands, to pay him back by making him weak and dependent on me and to kick Matthew out on half his allowance and see how he fends for himself. Then I look at you and tell myself not to do anything that would make you think less of me.'

There was a weight on top of her head, and she guessed he had rested his cheek there. What was it that his father had done? Whatever it was it must have been dire indeed to generate this much resentment and confusion.

'You are a very civilising influence on me, Miss Ellery,' Alex murmured. Warmth stirred her hair as his breathing steadied.

'The earl hasn't shown you the door,' Tess ventured, wondering why his father might do such a thing. Alex seemed quite content to stand there all night holding her. It was lovely, but not…*easy.*

'He knows he needs me. He is going to pretend he doesn't know my mother went against his prohibitions to write to me because if she had waited much longer he would have had to do it himself and this saved his pride. My father might be stubborn, belligerent and bigoted, but he is not a fool and he is devoted to the earldom. He will do his duty by it and he is not going to cut off his nose to spite his face.'

'It will make a great deal of work for you.' It would turn his world upside down, the world that Hannah said he had created for himself from nothing. 'You are going to do it, aren't you? You'll stay.'

'I don't see what else I can do. This is my duty. Not to him, but to the estate, and to my mother, of course. I will certainly not be able to concentrate on anything else. I'll have to stop my own business, stop travelling, stop dealing.'

'But you love it,' Tess protested, pulling back against his arms to look at him.

'I've had ten years of freedom.' Alex shrugged. 'Now it is time to bend my neck to the yoke.' He made a disgusted sound. 'Listen to me, full of self-pity for having to do my duty, for having to accept privilege and make some return for it. My family needs me, my inheritance needs me, our tenants and dependents need me. I can do some good for my mother and sister and for Matthew, if he'll let me. And heaven knows, there should be satisfaction in mastering something I should have been learning from my majority.'

'You are a good man, Alexander Tempest.' Tess lifted her hand to his cheek so she could turn his head and look into his eyes. 'A very good man.'

For a moment, as he met her gaze, she thought he was going to swear at her, throw her hand aside. When he spoke his voice was low and angry and fierce. 'No, I am not a good man. If I was, then I'd forgive him and I'd do this willingly. But I cannot forgive, I cannot forget and I want to make the old devil beg me to do both. Does that make me any better than he is? I doubt it.'

It cost her an effort of will to keep still, keep her tongue silent with the questions clamouring for an answer. 'I let myself dream about a life on my own terms,' he added. All the old cynicism was back in his voice, his expression. Once she had believed he genuinely did not care. Now... 'It was only an illusion, of course. This place, this title, was always waiting for me.'

'It is not all bad.' She made herself put into words the truths that had been haunting her. 'You will marry now, have a family.'

The shadowed face became even starker. He turned abruptly, went to the table, picked up the *Peerage* and slammed it back into a gap on the shelves, one hand lingering on the spine as though to trap it there. 'Go to bed, Tess,' Alex said without looking round.

'I wish I could help.'

'You cannot help, little nun.' His back was still a blank barrier. All she had to read was his voice, and that had lost all its flexibility, all its music. She ignored the words, answered only the pain under them, went to him, pressed herself against that long, strong spine and held on to the broad shoulders, her cheek against his shoulder blade. She could hear his sharply indrawn breath, the hammer of his heartbeat.

'I am not a nun.'

'I wish you were.'

'Why? Why on earth should you want that?' She stayed wrapped around him as though touching would make him easier to understand.

'Because then you would be out of reach, forbidden, protected by your vows. I want you too much, Tess. I want you in my bed, I want you naked under me, to be inside you, possessing you. Is that clear enough?

'Yes.' *Oh, yes.*

'Then, run. Cling to Dorcas, stay at my mother's side, make Maria your inseparable companion, because I am just about at the end of my tether, Tess, and I want you to be safe.'

I love you. Her lips formed the words, silently. Why had she not admitted it to herself before? It wasn't simple desire, or even liking that she felt for him, it was love. Should she say it? No. *Alex is not for me and never could be, not forever. But for one night, two or three, while he needs me...*

It went against everything she had been taught about morals and virtue. But where was the morality in denying Alex comfort? Where was the virtue in denying her own feelings for him? Tess lifted her hands from his still body and stepped back, away. 'I would never run from you, Alex. I would never feel I had to. But I will go now.'

In the luxury of the Chinese Bedchamber, with its painted scenes of exotic gardens and groups of figures, Tess surrendered to the ministrations of the highly trained lady's maid that the countess had allocated to them. She wondered how Dorcas had coped with being waited on for the first time in her life. Well enough, she supposed, for when she eased open the door and looked into the Rose Chamber Dorcas was fast asleep in a nest of pink satin bedcoverings.

After she had washed and undressed, the maid helped her into her nightgown and robe and then proceeded to let down her hair and brush it. 'One hundred times, Miss Ellery?'

'Yes, thank you.' It would give her time to gather her courage. There were bottles of scented waters on the dressing table and she sniffed each in turn and wondered whether to dab something more exotic than her usual lavender water behind her ears. No, it was the unsophisticated Tess whom Alex seemed to want, not some elegant lady. It was going to be nerve-racking enough without pretending to be anything but what she was.

The first thing was to find Alex's bedchamber, otherwise she would be wandering about blind and, knowing her luck, would probably end up in the earl's room. 'This is such a large house,' she remarked. 'I have never been in one so extensive. I suppose all the family rooms are clustered in the middle for convenience and the guest rooms out in these wings.'

'Oh, no, miss, they are all spread out. Lord Moreland has his suite in the West Wing, her ladyship and Lady Maria are in the central block and Mr Matthew prefers the tower rooms. Lord Weybourn has the suite with the park view, just at the other end of this wing.'

Hardly a close and loving family, Tess mused as she made conversation about the lovely views from all aspects. But it was wonderfully convenient for her. She had been quailing at the thought of tiptoeing through the silent corridors, no doubt patrolled by attentive servants, but now she knew exactly where she was going.

The maid tucked her up in bed, moved the Argand reading lamp to the most convenient side and tried Tess's patience to screaming point by enquiring if Miss Ellery required some hot milk? Or some biscuits? More blankets, perhaps?

Alone at last Tess lay still, listening to the clock ticking. Finally it struck the half hour. Past midnight. Surely everyone would be in bed by now? Alex always sent Byfleet off once he had changed for dinner, apparently preferring the solitude to having someone help him out of his evening clothes, so there was not even that to worry about.

When she opened the door all was quiet, the corridor dimly lit by a shielded lamp on a table. Tess walked rapidly, her bare feet silent on the polished boards. She found the door, eased it open and tiptoed into a dressing room. It was unoccupied and she stood listening, inhaling the faint aroma of Alex's cologne. When she plucked up the courage to try the door the bedchamber was deserted, also. She crossed to the far side and found a sitting room, equally empty.

Where was Alex? Surely not still in the library? The room was lit by three Argand lamps, the fire was banked up behind a guard and decanters were ranged on a dresser, so he was obviously expected to be sleeping there. Tess unfastened her robe and folded it on to a chair, climbed into the bed and sat there, prey to nerves. Should she take of her nightgown, as well? That seemed very bold, but then, being here in the first place was so shocking that nudity could hardly make things worse. Besides, it was hardly a very seductive garment—always assuming Alex would need seducing. Tess wriggled out of it and got back under the covers. She had never slept naked before.

The clock struck one. It felt very…gauche, sitting there bolt upright, the sheets clutched under her chin. Tess lay down. She could try to relax, just close her eyes. He wouldn't be much longer, surely?

She woke to the sound of someone moving around the room. Glass clinked against glass, someone sighed, as though weary, there were two thuds that she recognised as shoes being tossed aside. *Alex.*

Tess eased herself up against the pillows and found he was standing with his back to her. He took off his coat, dropped it on a chair and began to untie his neckcloth one-handed while the other held a glass with a finger of dark liquid in it. He set down the glass, took off his waistcoat and then started to unfasten his evening breeches.

I should say something. But her mouth was too dry. The breeches dropped to the floor and, thank heavens for maidenly nerves, the hem of his shirt dropped, too. Even so, even covered to mid-thigh, the sight of a pair of strong, muscled, hairy male legs was shocking. *Exciting...* *I cannot sit here spying on him.* Tess cleared her throat.

Alex spun round. 'What in Hades are you doing here?'

He sounded both angry and confused, but there had been one moment, one blink of an eye, when his face had lit up with welcome, with pleasure. It gave her the courage she needed to speak. 'I wanted to be with you. I need to be with you, Alex.'

Now she could not read his face at all. Alex grabbed a robe from the end of the bed and dragged it on, yanked the sash tight. 'If anyone discovers you are here, even if I come no closer than this, then you are ruined, Tess.'

'Ruined for what, exactly? I am not some young miss about to embark on her Season, someone whose virtue and purity is as important as her bloodlines and her dowry. I am destined to earn my living, not to wed. Will knowing what it means to lie with a man make me any less able as a companion, any less competent as a teacher?'

'No.' Alex picked up his glass again, stared at it, then slammed it down.

'I will not go from your bed to some den of vice to take part in wild orgies,' she said. 'I am not going to sell my body as a result. I know you desire me. I did not need you to tell me that in the library this evening. I desire you, too, and you know that, also.'

'What if I get you with child?'

'Then, you will provide for us, I imagine.' She felt calmer as his vehemence grew. 'I would never make any further claim on you and you are not betrothed, or even courting another woman, are you?'

'Tess, desire is not enough reason to risk your reputation.' Alex stood at the end of the bed, his hand on the post supporting the canopy. She knew him too well now to believe he was furious with her for being there, or that he wanted her to leave. But he was angry with himself for wanting her to stay, for wanting her at all: that she could believe.

'No, it is not,' she agreed, her fingers cramping on the edge of the sheet. 'But the need for comfort is, the need to be with someone. Curiosity is, too. I am never going to marry, Alex. I am never going to find another man I trust as I trust you, one that I could risk an affair with. I would wish for memories to warm my future dreams and I think you would welcome some warmth now.'

He was so still that time might have stopped if it were not for the tick of the clock, the crackle of the fire, the beat of her heart echoing the pulse she could see in his throat.

'No,' Alex said.

She had one card left in her hand, and she had no idea whether it was an ace or worthless. It cost enough to hazard, so perhaps it had some value. Tess released the sheet, threw back the covers, slid from the bed and stood naked before a man for the first time in her life. She closed her eyes.

'Tess.'

Was that good or bad? She was no beauty, she knew that. She was skinny and her breasts were small and she knew men liked breasts. But her hair was down and perhaps that covered some of the sharp angles.

'Tess.' Right in front of her. She could smell him now, smell his warm skin, his familiar citrus cologne, the plain soap from the bath he must have taken before dinner. 'Look at me.'

She opened her eyes, knowing she must be one whole blush, not having any idea what to do with her hands. Alex was so close she could see his irises were dilated, so close she could hear his breathing, see his slightly parted lips.

'I told you to run.' His hands were on the knot of his sash.

'I did. I ran here. I am a grown woman, Alex. I know what I want, what I need. Must I plead with you?'

'No. Never that.' He untied the knot at his waist, shrugged off the robe, pulled the shirt over his head and stood in front of her as naked as she was. Behind him the glow of the fire cast a nimbus of gold around his body. From in front the steady light from the little lamp threw sculpted muscles, long bones, taut tendons into sharp relief.

He was beautiful. Her exploring, fascinated gaze moved lower, stopped. This, then, was what an aroused man looked like. The fashion for tight evening breeches was revealing enough to demonstrate to even the most ignorant young woman that there was a difference between the man who had been at dinner that evening and the same man now. *Magnificent.* She managed not to say it aloud. There were other words—*alarming, impossible*—she did not say those, either.

'Do I frighten you, Tess?' His voice was husky with repressed emotion.

'No. Another man would, I think. Never you. Tell me you want this, too, that you are not doing this because I asked you.'

He laughed, a gasp of pure amusement. 'Tess, I can't feign this.' His gesture was graphic enough not to need words. 'Are you sure?'

'Nothing, except the most dire need, would have me standing in front of a man without a stitch of clothing on,' she assured him. *It is going to be all right. He wants me, I want him, we can be together, like this, for these few days.*

'You are smiling.' So was he. 'Come to bed, Tess, before you get cold.'

Chapter Sixteen

Such a prosaic thing, to scramble into bed, to feel the mattress dip under Alex's heavier body, to see his big, capable hands pull up the covers.

'I was quite nervous,' she confided. 'I still am. I have no idea what I am supposed to do.' If she wasn't careful she'd be chattering with nerves and that was the last thing he wanted, she imagined. Bad enough a gauche innocent; a wittering female would be even worse.

'Then, spare a thought for the virgin male.' He slid farther down the bed and pulled her with him to snuggle against his side. The slide of warm skin against skin was delicious. She itched to explore with her hands, but did not want to be clumsy.

'You know the theory, or at least, you think you do,' Alex said, his tone reminiscent. That was good, nothing was going to happen quite yet, not until she had her breath back. 'But the fellows who impart these facts are probably boasting. You hope they are. And you're the man, even if you are only fifteen and you haven't grown into your feet yet and your body and its reactions are certainly not under your control. So you think you ought to know what you are doing, you are sure you have it all straight…and then you encounter the female body.'

The hand that was curved around her ribs began to stroke, the fingers caressing slowly down the side of her breast. Alex continued speaking as though unaware of what his hand was doing. Tess kept very quiet and still in case he noticed and stopped.

'So soft, so responsive and so…complicated. There are curves, you know that, you have ogled them secretly for long enough. But then you discover the weight of a breast in your palm.'

He shifted, moved his arm and her small breast was lying cupped in his hand. 'It is heavier than you imagine it will be and so unexpectedly erotic it takes your breath away. Then you discover this.' His thumb moved, fretted back and forth across her nipple.

Tess gasped as the sensation arrowed down into her belly and her flesh became hard under the pad of his thumb.

'You see?' Alex shifted again so that he was half over her, his weight on one elbow. 'Not only does it feel good, not only are you rewarded by that little miracle of a reaction, but you discover you have given her pleasure, too. So you try the other breast, only this time you find yourself doing this.' He bent and took her other nipple between his lips, his tongue rubbing against her tight flesh while his fingers continued to tease the other nub. 'And you discover for the first time how good a woman tastes and you wonder if she tastes the same all over. You forgot to kiss her at first because you were so nervous and so clumsy in your eagerness.'

He moved until his mouth was a fraction from hers. 'So you taste her mouth.'

Tess arched against him as their lips met. He squashed her breasts into his chest, squeezed the nipple he was still fondling tight between his fingers, which should have hurt, but strangely only made the deep ache inside better, and worse. His tongue was talking now, showing her how he would go about exploring her taste, sweeping over hers, teasing the inside of her cheeks, withdrawing to stroke along her lips. He nibbled at them until she began to shift under him, restless, aching, and he lifted his head.

'You discover that her mouth tastes different from her skin. Delicious, uniquely her, but different. So you want to taste more and you go adventuring.' He slid down, pausing to lick across her breasts in great, wet, sweeping strokes of his tongue that made her want to giggle and moan all at once. Then down to her belly. His tongue traced her hip bones, her bony hip bones, she thought in despair. It tickled impertinently into her navel, which did make her giggle.

Alex shrugged off the bedcovers, which had tented over his head, and looked up, his face alive with the old familiar smile that she had despaired of seeing again. 'And this is different again. But now you are getting impatient because you haven't learned that restraint increases pleasure and you are still terrified that you are going to get this all wrong, so you start to shift, thinking about what has to go where and worrying that you aren't the right size, or shape or...'

'Or?' She could still speak. Just. Something was happening to her body and whatever it was, she seemed to have no control over it at all.

'Or...you don't know, just that you are scared to death and in heaven, too. So she, this beautiful, generous, wise, woman gives you a nudge in the right direction. Put your hand on my head and push.'

'Push?' His head? Confused, she did as he asked.

Alex slid down another foot or so, pressed her thighs apart and kissed her.

Tess opened her mouth to scream, but all that emerged was a long, groaning purr of pure, wicked pleasure. His tongue foraged into the secret folds, his teeth nibbled, his lips sucked and kissed and... *'Ooh!'*

Tess came to herself to find Alex lying on her, his weight on his elbows, his legs between her spread thighs. He lodged perfectly in the cradle her body made. 'That was...'

'Good, isn't it?' He grinned, obviously pleased for both of them.

'I had no idea. I thought you just...' She blushed. 'Um, put it...'

'We can do that next.' He shifted his hips and something pressed against her. Alex frowned when she wriggled, eager. 'It might not be so good, not the first time, I understand.'

'Have you never made love to a virgin before?' The pressure was more of an intrusion now, but this was Alex, she told herself, he would be as careful as he could be.

'No, so this is a first time for both of us. I think...' He nudged forward a little. 'Yes, quick might be good.'

'Ow!' They both went still. Tess considered how she felt. 'Go on.'

So he did. Things went from tight and sore to tight and wonderful to a glorious confusion of sensation and movement. 'Oh, Alex! *Yes.*'

She felt him go tense, then pull away and then groan as he held her and she slipped into a haze of pleasure.

'Tess, sweetheart.' A whisper in her ear, a hand gliding over her hip, then settling between her thighs.

'Hmm.' She wriggled against Alex's fingers. 'Again?'

'No, wicked one. Time for you to go back to your own bed.'

She sat up and found the beside lamp still burning and illuminating the very gratifying sight of one large naked man stretched out on the bed beside her. Alex even managed to look elegant with morning stubble and not a stitch of clothing. *My lover. My love.*

He got up and bent to retrieve her nightgown, affording a magnificent view of taut buttocks and trim waist. 'What?' he enquired as he turned.

'I was ogling you.' Tess put on the nightgown. 'You are a very pleasing shape.'

To her delight colour slashed across his cheekbones as he reached for his robe, then made a business of finding hers. 'No slippers?'

'No, I was tiptoeing. Look at all those muscles.' She reached for his arm and curled her fingers around his biceps as far as they would go.

'I think I was seduced by your shoulders from that first evening.'

'I was trying very hard to think of you as a nun,' he confessed as he removed her hand from his arm and pulled her to her feet. 'It was overly exciting to discover that nuns do not wear corsets.'

'I do now.' Tess tied the sash of her robe.

'That can have its moments, too. Now hush.'

He delivered her back to her door. As she closed it she heard a muffled sound as though a hand had been laid against the panels, then the soft pad of his footsteps.

'I love you,' she whispered. 'Sleep well, Alex.'

Alex strolled along the corridor to the study, consciously slowing his pace to distance himself from the anxious scurry of the nervous youth he had been the last time he'd been ordered here.

He had given up on sleep at the first faint sound of servants moving discreetly around the house. Before he had taken her back to her room he had dozed with Tess in his arms, too shaken by the experience to lose himself in unconsciousness. Besides, it was a new pleasure to lie like this with a lover and to watch over her, observe the flicker of her eyes beneath those fragile lids as she dreamed, the soft, parted lips, the way her hair lay like silk on his shoulder.

She had been right; this had made them both happy. Now he had to make certain nothing went wrong for her. He was most certainly not going to allow her to go off to some employment agency in the new year and tie herself to some form of genteel drudgery. Somehow he had to persuade her to accept his support without her firing up and declaring it was payment for coming to his bed.

Now, despite the lack of sleep, he felt alert and much calmer than he had last evening. More accepting of a fate he could not, in all honour, avoid, he supposed, although a desire to forgive still eluded him.

The clock struck ten. He knocked and entered. 'Good morning, Father.' He would not give way to the urge to say *my lord*. The man was his parent.

'Sit down.' His father sat behind the great mahogany desk that still looked vast, even from an adult's viewpoint. 'Let us not beat about the bush. Your mother would have me understand that you are not the effeminate pervert I accused you of being.'

'Well, that is certainly to the point.' Alex settled himself in the chair opposite. 'Let me be equally clear. I have never been attracted to my own sex. I have never been with a member of my own sex. However, I do have—and had—

friends who have that sexual inclination and I will not stay in this house to hear them insulted in the terms you have just used.'

His father's pale face flushed an unhealthy red. 'It is a hanging offence.'

'Indeed it is. And let us be clear about something else, as well. You accused Peter Agnew, my best friend, of being my lover.'

'He was older than you, he had a reputation—'

'He was my friend. Never my lover.' Alex fought to keep rational, not to shout and rant, throw all the anger that had seethed inside over the blind prejudice that had led his father to leap to conclusions. 'We had grown up together and he was like an older brother to me. He knew very well that I was attracted to women, and only women. God, I must have bored him to tears, pouring out all my youthful infatuations with this girl and that, confiding all the things that worried me before the first time.

'He would have no more tried to seduce me than any man of honour would attempt to seduce the daughter of a friend. In my ignorance, I had no idea how he felt about me until I read the letter he sent me before he blew out his brains. And he did that because you'd broadcast his name around the neighbourhood. Would you have had the restraint and the decency to suppress everything you felt for someone because it was for their own good? Would I? That keeps me awake at night sometimes, wondering. I have no idea if I can ever forgive you for it.' Somehow he had said it without losing his temper, without raising his voice.

He had never spoken of it except to his four friends at university. He had fled back to Oxford, angry, guilty, racked with shame and grief. They'd listened, Cris and Grant and Gabriel. Cris had simply flung his arms around him in a bear hug and then Gabe handed him a large brandy and Grant had said, 'Whatever you want to do, we're with you.' He knew then he could stand on his own two feet and that they would always have his back, just as he would have theirs.

His father was still glowering. Strangely it made it easier to stay calm. 'I really do not understand why you feel I had to fit into the mould of hunting, drinking, wenching masculinity you favour in order to be an adequate heir to the earldom. I was bookish, interested in art. That was, apparently, enough to label me less than manly.' Alex shrugged. 'If you had taken the trouble, you might have discovered that I am an excellent fencer, a more than adequate rider and that I actually perform quite well in the boxing ring. I just tend to do it all rather quietly and while dressed with elegance.'

His father glowered at him. 'You had no idea

about young Agnew? Damn it, rumours were flying about his behaviour at Cambridge. I assumed…'

Alex stared back at the red face opposite him. If his father was going to bluster and rant, refuse to accept he had been wrong, then he was going to walk out of this house and never come back.

'I was wrong.' Gradually the hectic colour in his father's face subsided.

Alex let out the breath he had been unaware of holding, unclenched his hands from the arms of the chair. *You stubborn, thickheaded old devil. Why not just* ask *me?* Alex got up, poured a glass of brandy and set it by his hand. 'You look as though you could do with that.'

'What are your debts?' the earl snapped.

'Debts? None at all. I am a rich man, Father. I don't need your money. I most certainly do not need this aggravation.'

'So doing your duty is an aggravation, is it?'

'Certainly. I doubt I'll have any time for my own business or for travelling, not if I'm to do this properly.'

'You'll need a wife. Time you were setting up your nursery.' He narrowed his eyes in calculation. 'Not that young woman you've brought with you. Pleasant chit, unspoiled, I like that. But no family from what I could extract from her.'

'No.' No family that would acknowledge her,

that was certain. The heir to an earldom did not marry an unknown miss straight from a convent. He certainly did not marry the illegitimate offspring of the daughter of a near neighbour. It had not struck him that he might want to marry Tess until he had seen the evidence of her parentage in black and white in the *Peerage*. Foolish that, to be so attracted to a woman, to feel so protective of her, so aroused by her and not realise that he was developing feelings that went far deeper than affection. Foolish and damnably painful.

It was tempting to announce that he would never marry and to stick the knife in that way, but that, too, was foolish. He had to wed; he knew that now. All he had to do was accept it.

'I'll squire Maria around for her Season. That will expose me to all the eligibles.' It would make him feel like a buyer at a cattle market. How the devil did you come to *know* a woman that way? He knew Tess right through to her heart, and after last night he thought he probably knew her soul deep, as well.

He couldn't just abandon her, not after she had given him everything, and all because she saw him as another stray to care for, like Dorcas and Annie or that damned kitten. Somehow he had to get her to accept an allowance.

'What's making you look so sour?' The earl tossed back a mouthful of brandy.

My guilty conscience. And this damn pain round my heart. 'The thought of Almack's.' Alex looked at his father and dug deep into his reserves of patience and diplomacy. He was far from forgiving, an infinity from accepting, but he had to make this work for the sake of his mother and sister, for the earldom. 'Tell me what needs doing and we'll work this out.' *Somehow.*

Tess made her way to the drawing room, feeling absurdly conspicuous. No one had observed her whispered consultation with MacDonald, Dorcas and Byfleet, but she was sure Lady Moreland would thoroughly disapprove. What she would think about how her son had spent the previous night, Tess shuddered to think. The shudder turned into a *frisson* of remembered delight at the thought of Alex's hands on her body, just as she turned a corner and walked straight into him.

'*Alex.*'

He pulled her close and bent his head. 'I need you.'

'Alex, we can't—not here.' *Yes, please, right here. Kiss me...* 'But we must talk, urgently.'

'What is wrong?' He opened the nearest door and bundled her into what proved to be a small, cold sitting room. 'We shouldn't be disturbed here, it was never used except in the summer.'

He sat down on a settee and pulled her on to his lap. 'Snuggle up, you'll get cold. Now tell me what is wrong. Is it about last night? I can't regret it, although I know I should. Are you sorry this morning, Tess?'

'No, certainly not. It was very…'

'Nice? Adequate? Alarming?'

'Stop fishing for compliments.' She curled into his embrace and butted him gently under the chin. 'It was surprising and wonderful and I feel very *womanly* this morning.'

'Hmm.' He nuzzled against her neck. 'I think you feel very womanly, too. So what is concerning you?'

'Christmas and our—your—staff. We had promised them a whole day to themselves—now what do we do? The staff here seem to expect to have to spend the entire day looking after the household.'

'I suppose they do.' She could hear the frown in Alex's voice. 'I never thought about it as a child, or a thoroughly selfish youth. Christmases just happened and they were crowded, noisy and involved a lot of people who spent most of the time arguing and eating and drinking too much. Are you sure you want to bother with this?'

She sat up straight and frowned at him. 'I thought you'd accepted that we were going to celebrate Christmas. You bought presents, you let us decorate the house…'

'That was back in London. You could have your Christmas downstairs, do what you like. If we start something here, goodness knows where it will end—the entire family glowering at each other around the dinner table while the carol singers serenade us, I expect.'

'It might help bring everyone together,' she ventured.

'I don't want bringing together.' There was silence. 'I suppose you are going to be disappointed.'

'Yes.' She was not letting him wriggle out of this.

'Very well. I'll talk to Mama. In fact, we'll both talk to her. I'll explain that you were organising it for me because Hannah was sick.'

He did not seem to be in any hurry to move. 'Alex?'

'Wriggle like that again.' His huff of laughter tickled her ear, his good humour apparently resorted. 'Come on, then, let's find Mama.'

Lady Moreland was in her sitting room with her household accounts spread out before her. 'Alexander, can you explain why we appear to be consuming three times more wax candles than this time last year?'

'No idea, I'm afraid. Mama, I brought my household staff with me as you know. I had promised them the whole of Christmas Day off for their own celebrations, now I find myself in a difficulty because we are here.'

'The entire day? You are very generous, Alexander.'

'I normally just have a cold meal that day. Miss Ellery and Mrs White profess themselves willing to make do, as well.'

'We wondered,' Tess ventured, 'if perhaps a hot luncheon would be sufficient for above stairs, with a cold buffet laid out for the evening. All of the downstairs staff could then celebrate together.'

'We could forgo dressing for dinner, just this once, Mama,' Alex said. 'An afternoon and evening doesn't seem too extravagant, once a year.'

'Unless that would be too disruptive for Lord Moreland?' Tess said, suddenly wondering how that sickly and irritable despot would take to the idea.

'If Alexander can persuade his father, then I have no objection. To tell you the truth, a quiet Christmas would be a blessing just now.'

'Forgive me, Lady Moreland. I do not wish to presume, but would it be helpful if I speak to the staff about it—provided we have his lordship's consent? I would wish to be of assistance.'

The countess looked at Tess, a small, considering smile on her lips. Tess shifted under the gaze. Was *no longer a virgin* emblazoned on her forehead? Or perhaps she was allowing her feelings for Alex to show. But his mother was definitely smiling. 'Thank you, my dear. I think that would be very…appropriate. Alexander, tell your father I am in favour of this scheme.'

Tess glanced at Alex, relieved, but surprised, and found that he was looking at his mother with a quizzical expression as though he, too, was taken aback by those smiles and her agreement. She shrugged inwardly. Provided no one found out that she was sharing Alex's bed and no one discovered who she was, then there was nothing to worry about.

Chapter Seventeen

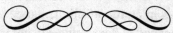

'We will go and find Garnett and take his advice on how to proceed with our party.' Alex steered Tess in the direction of the main hall.

'Your mother… I expected her to be reluctant,' Tess confessed. 'And yet she seemed quite approving of it.'

'I suspect the approval is for you rather than the scheme,' Alex said.

She wished they were in private so she could rub away the lines from between his brows. It took her a moment to realise just what he was frowning about. 'For me? She thinks you and I… But surely she knows I am a nobody?'

'Does she? Besides, you are not a nobody, you are very much yourself.'

How could he pretend to make light of it? 'I mean, does she realise that I am quite ineligible?'

'Probably not,' Alex conceded.

So there goes that foolish little daydream, the

*one where your King Cophetua falls for you, the
beggar maid, marries you and defies all conven-
tion. Of course Alex has more sense than that.*
'Then, you had better tell her before she comes
to any embarrassing conclusions,' Tess said,
more snappishly than she intended. It wasn't
Alex's fault that he was heir to an earldom and
she was the illegitimate child of a scandalous liaison. *Not that he knows that,* she mused as they
came out into the hallway. *He knows I am ineligible enough, even if he believes I am legitimate.
No money, no connections...*

'Alex! What in blazes do you think you are
doing?' Matthew thudded down the staircase, his
boot heels like thunder on the old polished oak.

'Organising Christmas dinner, since you ask,'
Alex drawled, coming to a halt under a trophy
arrangement of swords and rapiers that fanned
out across the entire wall.

'To hell with Christmas dinner. What do you
mean by thinking you can exile me to the other
end of the county, give away property—'

'You will kindly mind your language in front
of Miss Ellery. I have neither the power nor the
inclination to exile you anywhere and I certainly
do not have the ability to give away any of the
lands, although why you are objecting since they
would end up in your hands, I have no idea. I
merely suggested to Father that as you wanted

to set up your own estate, he give you one of the unentailed properties to the west.'

'To get me out of the way? And the old fool thinks that because you boast about your sword-play and your riding that you're a fit heir all of a sudden?' Matthew was pacing up and down, hands clenched, shoulders hunched, for all the world like an angry bull, Tess thought.

'Excuse me. This is obviously a family matter.' She stepped back into the passageway, then stopped behind the shelter of a screen. She did not want to eavesdrop, but nor did she like the edge of violence in Matthew's ranting.

'I *am* the heir. It is not a matter of choice.' Alex was hanging on to his patience somehow. 'I suggested he double your allowance, set you up with a good property in recompense for the fact you've been landed with all the work up to now. If you hate the idea, then stay here.'

'And watch you mincing around?'

'I do not mince.' It sounded to Tess as though Alex's patience was stretched to breaking point. Why his brother seemed to be constantly jibing about his masculinity baffled her.

'Of course, I was forgetting you were a great swordsman. So show me.'

There was the sound of metal scraping against metal, then Alex said sharply, 'Take care, Matthew, there are no buttons on those foils.'

'All the better to prick you with, brother dear.'

Tess looked round the screen in time to see Mathew, foil in right hand, throw a second at Alex. He caught it by the hilt and pointed it at the floor. 'Don't be a fool.'

'What, scared of a little sport?' Matthew was in a fighting stance, feet spread, left arm out behind, the unblunted foil pointing directly at Alex's heart.

'Not at all, but do tell me, are you attempting to alter the succession?' Alex enquired and lifted his own weapon, adopting the same position. Tess could not see his face, but his posture seemed dangerously relaxed. She recalled how he had looked just before he'd hit the sailor on the ship and felt reassured.

'Alter the succession? No, you're welcome to it, but I would be interested to see whether you bleed water or red blood.'

'At this time in the morning, coffee.' Alex moved suddenly, a flickering lunge with the blade, and Matthew jumped back. Tess winced at the clash of metal and the two stopped talking and began to fight, it seemed to her, in deadly earnest.

Matthew was more aggressive, stockier and heavier and, to her ignorant eye, far more serious. Alex moved less, but with more grace, and he used his foil with an economy and accuracy that seemed to expend far less effort.

His brother was panting now, with sweat on his brow. Alex, as the fight brought him circling round to face her, looked cool. Matthew lunged straight for Alex's ribs. Tess clapped her hand over her mouth to stop the scream as Alex stood stock still, let the blade come, then sidestepped at the last moment. His left hand came down to fasten on Matthew's wrist and with a twist the foil went clattering against the wall.

In the ringing silence Tess braced herself for Matthew to lash out at his brother, but he straightened, his wrist still in Alex's grasp. 'Where did you learn to fight like that?'

'Germany. Where did you?'

'Father. We've been wrong about you, haven't we?' Matthew seemed half sullen, half embarrassed.

'Because I can use the foils?' Alex grinned. 'You should get around more, little brother. The man who taught me swordplay fought, shall we say, for the opposition. So does the man who gave me that in Gentleman Jackson's boxing ring.' He touched a finger to the thin scar on his cheekbone. 'But yes, you were wrong about me. I hate to break it to you, but an interest in the arts and a disinclination to slaughter everything with fur, feathers or fins is not a reliable indicator of very much, I'm afraid.'

Tess wondered what on earth they were talking about. But whatever it was, it had changed Matthew's attitude. 'You've boxed with Jackson? *The* Jackson?'

'There is only one.' Alex stretched up to hook the foils back in their place on the wall. 'Come on, let's go and have a look at the maps, discuss which of those two manors you want and I'll show you a really tricksy cross-buttock throw the Gentleman taught me.'

He had certainly forgotten she was there if he was discussing buttocks.

Alex waited until Matthew closed the library door behind him and was looking at him before he knocked him on to his backside with a sharp right to the jaw.

'What the hell was that for?' Matthew stared up at him, rubbed his jaw, but seemed disinclined to get up and return the punch.

'Swearing in front of Miss Ellery, fooling about with unguarded foils and generally being an ass.'

'Fair enough.' His brother grinned, then winced. 'At least, for the first two, guilty as charged. But what am I supposed to think when

Father loses his temper, throws accusations at you and you walk out and are never seen again?'

'Let me think.' Alex leaned back against the edge of the long table. 'That he'd severely wounded my feelings? That his temper tantrum ended up with a young man blowing his brains out? That your seventeen-year-old brother didn't take kindly to having his manhood called into question? And I could have been easily seen if you'd bothered to look. There was no secret about where I was, and I've never been out of contact with our mother.

'You could have come and visited me in London any time you chose, when I was in the country. Or did you think the house would be full of macaronis and fops and we'd drag you off to some molly house and make you wear *macquillage*?'

'Er, yes, more or less.' Matthew got to his feet and showed admirable common sense, in Alex's opinion, by putting the width of the table between them. 'At least, thought it might be damned embarrassing.'

'Have you ever been to London?' Matthew shook his head. 'Long past time you did, then. Come and stay for the Season and I promise I'll protect your virtue.'

'Don't need it protecting.' Matthew hunched a shoulder, then burst out, 'I wanted to go, but the old devil wouldn't let me. Says there's nothing there for real men, no decent sport, just a lot of fancy balls and boring crushes.'

'Our father has an eye to his pocketbook. You'd enjoy London. I'll put you up for a couple of my clubs, introduce you around, get you some decent boots—'

'Hoby?' Matthew looked as though someone was waving gold coins in front of his nose.

'Hoby,' Alex agreed. 'Gentleman Jackson's, Purdey's or Manton's, some of the less stuffy places of entertainment. Just don't get into the claws of some Captain Sharp in gambling dens, because I'm not covering your vowels if you do.'

There was dead silence. Matthew opened and closed his mouth, then managed, 'I've been a bloody fool.'

Alex shrugged. 'So have I, I suspect. But I had a good time while I was at it and I don't think you have.' Matthew was growing up, wanting to achieve something of his own and emerge from under the shadow of his parent.

'Father approves of your sporting prowess, he thinks you are a real man in his image, but I'll wager he makes you feel you're second best because you aren't the heir.' His brother's face darkened. 'It's true, isn't it? He's obsessed with having an heir who is just like him. I'm not a sporting Nonpareil and you can never feel for the earldom as I do. Both of us miss being what he wants.'

Matthew stared at him, growing comprehension on his face. 'You're right. Damn it, I never could work out why nothing ever seemed to be quite good enough. And I'm bored here. I want something that's my own. And when he said you suggested just that, I suppose…'

'You were angry because I'd suggested it and it wasn't his idea? I think we had both better stop hoping that one day our father is going to declare himself proud of the pair of us. I suggest we just get on with our lives the way we think we ought to live them.'

He had surprised himself by how calm he felt when the realisation came into his head, and it seemed he had surprised Matthew, too. 'What has come over you? You have to be angry about the way you've been treated in the past and you've had a damn unfriendly welcome home from Father and me. Why are you being so forgiving?'

'I'm not, not about Peter. But…I don't know.' He shrugged. 'Christmas spirit, I suppose.' *Tess's influence is more likely.*

'The love of a good woman?' Matthew said with a grin. 'Miss Ellery's a very pretty girl, you lucky devil.'

She's more than that. The odd pain under his

breastbone was aching again, as though something was tight and fearful inside him. 'You know perfectly well I'm expected to make a good match.'

Matthew's grin became wicked. 'Who said anything about—?'

His brother flinched when he saw Alex's expression. 'Do not say it. Do not think it. Miss Ellery is a guest under our roof.' Perhaps the pain was simply his conscience.

'Yes, of course. Sorry. Shall we have a look at the estate plans? If I can really choose one of the unentailed manors, I've got some ideas.' Matthew began to unroll the maps from the end of the table and weight the corners with books. 'I'd appreciate your advice.'

Alex found, suddenly, that it was difficult to speak. His brother wanted his advice, wanted what he had been able to give him, wanted to work with him. He had thought he had all the friendship and companionship he would ever want or need but this, he discovered, was different. This was family.

'Sorry, frog in my throat. Yes, of course, although you know far more than I do, I've no doubt. Is this the one you favour?'

'There you are. I've been looking everywhere.' Tess kept her voice cheerful as she bustled into the library. Alex's silhouette against the darkening grey sky beyond the wide windows looked bleak and brooding, and she made herself straighten her suddenly sagging shoulders as the flame of the candle she carried dipped.

She had been worrying about Alex and what was happening between him and his brother all afternoon, braced for the sounds of a fight or even, in her more anxious moments, a gunshot.

But as she touched the flame to the wicks of the unlit candelabras that stood around the room he turned and smiled at her, and the relief was enough to make her sit down with a thump on the nearest chair.

'I'm sorry, I have been neglecting you.'

'Not at all, only I have so much to report about my discussion with Garnett, Mrs Garnett and Cook that I wanted to tell you as soon as possible. I have a list, but essentially they think it an excellent idea and the staff are very enthusiastic. I spoke to your mother again and promised I would help organise the buffet upstairs in the evening, but we will have plenty of time to spend with our people. I mean your people.' *Lord, what a slip to make!* 'Handing out presents and so forth.'

She produced a notebook and Alex came over and sat next to her. 'Ah, the infallible notes.' Tess passed it over and watched him covertly while he read. He looked different, she realised. Younger almost, as though years had been lifted away.

'Is everything all right?'

'With this? Yes, excellent as far as I can tell—you know I have no recent experience of Christmas festivities. I have no doubt everyone will have a splendid time. You are a born organiser, Tess.'

'I meant with your brother. I was rather worried. He seemed so angry.'

Alex gave a snort of laughter. 'A masterpiece of understatement given that he made a spirited attempt to spit me on a blade. Yes, everything is all right with Matthew. I've found my way back to my little brother, Tess, and he needed me.'

'I am so glad. Oh, Alex, that is such good news.'

'It is all because of you, little nun.' His smile was decidedly lopsided now, as though he was attempting to cover deep emotion with a joke. 'You've infected me with your Christmas spirit. I am probably doomed. It will be handbell ringing and carol singing next and then I will be beyond help.'

'You are such a good man.' Tess leaned over to emphasise the warmth of her praise with a kiss on Alex's cheek just as he turned his head towards her. She found herself on his knee, twined in his arms, his mouth on hers, not returning the warm affection she had intended, but with the hard demand of a lover.

It seemed a very long time since he had taken her back to her bedchamber in the pre-dawn gloom. It seemed an endless evening stretched before they could be alone together again.

'I'll come to your room tonight, if you still want me to.' Alex traced the line of her eyebrows. 'Don't frown at me, little nun. If you don't want me I will stay away. My heart will break—'

'I am not a nun and your heart will do no such thing,' Tess snapped. She got up and paced down the library. 'Don't give me all that flummery. There is a mutual attraction, that is all it is. I am not one of your society flirts who needs seduction wrapped up in sparkly ribbons.' *Of course I want you, you darling man. Are you blind? And I want your heart, not your teasing. And if I got it I would have to give it back*, she thought drearily.

Safely on the other side of the table she took a deep breath and found a smile. 'Now, we haven't talked about all the details for the Christmas arrangements. We require a cartload of evergreens and then I'll need to know when you'll be coming downstairs to give your staff their presents. Do you think your family would enjoy it if they came upstairs at some point and sang carols? They've been practising.'

'If you need evergreens, ask Matthew.' Alex was on his feet, his face stony. 'I don't imagine for a moment that the staff want me down there, they'll have much more fun if left to their own devices, and if you organise carol singers then don't expect me to stay and listen to the cater-wauling.'

'Then, that will be your loss. I will go and speak to Mr Tempest.' *Pull yourself together, Tess,* she scolded as she picked up her candle and left, managing not to sniff until she was outside the door. *You knew he only tolerated your interference to be kind.* Lady Moreland had been enthusiastic about the idea of evergreens and this was her house. She set out to look for Matthew.

Chapter Eighteen

Alex arrived five minutes late at the dinner table in a mood that more than matched his father's.

'You are late,' the earl snapped.

Alex inclined his head to his father and smiled at his mother. 'My apologies, Mama, ladies.' He took his seat and slapped his best amiable mask over an inner scowl. An afternoon of mingled sexual frustration, irritation, awareness that he had blundered with Tess and the necessity to write a ream of instructions to his secretary was enough to both kill his appetite and leave him longing for the brandy bottle.

Tess spared him a glance and a smile, then turned back to Matthew, with whom she was apparently deep in discussion about holly.

'I gather we're to have a traditional Christmas.' His father regarded Tess from under lowered brows and, as she answered, Alex braced himself to come to her rescue.

'Only if it will not disturb you, Lord Moreland.'

'Not at all, my dear.'

My dear? What had come over the old curmudgeon? It appeared he approved of Tess.

'The best berry-bearing holly are those trees along the west boundary of Tom's Covert,' his father said to Matthew. 'You should find something for a yule log in that area—three oaks went down in the big storm last year.' He stared down the table at Alex. 'What are you snorting about?'

'Was I? I am sorry. But yule logs, Father?'

'If Miss Ellery wants a proper traditional country Christmas, then we need a yule log. I gather she's not seen one in all that time she's been in Ghent. Don't do these things properly over there. Foreigners.'

'Their traditions are simply different, Father.'

'I suppose it is too much to expect you to be getting your expensive boots dirty.' Alex resisted the temptation to produce an artistic shudder. 'You can go and tell the vicar he's welcome to bring the carol singers round on Christmas Eve, that'll liven the place up.'

'And the handbell ringers, too, I suppose? Father, you should be resting, not having half the village in to create a racket.'

'We haven't had a proper traditional Christmas since you left. I think I'd like one this year.'

As if they were days of joy and harmony before! Alex took in the set of his father's mouth and realised this was more than the desire to give orders. *Hell, he thinks it will be his last one.* 'Of course, sir, if it would please you.' He was rewarded by a speaking look from his mother and warm smiles from Maria and Tess. He still thought it sentimental nonsense, but if it gave his family pleasure he would smile and pretend. Which might put Tess back in charity with him, too.

Alex scratched on Tess's bedchamber door as the clock struck one, slipped inside and braced himself for a thrown slipper.

'Alex?' She had blown out all the candles and the room was lit only by the glow from the banked fire. It turned the white bedcovers patchily to rose and gold and threw her shadow flickering across the bed hangings.

'No, the headless ghost of the first earl. Who do you think?' He turned the key in the door and padded over to the bed.

Tess gave a little snort of amusement and sat up. 'I thought you wouldn't come after we quarrelled.'

'Was that what it was? A quarrel? I thought I

was being chastised for insensitivity and a lack of Christmas spirit.'

'And I was being snappish. You were kind to your father at dinner tonight.'

'He may not see another New Year. I'm still angry with him, but barring the door to carol singers isn't going to bring Peter back.'

'Peter?'

Hell and damnation, she doesn't know why I left home. She doesn't know about Peter. 'He was a friend of mine and he had a secret, rather a dangerous one. When I left home my father said things about him that led him to commit suicide.'

'*No.* How dreadful.' Tess reached out and caught his hand, tugged him towards the bed. 'But what on earth could the earl have said for him to do that? Had he committed some crime?'

'No, but he had wanted to. Tess, I can't explain.' He looked down on her bent head as she studied their joined hands and felt her concern and kindness like a caress.

'Was he in love with you?' she asked.

'What?' Alex realised he had almost shouted it and dropped his voice to a whisper. 'What did you say?' He tried to tug his hand away, but Tess held tight.

'There was a scandal last year, the brother of one of the boarders. He wrote a very indiscreet letter to his sister and told her what had happened. He ran away to Italy with his friend.'

'I had no idea sheltered young ladies knew about such things.'

'Some of us do, and we aren't idiots, Alex. It makes sense of the way Matthew was goading you. But they were wrong, weren't they? I mean, you and I…'

'Yes, they were wrong. My father's an intolerant old bully and I was too artistic, too neat and precise for his liking. Then when he realised what Peter felt—which was more than I did in my innocence—he put two and two together and made fifty. I stormed out full of thoroughly embarrassed righteous indignation, stopped on the way to rant at Peter about the stupidity of my father, then left for Oxford without any idea of the bombshell that I'd dropped at his feet.'

'If that hadn't happened, then both you and your father would have calmed down, reconciled,' Tess said.

The sadness in her voice was like a jab in the solar plexus. What had she to be sad about? Was he just another of her lame dogs to be taken in and cared for? It was *his* grief, *his* anger, and he hadn't asked her to care, certainly hadn't asked a sheltered young woman to understand variations of sexual preference that should have sent her into strong hysterics. Alex found he was becoming weary of maintaining an unruffled front, of not revealing his feelings, of appearing tolerant and self-assured and all the things that right at that moment he most certainly did not feel.

'Are we going to bed or am I going to stand here all night discussing my family?'

Tess blinked at him, obviously startled by the harsh edge to his voice. Well, damn it, it was about time she realised that he wasn't a nice man hiding bounteous goodwill to all God's creatures behind a cynical exterior. Nor was he some hapless victim of cruel fate. Just at that moment he was a man who wanted a woman and who was on the edge of losing his temper for reasons he was not at all sure he understood.

'Yes, of course.' Tess flipped back the covers and moved across. She was wearing a nightgown tonight, he saw. A prim and proper flannel abomination, tight to the throat and the cuffs without a single frill or ornament to its cream plainness. 'I hoped you would come,' she added as he tossed his robe aside.

Her eyes widened. Had she seen him erect last night? Surely she had. Was she frightened? Then Tess ran the tip of her tongue over her lips and a surge of primitive power jolted through him. When he joined her on the bed she reached for the hem of her nightgown and pulled it over her head without hesitation, turned into his arms and lifted her face for his kiss. No, not frightened.

He took the lips that were offered to him, caressed the quivering, urgent body, found, without conscious intent, that he was already over her, nudging against the wet heat that was so ready for him. There was a rushing in his ears, a thunder of blood mingling with their panting breaths. Her mouth was open to him, sweet and fierce, her body closed around him, urgent, yielding, demanding. He surged in her, riding the pleasure like a wild horse, focused only on the turmoil of their two bodies, heard her cry and, somehow, found the focus to pull from her body before he crashed into his own shattering climax.

Pleasure, exhaustion, sticky heat, softness, the beat of a heart under his. Alex lay still, let his lax body come to itself while he gathered his wits, rubbed his cheek against the soft one next to it.

Gradually the human part of his brain gained some ascendancy over the triumphant, sated, animal part. He was sprawled with all his weight on the slender figure beneath him.

Tess. God, what have I done. He rolled off with a contraction of muscles that almost sent him off the far side of the bed. *She was as near as, damn it, a virgin, and I used her like a courtesan.*

* * *

'Alex?' Tess blinked her eyes open onto a chilly world where the lovely, big, muscled body that had been squashing her so deliciously was gone. Alex's lovemaking had been a revelation. The excitement, the urgency, the sheer vibrant sexuality of it, had shaken her in a different way to his tenderness and care the night before. That lovemaking could be so varied had never occurred to her. What would it be like tomorrow?

He was staring at her across the width of the bed. 'Tess, I am sorry. I hurt you.'

'No, not at all.' Why wouldn't her come to her, hold her?

'I was a brute. An animal.'

'Alex, don't—'

'I won't, don't be afraid that after that I would touch you. No, don't try to tell me it is all right, you are too forgiving, Tess.'

I will come over there and show you the opposite of forgiveness if you won't let me get a word in, Alex Tempest! She opened her mouth to override him, shout him into being forgiven for whatever male sin he thought he had committed, if that was what it took to wipe that look from his eyes.

'I meant to say this after Christmas, but it is best now. Tess, I can't have you going back, dragging round agencies, finding yourself a position as some sort of drudge to a cantankerous old lady or a house full of screaming brats.'

'But—'

'I will find you a house somewhere, a pleasant market town, perhaps. Somewhere you and Dorcas can settle down respectably. I'll give you an allowance. You won't have to see me again. My man of business will handle it all discreetly.'

You won't have to see me again. At first her brain could not make sense of what he was saying, then it was as though her body realised at some deeper level. She began to shiver. 'You are paying me off? A house and an allowance is very generous in exchange for two nights in my bed, especially considering my complete lack of skill or experience. My goodness, what might I ask for if I acquire some more tricks?'

'Tess, it is not like that.' Alex swung off the bed and stood up, over six feet of naked, angry male. 'You didn't expect me to marry you. We talked about that. And don't flinch. Do you think I am going to hit you next?'

'I am not flinching. I am recoiling from a man I thought I knew and now find I do not. How dare you treat me like a whore! How dare you offer me money!' She scrambled from the bed in an ungainly lurch, picked up his robe and threw it at him. 'How dare you suggest that I am angling for a marriage so far above my station!'

Alex caught the bundle of red silk one-handed. *'Tess.'*

'Miss Ellery to you, my lord.' The shivering had stopped, replaced by a strong desire to be sick. 'Now get out of my bedchamber.'

At least he had the sensitivity to go without saying another word. It was difficult to move after the door closed behind him. After a while she became conscious that she was cold, so she moved round to the side of the bed nearest the fire and stood there, watching the dull glow of the coals. Then it occurred to her that she would like to wash, so she did, all over, in the water that had cooled almost to the temperature of the room.

There were marks on her body, red pressure marks where Alex's weight had lain on her, a roughness on her shoulder that his evening beard must have left. Yesterday the slight soreness and stiffness that lovemaking had created had been exciting, welcome. Now she moved gingerly as though she were ill, trying not to send those aftershocks of pleasure through her belly, through her limbs.

When she was sure she had scrubbed the scent of his body from hers she turned to the bed, pulled on her nightgown, flapped the sheets, found several brown-gold hairs that she threw on the fire. Then she climbed back into bed on the far side from the one they had made love on and curled into a tight ball while she waited for sleep.

'Miss Ellery, are we overworking you?' Lady Moreland put down the teapot and looked at Tess in a way that made it quite clear that her mirror had not lied. She *did* have dark circles under her eyes and she was pale and, try as she might, her cheerful expression looked as though she had cut it out of a print and pasted it on.

'No, not at all. I simply had one of those inexplicable sleepless nights. You know, I am sure, the kind where you toss and turn and can't drop off.'

'Oh, dear, that is so annoying when it happens. I wouldn't mention your looks if any of the men were down to breakfast of course, but Alexander and Matthew have gone out with the workers from the Home Farm to cut evergreens and my husband is staying in his room.'

'Alex—Lord Weybourn has gone out to cut evergreens?'

'Yes, and I hope some fresh air and exercise will put him in a better mood,' Maria said as she heaped eggs on her plate. 'He looked positively grim this morning. I thought he and Matthew had been arguing again, but they seem perfectly in charity with each other.'

'I think perhaps he is a little low because of having to give up his art business,' Tess suggested. 'It must be making a great deal of correspondence.' She wanted to throw the entire contents of an art gallery, preferably one full of marble busts, at his head, but it would be unfair on the rest of his family if she let her misery show. They had to live with Alex and she did not want their reconciliation spoilt by a sordid squabble.

'That will be it,' Lady Moreland agreed as she passed a cup of tea to Tess. 'It must be very difficult, and I never expected him to make as much of an effort to be civil to his father.' Tess's expression must have betrayed something of her feelings for she added, 'I do not scruple to mention the estrangement in front of you, Miss Ellery. I can tell you will be most discreet.'

Tess mumbled something that she hoped conveyed discretion, sympathy and a total disinclination to hear more. Lady Moreland steered the conversation on to London fashions and plans for Maria's wardrobe for the Season and Tess was left to make interested noises and look out of the window onto the carriage sweep at the front of the house for the return of the brothers.

When they did come back it was on a wave of cold air and a bustle of servants all loaded with branches to heap in the entrance hall. Matthew was in high spirits and Alex's unsmiling face was a healthy pink from the chill. He glanced at Tess and then looked back again, a long stare while, she supposed, he took in just how dreadful she looked. She nodded politely, then joined Maria and Matthew in a discussion of what needed to go where. Alex stalked off.

'Don't know what the matter is with Alex,' Matthew commented as soon as the sound of boot heels on stone had died away. 'Like a bear with a sore head.'

Maria offered Tess's suggestion about the heavy workload with the art business and Tess was able to retreat into a corner with a pile of holly, stout scissors and wire to fashion some wreaths. She wanted to think calmly about Alex, but she was so tired that the same hurtful, jangling thoughts just kept circling and knotting in her head until all she was conscious of was pain and a deep sense of loss. *Which is irrational*, she told herself. *He was never yours. You know there never was any hope of that.*

At luncheon she managed to sit between Maria and Dorcas and listened to Maria's anxieties about Almack's, her hopes that she would make friends easily and her despair of ever winning her dancing master's approval. On the far

side of the table Alex endured his father's tren-
chant views of the government's foreign policy
and then politely demolished them.

Tess, conscious that the four women at the
table were all holding their breath, expected that
outright opposition would send the earl into an
apoplexy, but he grunted, 'You don't toad-eat,
I'll say that for you, Weybourn. You're a damn
fool Whig, of course, but at least you can con-
struct an argument.'

Alex took the backhanded compliment with a
wry smile and began to discuss felling some of
the Home Wood. Across the table Lady Moreland exchanged a knowing look with her daughter.

Last night had apparently made no impact on
Alex's thought processes or his intellectual alert-
ness. He obviously had slept perfectly soundly,
Tess thought resentfully. A touch on her arm
drew her attention to the fact that Matthew was
speaking to her. 'Shall we put up the mistletoe
after luncheon, Miss Ellery?'

'Why, yes. That would be fun.' She managed
a bright smile and was rewarded by a cold look
from Alex. *If he thinks I'm going to flirt with his
brother under the mistletoe, then more fool he*,
she thought. Although it might be soothing to her
bruised heart if Matthew wanted to flirt with her.

Chapter Nineteen

Alex told himself he was far too busy to waste time strewing greenery about the place, releasing spiders and earwigs and making every corner prickly with pine needles and holly.

If Tess wanted to giggle under the mistletoe with Matthew, then she was welcome to him. His brother was unlikely to offer her assistance that she could then wilfully misunderstand and throw back in his face, leaving him feeling like some kind of unsavoury rakehell preying on innocent young women and then buying them off.

Righteous indignation could only get him so far. Alex stopped halfway along the Upper Gallery and slammed his fist down on to a fragile side table, sending a vase rocking wildly. 'Hell and damnation!'

Tess had been an innocent young woman and, in virtually every way, she still was. Thanks to her gossipy schoolgirl friends she might have knowledge of some things that society thought were kept from unmarried ladies, but her understanding of the big, dangerous wide world was virtually nonexistent. He had surrendered to temptation and had taken her virginity, and now he had made that world far more perilous for her.

He steadied the vase, ran his thumbs over the fragile white purity of the Wedgwood medallions that decorated it. Tess had rocked his life, unsettled his certainties. She had taught him a tolerance and forgiveness that made this painful reconciliation with his family negotiable. She had burrowed into his affections and curled up there, trusting and straightforward, just like that accursed kitten.

His offer of financial support had shocked her in a way that his uncontrolled lovemaking had not, he realised as he paced down the Gallery. She had told him the truth when she came to his bed. She had wanted, and asked for, the right simply to be with him for a short while, to share whatever it was between them.

The portrait he was staring at came into focus. Lucinda, wife of the second earl. Beautiful, the daughter of a duke, well dowered and, by all accounts, a profligate little madam who had brought her besotted husband to the brink of financial ruin. He walked on a few paces to Wilhelmina, the first countess. Impeccable breeding, the face of a horse and the temper of a cornered cobra, so legend said.

For all their blue blood, what had those two carefully selected brides done for the Tempests, other than bring unhappiness? 'Damn it,' Alex said in the face of Wilhelmina's haughty disapproval. 'I'll marry the girl, bring in some affection and honesty and caring, and society can damn well think what it likes.' She might not think much of him any longer, but with good fortune he would give her children to love and, God willing, she'd stop him being such a disastrous parent as his own father had proved.

The prospect should have filled him with satisfaction, not a faint feeling of queasy foreboding. Nerves. He turned on his heel and strode towards the double doors. A man proposing marriage had a right to feel a degree of anxiety. He would sweep her off, down to the stables, take her up in front of him and ride off to the old castle, propose there. Tess would like that, enjoy the romance of it.

He diverted to his room, shrugged into his greatcoat and took his hat and a heavy cloak for Tess.

'My lord?' Byfleet hurried out of the dressing room. 'I'm sorry, I did not hear you ring.' He stopped at Alex's gesture of dismissal. 'Are you quite well, my lord? Only you seem a trifle pale.'

'Need some fresh air.' Was he coming down with something? Alex caught a glimpse of himself in the mirror, dark under the eyes, white around the mouth. He hadn't looked as bad as this, or felt as bad, before his one and only duel, an affair involving an Italian contessa, a dubious Old Master drawing and a jealous husband.

Then his life had been at stake, reason enough to feel a cold lump in the pit of his stomach and an encroaching sensation of dread. Now there was no excuse. All he had to do was make his peace with an intelligent, sweet and forgiving young lady who would be swept off her feet with joy at the thought of finding herself a future countess.

Tess was in the dining room, filling vases with holly and trails of ivy. No servants, he was pleased to see and, thankfully, no sign of Matthew, either.

She dropped the ball of twine from which she was cutting lengths when he marched up to her and stopped in a swirl of coat-skirts and cloak. 'My lord.'

No one who did not know her as well as he did now could have told that she was unhappy. Her self-control was as impeccable as ever, and it gave him no pleasure to see the tension in the way she held herself, the slight droop of her mouth. 'Tess, come riding with me.'

'I cannot ride.'

'I'll take you up in front of me. Tess, I am sorry, I should not have offered you what I did. I should have offered you marriage.' So much for a romantic interlude on horseback, a gallant knight making a powerful declaration to his lady in the castle ruins.

Her eyes were huge and dark and deep. A man could drown in those eyes. She was amazed that he had offered marriage; she was in shock. At any moment a smile would dawn and she would be in his arms.

'No,' Tess said. *'No.'* She backed away from him, her hands clenched tight by her sides. 'You must not. No.'

Alex made no move to stop her when she ran from the room. From him. So that was that. He had disgusted her with his violent rutting and insulted her with his crass offer and she had punished him in a far more effective way than she could ever have dreamed, leaving him unable to do the honourable thing.

I can't. I mustn't. Tess ran blindly away from temptation, ran as though all the devils in hell followed after her whispering inducements and false promises. She pushed open panelled double doors and found herself in a long gallery. It was mercifully empty, so she sat in one of the window seats and uncurled her cramped fingers. There was blood in her right palm where the nails had bitten in. She had wanted to say *yes* so much. Had wanted to reach for him, be held close, kiss that tight unhappiness from his face. She wanted to have her Alex back, her knight in slightly tarnished armour, her cynic with a soft heart, her lover with magic at his fingertips.

'No,' she told herself again. 'You will not take advantage of his honour.' She was being watched. The uneasy feeling stole over her as she sat there and she sat upright, got her face under control. How shameful to be found huddled miserably in a corner by the servants, or worse, her hosts.

When she looked around her the long chamber seemed empty, peopled only by the ranks of portraits with their guarded, careful expressions. It was foolish to imagine they were all staring with disapproval at her.

Chin up, back straight, Tess walked over to confront one particularly haughty dame. 'Wilhelmina, Countess Moreland', the gilded label on the frame read. 'Daughter of Hugo de Vane, Third Marquess Peterborough'. Wilhelmina stared down at Tess as though she was a junior housemaid who had upended a chamber pot on the best Wilton carpet.

Her bloodlines would be traceable back to some uncouth and sweaty Norman baron who had come over at the Conqueror's heels, Tess had no doubt. The countess would have been the culmination of centuries of dynastic breeding, careful alliances, political manoeuvring. There could have been no blots on her escutcheon or the earl would not have wed her. *She* was not illegitimate, let alone the product of a scandalous union.

Tess wondered rather drearily if she was ever going to find a place where she actually fitted, belonged. Everyone else knew their place, it seemed. She only wished Alex would let her find hers and stop filling her full of hopeless dreams.

She pulled a face at Wilhelmina. It was juvenile, but it relieved her even more childish desire to fling herself down and have a tantrum about the sheer unfairness of life. She had experienced what she had wished for—to lie in the arms of the man she loved and to share physical passion with him. Now she had to live with the consequences.

'What I need,' she informed Wilhelmina, 'is a baby to cuddle and a kitten to play with. I will wager you never said that in your life. And I know where I can find both of those things.'

* * *

Baby Daisy was in the nursery with Dorcas and Annie. She had just been fed and changed and was at her adorable best, all gummy smiles and tiny waving fists. Ten minutes of cuddles and cooing restored Tess's spirits enough to pay some attention to her companions. Dorcas looked plumper, healthier, happier than Tess had ever seen her and little Annie was acquiring quite alarming confidence with her new role of nursery maid.

Tess cradled Daisy and watched the other two women together. Annie had the rudiments of reading and writing, but Dorcas was encouraging her to read the newspaper and to keep basic nursery accounts. What was going to happen to them when the new year came? It would be a criminal waste for Annie to go back to her role as Alex's scullery maid and Dorcas, with no references and the baby depending on her, could never hope for respectable employment.

'Dorcas, may I tell Lady Moreland about your circumstances? I hope she may give you both a reference, and I will ask Lord Weybourn if you may both stay at the Half Moon Street house until you find employment.'

They both shot her startled glances. 'But, Miss Ellery, won't you be staying here? So can't we stay, too?' Annie said and was promptly nudged in the ribs by Dorcas. 'What?' she demanded inelegantly. 'Miss Ellery and his lordship are all April and May, anyone can see there's a wedding coming.'

'I cannot marry Lord Weybourn.' Annie opened her mouth so Tess snapped, 'Because I am not eligible. I am illegitimate.'

'But you love him,' Annie protested. Little Daisy began to grizzle and she scooped her out of Tess's arms. 'And he loves you.'

'He doesn't and my feelings have got nothing to do with it,' Tess stood up, the good effects of cuddling Daisy vanishing. All she could think of now was the children she could never have with Alex. 'Lord Weybourn has his duty and he is perfectly well aware of it.' He would be, and be relieved, once he had got over his momentary fit of gallantry. And as for the suggestion that he loved her, why, that was simply Annie's romantic nonsense.

'I am going down to the kitchens and then to find Noel. I will see you at dinner, Dorcas.' She was running away, she knew that.

The kitchens were all a bustle with preparations for the Christmas Eve dinner, but Cook assured her that the sweetmeats she had made as gifts for the family were safe and sound in the coolest larder. One skill that Tess possessed to the satisfaction of the nuns was making the traditional candies that they sold in the town. She had created strong peppermint drops for Lord Moreland and Matthew and delicate rose pastilles for Lady Moreland and Maria, and Cook had found some pretty paper boxes for her to pack them in.

That just left Noel to find. He was drawn to the stables, but Tess worried that the bigger, fiercer stable cats would hurt him and fetched him back whenever he strayed.

She left by the kitchen door into the service yard, dodged the laundry maids lugging wet washing into the drying rooms, waved to the woodsmen delivering a load of logs and went through the archway into the stable yard. There was no sign of the kitten but she could hear Alex's voice coming from the tack room and went close to the door to listen. She should go before he saw her, but she needed to find out how he was after that last, fraught declaration.

'I think we'd do better running them unicorn.' When she peeped though the gap between open door and hinge she saw Alex was sitting on a saddle horse, his back to her as he spoke to one of the Tempeston grooms.

'Showy, my lord, I'll give you that, especially with the three greys. But Mr Matthew's been having a devil of a time with them and unicorn is a tricky configuration.'

'But it will remove the gelding who's proving most troublesome. The remaining three work well together.'

Obviously he wasn't nursing a broken heart, or even wounded pride, if he could chat so casually about carriage horses.

Tess began to back away, then her heel caught an upturned bucket and it tipped over with a clang on the flagstones.

The groom leaned sideways and saw her. 'There's Miss Ellery, me lord.'

Alex swung one long leg over the saddle horse and turned to face her. 'So I can see. I wondered what had happened to you, Miss Ellery. You had seemed a little discomposed earlier.'

'Oh, I have been busy, my lord.' Tess smiled politely. 'A little art appreciation, a visit to the nursery and the kitchens, then I thought I must see where Noel had got to.'

'I saw him in the hayloft a while ago,' Alex said. His voice was calm, his eyes were stormy.

Tempest eyes, Tess thought. 'I was concerned, but I see I was mistaken to be so. Life goes on, does it not, whatever emotional distractions confuse us.'

'You can call what there is between us an emotional distraction, Tess?'

She threw up a warning hand to remind him the groom was somewhere close.

Alex turned and called, 'Hodgkin, see if you can find Miss Ellery's ginger kitten, will you?' The sound of booted feet faded away. 'You have it all worked out now, do you, Tess? I cannot say I have.'

'You are suffering from a fit of quixotic gallantry. I am utterly unsuitable for you, you know that. It is not just that I am an orphan with no connections, no dowry and no qualifications whatsoever for a place in society.' She braced herself. Time to tell him, time to see the shock and distaste on his face. Time to watch the man she loved disentangle himself from this coil with cool finality. 'I am—'

'Illegitimate, I know.' Alex looked impatient, as though that bombshell was merely a minor irritation, a firecracker going off.

'But my mother—'

Again he cut in before she could finish. '"Jane Teresa Ellery, born 1775, died, unmarried, 1809." Yes? That is what the *Peerage* says and she was your mother, I assume? The date and her middle name seem too coincidental.'

Silence. 'Am I allowed to finish a sentence now?'

'Of course.'

'There is no *of course* about it. You do not

listen to me. You have not right from the beginning. If you had, I would never have missed that boat, none of this would have happened. Now you will not allow me to finish a simple explanation when you must see how difficult it is for me.'

'I'm sorry.' Alex moved away abruptly, as though to leave, then swung back. 'I am unused to difficult discussions with women. With a lady,' he corrected himself. 'But James Ellery, third Marquess of Sethcombe, is your grandfather, is he not?'

'Yes. Is he still alive? My grandmother? I never met them, you see, or my aunts or uncles.' And that sounded pathetic, as though she was pining for a family to love, whining that she wanted their love, admission to their charmed circle of belonging. *Pathetic and true. Yearning for the moon.*

'Your grandfather is alive and, from what I gather, in his usual state of unarmed combat with my father over fishing rights on the river between the two estates, over fences, straying cattle, poaching tenants. My father said he inherited Sethcombe as a neighbour along with the title—like a bad debt or a mad relative in the attic. The old man was a cantankerous so-and-so even then. He must be a considerable age now if your mother was his youngest child. Your grandmother, I'm afraid, died some years ago.'

Tess blinked away the tears. She would never know whether her grandmother had cast her own daughter out and never forgiven her the horrible scandal or whether, like Alex's mother, she had secretly tried to keep in touch, to send her loving thoughts. 'It is a malign coincidence that your family's lands march with the Ellerys', is it not?' She kept her voice hard.

'Not really.' Alex shrugged. 'The aristocratic families are so entwined that it would be surprising if we did not adjoin some relative or another of yours.'

'For my grandfather to be the enemy of your father, that has a certain…inevitability about it.'

'Only if you are writing some damn stage melodrama,' Alex snapped. 'The gods and Fates are not hovering about trying to make life as difficult as possible for us with some pre-ordained doom. If you want to insist on making a production out of this, then let us assume we are supposed to bring about a reconciliation.'

'*Making a production out of this?* What is *this*? The unfortunate fact that I have lost my virginity to you and now you have an attack of conscience about it?' Loving someone did not stop them being hurtful, it seemed. *I love you.* She wanted to scream it at him, throw it in his face, watch him deal with that along with all the complications of male honour, family honour, love affairs real and imaginary, sexual scandal.

'Miss Ellery, I've found your kitten.' The groom came into the tack room, Noel clinging like a furry ginger burr to his shoulder, and stopped dead. 'I'm sorry, my lord. I'm interrupting?'

'Not at all,' Tess said. 'Please could you take Noel to the kitchen for me?'

Alex slammed the door behind the man and shot the bolt. 'You are illegitimate, that is unfortunate, but if your mother's family will recognise you, even as a distant relative, things will not be so bad,' he said. 'Who was your father?'

'George Fenton, the younger son of Lord Melford.'

'Why the blazes didn't they get married then? I don't know Melford. I think they're a Cumberland family, aren't they? Perfectly good match for the youngest daughter of a marquess.'

'My father was married.' There, she had said it.

Alex frowned. 'Married? Then, you aren't illegitimate. Tess—'

Her turn to interrupt now. 'Married to someone else. And then he married Mama. It was bigamous. They were criminals.'

Chapter Twenty

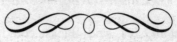

'Bigamous? But I heard nothing of that.' Alex stared at her as though she had announced she was the love child of the Prince Regent.

'I think the Ellerys managed to hush it up,' Tess said. 'Mama didn't know, you see, that Papa's first wife was ill, with a disease of the mind. Apparently she became ill quite gradually and Papa tried to find medical help for her, but in the end she was completely deranged. He had her looked after in a quiet country house of his. It must have been awful for him. There was nothing he could do for her except give her good care. That's where all the money must have gone, I think. Then he met Mama and they fell in love.

'She thought he was a widower and couldn't understand why her father forbade Papa to even speak to her. If he had only explained it would have been a heartbreak for her, but at least she would have understood before it was too late. I suppose in those days daughters were supposed simply to obey and not ask questions.

'They loved each other. I do not know when Mama found out that his wife was still alive, but she must have forgiven him and they never told me, only that Papa had been married before and had loved his first wife, but he'd felt blessed to have found a new love with Mama. I think it must have been true. He was such a kind man he must have loved her until she changed into someone he no longer knew.

'I had seen their wedding lines, but I had no idea they were invalid until Mother Superior told me when I was sent to the convent.' *Bastard, child of sin, daughter of depraved criminals. Unworthy.* The words still rang in her ears. *Only through hard work, humble acceptance of who and what you are, can you aspire to move in respectable company. You have no rights to the place where your parents were born, you have no place either amongst decent, God-fearing humbler folk...*

Tess took a steadying breath. 'I thought my name was Fenton until then, but of course, as the marriage was illegal then I am a bastard and must use my mother's surname. So you see I am utterly impossible as a wife for you, or for any respectable man.'

She thought she could read Alex's face now,

but all she could discern was furious thought. Perhaps he was trying to work out a way to remove her from the house before his mother discovered just what she was harbouring.

'Why didn't you tell me before?'

'Before you slept with me? Before you brought me into your family home?'

'Before I fe— What's the date?'

'The *date*? Why, the twenty-third, of course.' Perhaps she had tripped and banged her head and not realised. Or perhaps the shock had turned Alex's brain.

'No damned time,' he muttered. He looked at her, his expression unreadable, then he took her by the shoulders, pulled her towards him and kissed her with a hard, possessive urgency.

That was goodbye, Tess thought as he released her as abruptly as he had taken her.

'I knew Christmas was a bad idea,' he said, turned on his heel, shot back the bolt and was out of the door and across the yard before she could speak.

Christmas Eve had been a strange day, Tess decided as she waited in the drawing room for the family to assemble for dinner. The earl had kept to his bedchamber, resting, because he was determined to go to midnight service. Lady Moreland and Maria had been out visiting friends and neighbours with gifts, calling on tenants. The servants had been busy with preparations and Alex and Matthew simply did not appear.

Annie reported that they had ridden off early together. 'I heard Mr Matthew say, "I don't blame you for running out on all the fuss,"' she confided. 'And his lordship said, "I need to think and I'm damned if I can do it in the house, so come and act like a brother for once and keep me company." And Mr Matthew said a bad word and laughed and off they went.'

The earl, Maria and Lady Moreland came in as she was puzzling, yet again, about Alex. Was he simply finding excuses to avoid her? Tess stopped fiddling with her fan as she and Dorcas stood and curtsied, and then forced herself to make conversation while Dorcas retired to her usual corner.

'Where are those boys?' Lady Moreland said after half an hour of everyone avoiding staring at the door.

'My apologies, Mama.' Alex strode in, elegant in immaculate evening dress, Matthew, less polished but still correctly attired, at his heels. Both faces had high colour from having been rapidly warmed after long exposure to cold. 'We have only just got back.'

'From where?' Lady Moreland demanded. 'I

shudder to think what state the goose will be in. Cook will probably hand in her notice this very night.'

'I wanted to look at the estate, Mama. It has been a long time.' He looked at his father and then at Tess. 'I found it put things in perspective. I apologise for leaving our guests, but I see the house is most festively garlanded, so I assume you must have found occupation, Miss Ellery.'

'I…I am sorry, Lord Weybourn, I did not quite catch what you said.' *Not with you smiling at me like that.* The curve of his mouth was tender; the look in his eyes was regretful… *Stop it. It means nothing. He is simply apologetic for leaving me all day without a word. That look is not…*

He had been out all day thinking, looking at the estate with his brother. He had been reminding himself who he was, what was owed to his name. She could not deceive herself by choosing to see only that smile. Because she was fraught and nervous and aching for him, she saw in his expression what she longed to see. And that was impossible. Must be impossible.

Alex took her into dinner and Tess got through the meal somehow. It was true what the nuns had drilled into the girls: good manners and polite observances would carry you through the most difficult social situations. They would even cover up heartbreak.

Alex sent her no more of those achingly tender smiles. He, too, kept to polite conversation, teased his sister gently, drew out Matthew on the subject of horse breeding and endured his father's observations on the state of the nation.

Finally Lady Moreland rose. 'Gentlemen, if you are willing to forgo your port, shall we all retire to the drawing room for an exchange of gifts?'

She received no protests. Even Alex went meekly, Tess noted with relief—and promptly walked straight into Matthew's arms. 'Mr Tempest!'

'Miss Ellery, behold, the mistletoe.'

She glanced up. 'That is not where I told the footman to put it.'

'Indeed not, but it is where I moved it to.' He bent his head, his intent obvious, and then Tess found herself whirled round into Alex's embrace.

'Poacher,' Matthew protested. 'I would call you out for that, brother, if I were not so dazzled by Mrs White's new Christmas finery.' He caught Dorcas's hand and, despite her squawk of alarm, pressed a bold kiss on her lips.

'No,' Tess whispered, caught in the circle of Alex's arms. 'It is not…kind.' He was strong and hard and so wickedly tempting. Just one kiss, a kiss his family would think of as innocent Christmas fun. One last kiss to break her heart.

'On St Stephen's Day, if you want to leave me, Tess, I will let you go. I will send you back to London, somehow find you respectable employment. But you gave yourself to me for Christmas and until then, you are mine.' His whisper was urgent, fierce against her lips. And he kissed her, a kiss as light as a breeze, a mere brush of his mouth, an exchange of breath that left her trembling and close to tears. Then he released her and kissed Dorcas, a wicked smacker that made her laugh and blush before he passed on to kiss his mother and sister on the cheek.

St Stephen's Day, the twenty-sixth of December. She had not agreed to any length of time to stay. But she had gone to his bed, given herself to him, agreed to come with him to his family for Christmas, so perhaps he was within his rights to make demands. Although to what end, she had no idea. Surely he would not want to make love to her now, not when he knew she was the skeleton in the neighbours' closet, not when he had settled in his own mind where his duty lay.

And she had not helped the family much, not as she had intended. The earl was not bedridden, Lady Moreland seemed to need no assistance and Alex and his father were on speaking terms, of sorts, without any intervention from her.

'Are you unwell, Miss Ellery?'

The earl's abrupt question made her start

guiltily. *If he only knew who he is harbouring under his roof.* 'Not at all, Lord Moreland. I was deep in thought, that was all. This is all very different from what I am used to.'

'A nunnery, eh? Not much mulled wine there, I'll be bound.'

'No, my lord.' The footman opened the door on to a blaze of candlelight and a table laden with parcels and packages. The servants had been hard at work while the family ate. 'Oh, this looks so festive!'

Alex found he was smiling. Not at the decorations or the presents, but at Tess's obvious delight. She looked like a child for a moment, hands clasped to her heart with delight—and then she was a woman again, the woman he desired, the innocent whose life he had almost ruined. Might still, if he was not very careful, very lucky.

There had to be some way through this. He found he was looking at the portrait of his grandmother above the fireplace. Another dynastic alliance, another proper match for the Earl of Moreland. He had been infected by Tess's ridiculous fantasy world of Christmas love and magic into thinking that, somehow, there was a happy ending to this. But if there was, he had to find it. He had fallen in love with a daughter of scandal, a woman disowned by her family who could bring nothing to the earldom.

Then his brain caught hold of his thoughts. *In love. So that is what it is, this pain in my chest, this ludicrous optimism and plunging despair. Not just liking, not simply lust. I love her.*

No one appeared to notice him standing like a stunned ox in the middle of the room. Alex shut his mouth with a snap and looked about him. His mother was ordering everyone to their places, grouped around his father like a conversation-piece portrait of a happy family. Maria had thought to send for little Daisy, so there was even the obligatory charming baby, he thought with a flash of his old cynicism. Even the dratted kitten had managed to find its way upstairs and was stalking a trailing ribbon on Maria's gown.

Matthew had apparently been chosen as the distributor of gifts. Alex squeezed into a place on the sofa between his sister and Tess and was rewarded by a sharp elbow in the ribs.

'You are squashing us,' Tess whispered. 'It is not kind.'

'To squash you or to sit with you?' he murmured back. Against his side she was warm and soft and smelled deliciously of rosewater and Tess. 'Trust me, Tess.' *To do what?* the cynical voice in his head jibed. *Ensure her ruin? Make her unhappy?*

'To do what?' Her voice cracked as she echoed his thoughts and he saw her hands clench together. 'To set me up as your mistress? To keep my secrets?' She had as much faith in him as he did in himself. Or perhaps she was just more realistic.

'I have no wish to make you my mistress,' he said, soft voiced in her ear. The soft curls tickled his nose; the scent of her was almost intolerably seductive. *I can't give you up.*

'Then, why keep me here—?' Tess broke off as his mother clapped her hands and ordered Matthew to begin.

Tess seemed flustered to be presented with a Kashmir shawl from his mother and a fan from Marie. Her own sweetmeats were received with expressions of delight, Daisy's doll was instantly seized and sucked and Dorcas expressed delight with her parcel of novels. The floor was soon strewn with sheets of torn paper and tangled ribbons and Noel was in kitten heaven, chasing imaginary mice through the crackling heap.

When was Matthew going to get to his own gift to Tess? She had retreated as far into the corner of the sofa as possible, the tension crackling off her until he felt as though a thunderstorm was about to break. *She'll hate it*, he thought with a fresh plunge into pessimism. *She'll think I am laughing at her.*

'For Miss Ellery!' Matthew produced a rectangular package with a flourish and peered at the label. 'With Christmas wishes from Alex.'

'Thank you.' Tess's smile was warm as she took the package, but she was biting her lip when Matthew turned away.

'Open it,' Alex urged as she sat there making no effort to untie the knots.

It was almost the last parcel. She seemed to realise that all eyes were on her and scrabbled at the wrappings with uncharacteristic clumsiness. The lid came off the box and she pushed back the tissue paper and lifted out the contents.

'A doll? Alexander, you've addressed a present for the baby to Miss Ellery,' his mother said with a laugh.

'No,' Tess said before he could speak. 'No, he hasn't.' Her hands were shaking as she held the stiff wooden figure with its froth of blue skirts and painted black hair. 'It has sentimental meaning for me…something I told Lord Weybourn about. A memory from my childhood. Thank you.' She turned to him and he saw her eyes were brimming with tears.

'Tess,' he said softly, taking the doll from her and making a production out of settling it back in its box to give her a moment to recover. 'I never meant to make you cry.'

'It was a lovely thought.' Her hand on his was

steady now, but he could feel the pulse hammering as he closed his fingers around her wrist. 'And I know you do not mean to make me cry.'

It was not the doll that she referred to, he knew, as she set the box firmly on her knee and looked back at Matthew and the others with a determined smile. He had made her cry, even if she would not allow him to see it, even if she acquitted him of deliberate cruelty, or careless disregard of her feelings.

'One last package, and it is for Alex,' Matthew announced, handing over a small carved box.

Alex took it, puzzled. There was no wrapping, no label, just old dark oak rubbed smooth more by handling than from any refined finishing. He opened it and stared. 'This is the Moreland signet ring, the seal.'

When he looked up his father was watching him, his left hand spread out, the fingers twisted and cramped and unadorned. 'I cannot wear that ring any longer. I would rather give it to you now than have you take it from my dead hand. If you will stay, take on the business of the estate, then you will need it, Alexander.'

He found he could not speak. Beside him Tess made a little choking sound, perilously like a sob. Alex tugged his own signet off, moved it to his right hand, then slid the ancient ring onto his finger. It fitted easily. Looking down, he saw his grandfather's hand, his father's, and he found he could speak. 'Thank you, Father. Of course I will stay.'

For a moment he thought his mother would weep and, to his horror, his father, also. Then the door swung open, there was a scrabbling of claws on the polished wood, Noel shot up his leg and onto his shoulder and James the footman skidded to a halt on the rug in front of him, both hands clinging to a leash with a panting hound puppy on the end of it. 'Sorry, me lord, only I couldn't stop her.'

The pup rolled over onto her back, waving huge paws and ungainly legs in the air. She grinned upside down at him, all teeth, tongue and slobber, wriggling with excitement, a ludicrous pink satin bow tied to her collar.

'What the blazes is this?'

'Your Christmas present from me,' Tess said faintly. He realised she was suppressing laughter, probably hysterical. 'Her name's Ophelia.'

Chapter Twenty-One

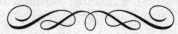

'*Ophelia?*' Alex leaned down and scratched the fat pink stomach and the puppy writhed ecstatically. 'What sort of name is that for a hound? If it is a hound,' he added dubiously.

'I think there is some hound in there,' Tess said. 'She's *mostly* hound. Perhaps the rest is mastiff. Look at the size of her feet.'

'I am looking.' And looking at the sullen gleam of the intaglio bloodstone in the ring on his hand. If he had been drinking hard all day he could not feel more dislocated from reality. He dragged himself back to the present, to one mongrel hound puppy busily licking his shoes. 'The thing is going to be as big as a horse.'

'Don't call her a thing.' Tess was still laughing, he could hear it in her voice. But she was wary, too. 'The poor creature has had a hard life and deserves a proper name. She was found in a sack in the cattle pond. She would have drowned if one of the grooms hadn't gone in and rescued her. That is why we called her Ophelia.' She shot him a sideways glance. 'All small boys should have a puppy. I thought a grown man might like one, too.'

He had never had a dog as a child. His father kept pedigree fox hounds, Matthew had been given a lurcher to go rabbiting with, but Alex had not expected to be allowed a dog, had not asked. He had never thought he wanted one. Ophelia rolled over and began to chew his shoe.

'Stop that.' He clicked his fingers at her and she sat up, tongue lolling out comically as she put her head on one side. 'I don't suppose you are house trained, are you?'

'Er, no,' Tess said. 'In fact I think it would be a good idea if James took her out for a walk now.'

'Thank you, Miss Ellery, for my present.'

The hound puppy gave his hand one last slobbery lick, then towed the footman out as his family got up, began to move about the room looking at each other's gifts, talking. Beside him Tess sat, cornered by his body, the doll in its box on her knee.

'I should have given you gloves or a reticule,' he said, twisting the unfamiliar ring on his finger. A week ago, if someone had told him he would be wearing it, that his father *wanted* him to wear it, he would have thought them insane, or that he was drunk.

'I should have given you a book or hemmed some handkerchiefs.' Her fingers stroked the doll's skirts and he imagined their caress on his skin like a remembered breeze.

You gave me something you knew was missing from my childhood, because you understand me. And you have given me something far more precious—your trust and your innocence. I only hope I can make this right for you, Tess. For us. Why couldn't he talk to her? Why were the words so hard to find, so difficult to say, even in his head? *I love you. I want to marry you. Can I make you happy?*

No one was attending to them. 'Tess, I wish you would let me do the right thing.'

She turned, her body shifting against his, firing all the memories of her naked in his arms, the passion and the trust. Where had the trust gone? 'And I wish you would let me do the same,' she murmured. 'I do not want to marry you, Alex.'

'Why not?'

'Why not? To even ask that shows a great deal of self-confidence, my lord, if you cannot think of any reason that would outweigh your attractions as a husband. What can we put in the scale? On one side a title, wealth, a charming manner, kindness and, undoubted skills in the bedcham-

ber. On the other the fact that I would bring a
scandal into your family, that I can bring nothing else. You have only just begun to reconcile
with them, Alex. Why would you throw that that
away simply to do the *right thing*?'

'If it were not for your birth, would you marry
me?' he demanded, cursing himself for beginning this whispered argument in a room full of
people.

'If wishes were horses, beggars would ride.
A cliché, but a true one,' Tess retorted. 'I am no
one, Alex. I have no family, no roots, nothing. I
will not be your mistress and I cannot be your
wife.' She pressed a sharp, well-placed elbow
in his ribs and wriggled out of her corner and
onto her feet. 'I am going to my room.' As Alex
stood she added, 'And that was not an invitation.'

No, he could not make love to her again, not
without fearing that he was putting unfair pressure on her, attempting to seduce her into doing
what she did not think was right. Nor could he
use words of love to her, not when he had no plan
yet to counter the arguments she set out against
a marriage. Tess, he was coming to realise, had
as strong a sense of honour as he did.

It was all her fault for going to his bed. She
was quite clear about that. There was no possible
excuse. She had known that what she was doing

broke every rule of good, modest behaviour and now she was reaping the reward.

Tess propped the doll up on her dresser and returned the beady-eyed stare. 'I have no one to blame but myself. Mama had no idea she was doing anything worse than eloping with the man she loved. I knew perfectly well what I was doing.' And, like the dreamer that she was, she hadn't thought beyond that moment in Alex's arms. She hadn't realised she was in love with him and that being with him would make that love real and painful. And impossible.

'I suppose I ought to call you Patricia, not Patty. Patty was a child's doll. You are a foolish grown woman's, confessional.' So sweet of Alex to remember her words in the toyshop, so like him to buy her a doll to replace the one taken from her. He pretended he was a cynic, that he didn't believe in Christmas and gifts and traditions, but he did yearn after the magic, deep under that glossy shell of uncaring sophistication.

He would make a wonderful father to those children she could never have. She imagined them growing up, the children of scandal, the rejected relatives of the neighbouring great house. If Alex had not been so careful then she might be carrying his child now. Tess folded her hands over her stomach, over her empty womb, as hollow as her heart.

'I have lost nothing,' she told herself, willing the tremor out of her voice. 'I could never have Alex, never be anything else but his mistress.' Imagine the anguish of seeing him court and wed another woman. She knew Alex—he wouldn't keep a mistress then; his marriage vows would be sacred. Nor could she be with a married man. *I have lost nothing, just a few weeks with him, perhaps. You see, it is not so bad, I am not even weeping.*

She lay down on the bed and closed her dry eyes. It would be prudent to rest for an hour before they left for the church and the midnight service. No one must guess how she felt, least of all Alex.

She must have drifted off to sleep because Dorcas's discreet tap on the door woke her with a start.

'The carriages will be at the door in thirty minutes, but Lady Moreland says to come down as soon as possible. Will that gown be warm enough, Miss Ellery? Or shall I find your flannel petticoat?'

'Goodness, no.' Tess went into the dressing room and splashed cold water on her face. She would never undress for Alex again, but she was not going to appear anywhere near him in such a garment as a flannel petticoat. Which was totally illogical and, she supposed, he would say it was feminine nonsense if he knew of it. She could imagine the mischievous expression on his face as he teased her.

'I must have the muff and the heavy cloak with the hood.' Both were garments that Hannah had bought for her with Alex's money. Should she try to pay him back? Or return them, perhaps? But she would never find respectable employment without respectable clothes on her back. He wouldn't laugh about that, he would say it was foolish pride, and perhaps it was.

It was difficult at first to keep the smile on her face when she went downstairs to join the family in the hall, but the view from the door when Garnett flung it open took her breath away.

It had begun to snow and there, in a semicircle at the foot of the steps, was a group of carol singers. They launched into 'Adeste Fidelis' as the light spilled out down the whitened steps and illuminated their faces and beside her a fine tenor voice picked up the verse.

'"*Adeste fideles, læti triumphantes. Venite, venite in Bethlehem. Natum videte, regem angelorum. Venite adoremus...*"'

It was Alex. Beyond him Lady Moreland added her contralto and Maria joined her. Tess began to sing, translating in her head. '"Come all ye faithful, joyful and triumphant..."'

Soon they were all singing, footmen and butler as well, and even a deep bass rumble from Alex's father. There was silence when the last notes died away, then the singers began another carol, one that Tess, raised on the convent's hymns, did not know: 'Christians Awake!'

The rest of the staff had come out, too, and gathered round behind the villagers. Everyone sang and she stood and watched Alex, saw him smile at his mother, heard his voice, clear on the cold air, and knew she would remember this for the rest of her life.

One more carol and the staff were passing round glasses of punch, the farm wagon came round to carry the singers back to the village and the family coaches pulled up.

'You are a dreadful fraud,' Tess said to Alex as he helped her into the first carriage. 'The things you said about carol singers!'

She expected him to joke, to pick up her rallying tone, but his face was serious as he settled her in the seat and stepped down. 'I had forgotten the simple beauty of it,' he said. Then he did smile. 'Mama, mind that slippery patch.' He helped his mother to her place, then Maria and his father. Matthew climbed in, assisting Dorcas, and Alex shut the door.

'Is Alex—Lord Weybourn—not coming?' Tess felt something like panic, which was foolish.

'He has gone up on the box. Said something about clearing his head,' Lord Moreland said with a grunt.

At least mine is clear enough, Tess thought. *No room for daydreams now. Two days to get through, then I can ask Alex to send me back to London. I can go to Hannah's lodging house. I have enough money to support myself for a few weeks. Perhaps Hannah will give me a reference.*

The church was ancient and simple, its interior glowing with candlelight and made festive with evergreen swags along the pews. Up in the gallery the band was readying their instruments; there was a scraping from the fiddles, the deep boom of the serpent, the quick tootle of a flute.

Tess followed the family to the great box pew at the front of the nave and settled into a corner created by the pew butting up against a medieval tomb, an ornate box with the full-size effigies of a knight in armour and his lady lying on the top.

'That's Hugo de Tempest,' Maria whispered.

Tess was grateful for the embroidered cushion on the hard oak bench seat and the carpet on the stone floor. The hassocks were embroidered, too, and she knelt on hers and did her best to calm her thoughts and turn them in an appropriate direction. Then she sat and fixed her gaze on the haughty profile of the recumbent Hugo and tried not to think about his descendant sitting four feet away from her.

Alex sat, knelt, stood and sang with his mind fixed on one thing, one person. As the congregation settled down for the sermon he shifted slightly on the pew so he could see Tess's profile. She was no longer his little nun. She was groomed and well dressed and had found the confidence to fit in with his family. And she was beautiful, he realised, watching the still, calm profile set against the frigid stone carving of the tomb. He had fallen in love with a woman without once thinking about beauty, and yet he had always expected it of any of the women he had kept over the years.

He was dazzled by her body, there was no denying it, but it was Tess he had fallen in love with, not her face. His family liked her already, he had seen how competent, how caring she was with the staff in his own house. She would be a perfect countess—if only he could persuade her that she would be accepted. Damn the Ellerys. Why they had to build Sethcombe Hall next door and not in furthest Northumberland…

* * *

Alex was not certain afterwards when the idea had come to him. Possibly at some time between the end of the sermon and the blessing, certainly before he had shepherded his small flock down the aisle and abandoned his mother to Matthew's support while he took his father's arm.

'Stop fussing, Alexander.'

'As you say, sir. But I'd be grateful if you would be careful of your health. I have no wish to be using this signet except at your direction for many a long day.'

'Ha! Humbug.' But he smiled.

His mother hustled the earl off to his bed the moment they reached the house, Maria on their heels. Matthew had vanished. In front of him Tess was climbing the stairs slowly, back straight, cloak trailing behind her.

He followed her up quietly and caught her in the corridor. 'Tess.'

'Please, don't.' She did not turn. Her hood had fallen back and he looked at the nape of her neck. It was pale, vulnerable, soft. He knew how her skin felt under his lips, he knew how she smelled, just there, he knew the taste of her. Not to touch her now, not to pull her back into his arms so he could kiss that perfect place… that took an act of will.

'Tess, do you hate me?'

'Hate?' She turned abruptly, so close he could have pulled her against his body if he had not linked his hands hard behind his back. 'No, never. How could I? I—' She broke off as his heart gave one hard thump.

What had Tess been about to say? *I love you?*

'I wish I had never come here,' she said fiercely. 'I wish you had not skidded on those cobbles, that I had not fallen, that I had not overslept. I wish I was cold and lonely in that London convent because I knew my place there, I knew who I was and what I was. You made me dream impossible dreams.'

Alex dragged his hands apart, reached for her. 'Tess. Darling Tess.' She dreamed, he made her dream. Despite everything, despite her unhappiness, he wanted to cheer.

She stepped back. 'But I cannot blame you. It is all my own fault. Mother Superior in Ghent explained very clearly that I am not only a bastard, but the child of a criminal liaison. I am old enough to understand that and to accept it, you would have thought.'

'Is there a convent on the coast of Greenland, do you think?' Alex enquired. He could feel the anger boiling up, only just in his control. 'Or on the slopes of some volcano somewhere? I would like to see her transferred there, I think. You are the child of parents who broke the law and you are an innocent in all of this.'

'None of this is fair,' Tess said. 'But it is the reality. I will not be your mistress. I could not bear it. And I cannot be your wife, however often you gallantly offer to ruin your name and alienate your family for a woman who will never be accepted in society, simply because your honour demands it.'

'My heart demands it.' He could not believe he was saying it. Tess would laugh at him, just as she had when he had joined in the carol singing. He had worn the mask of cynicism for so long that surely no one would be able to see behind it now.

'Oh, Alex.' She reached up and caressed his cheek and he closed his eyes against the pain of it. 'You were right. I was a silly romantic and now I have infected you with my sentimentality and you will be hurt, too. I am so sorry.'

Her fingers left his face, but he kept his eyes closed, standing in darkness as her footsteps faded away. The clock struck one. It was Christmas morning already.

Chapter Twenty-Two

His father did not appear at breakfast, which was hardly surprising. Everyone except his brother and sister and Dorcas had taken it in their room, it seemed. Alex made himself eat his way through bacon, eggs and toast, all of which tasted like straw. He finished a second cup of coffee before he asked Garnett if he knew the earl's plans for the morning.

'I believe his lordship intends to spend some time in the study, my lord.' The butler gestured to a footman to replenish Alex's cup. 'Her ladyship expressed her concern that he should rest, but he remarked in my hearing that he intended to deal with some social correspondence and would not overexert himself.'

'Inform me when his lordship comes down, please, Garnett.'

The butler effaced himself and Alex reached for some more toast he did not want.

'Are you going to marry Miss Ellery?' Maria's question sent the strawberry preserve dish crashing from his fingers into the butter.

There was a flurry of attentive footmen. Alex waved them away. 'Thank you, you may leave.' When they were alone he rescued the spoon and dumped jam on the toast. 'Why should you expect me to do that?'

Matthew snorted. 'Because the pair of you look like agitated turtle doves, billing and cooing one moment and flapping about in a taking the next.'

Alex made himself bite off a mouthful of toast, chew and swallow. 'I do not bill, nor coo, nor, for that matter, flap.'

'But you love her,' Maria persisted.

'What do you know about love, Mar?' Matthew enquired.

'I have eyes in my head and I know more about it than you do with your raking about, I'll be bound. And don't call me *Mar*.'

'Stop squabbling, children. You make me feel old.' Alex found he was incapable of denying that he loved Tess. Even a prevarication refused to pass his lips.

'You are getting old,' Maria countered. 'And it is certainly time you married. Mama likes her.'

'I am not yet thirty and it is not that simple.' Alex pushed back his chair and retreated to the library. It *was* a retreat, a full-scale, cowardly rout, he admitted it, but he dare not risk meeting Tess before he had this settled.

He pulled the *Peerage* from the shelf again and sat studying it. There were no answers there; he had to rely on his own wits.

The clock was striking eleven before Garnett came into the room. 'His lordship has just entered the study, my lord.'

'Thank you.' This was it, then. Alex remembered the duel again and decided that had, in retrospect, been considerably less nerve-racking than this.

The study door was closed, as always. A cliff face of polished oak, armoured with brass knobs, massive hinges. The great gate to the ogre's fortress when he was a child and had stood here stiffening his nerve after the summons to yet another lecture on how inadequate, useless, unmanly and generally unsatisfactory he was as a Tempest.

Alex flung it open without knocking, then closed it behind him with a satisfying thud.

'What in Hades?' His father flung down his pen. 'Damn it, Weybourn, I've made a blot! What's wrong with knocking, might I ask?' He narrowed his eyes. 'Something's wrong.'

'You owe me a life, Father.' Alex made himself sit down in the great chair opposite the desk instead of leaning over and thumping his fist on the leather surface. He crossed his legs, smoothed a wrinkle out of his breeches. 'We have skirted around this, but it is time to confront it. A young man died because of you. My friend. There is a debt to be paid and you are about to pay it.'

He had prepared himself for a temper tantrum of monumental proportions. Instead, his father picked up the pen from the blotter and stuck it into the inkwell. 'That young woman, I suppose. Tell me. Tell me what you want.'

Alex resisted the urge to pinch himself. Apparently the reasonable tone was not an illusion and his father was actually prepared to listen. But this would be a negotiation and he would need all his skill. He took a long breath in through his nose, settled back in the chair and told his father what he knew about Tess and what he wanted the earl to do.

There was one explosion, a bellow of, 'You want me to do *what*?', a great deal of muttering and banging about, and then his father said, 'Order the carriage and ring the bell for my valet. And tell your mother we will not be home for luncheon.'

The earl hauled himself to his feet with a grimace that Alex saw as he turned from the bell rope. Before he could think he found himself at his father's side, his hand under the older man's elbow. He had come to the house never thinking to touch his father again, certain that he hated him. Now he realised he was anxious, fearful for his father's health. *I care about him*, he thought, confused by the rush of emotion.

'Perhaps this is not the way to go about it. I will go by myself. You should rest, sir.' His mother would never forgive him if he dragged his father out on a wintery journey and his precarious health suffered further as a result. 'You could write a letter, perhaps.'

'I'll rest in my tomb,' the earl snapped, even as he leaned his weight on Alex's arm. 'And I'll see this matter sorted out before I do.'

Luncheon was served at one o'clock as usual. And as usual all the ladies were present. Matthew also appeared, explaining that if this was going to be the only hot meal of the day he would forgo his usual pie and tankard of ale down at the Moreland Arms.

Tess assumed Lord Moreland and Alex would take luncheon also, for the same reason, but there was no sign of them. Her hostess did not comment and finally she could bear it no longer. 'I hope Lord Moreland was not too tired by the late night.'

'No, not at all. He and Alexander have gone out, apparently.' Lady Moreland sent Tess a disconcertingly straight look. 'Did Alexander not tell you where he was going?'

'I have not seen him since last night, after the service. And he said nothing then of going out this morning.' For a moment she thought that Alex must have gone back to London, then she realised that his mother knew where he was, but, for some reason, was being mysterious about it.

'Did he not?' Lady Moreland. 'No, I suppose he would not. He always was a secretive young man.'

'I would have said self-contained rather than secretive,' Tess said, more forcefully than she had intended. Lady Moreland's eyebrows rose slightly. 'But of course I have only known him as an adult.'

To judge by her faint smile Alex's mother was more amused than irritated by Tess's defence of her son.

Matthew removed his attention from a pile of lamb cutlets and potatoes. 'I saw them drive off in the coach. Father was looking dashed serious.'

'I hope Lord Weybourn returns before dinner time. His staff are expecting him to look in on their festivities below stairs.' Tess chased a slice of carrot around her plate and wondered where her appetite had gone. *Where Alex has gone, is more to the point. He is up to something.*

She missed him, even though it was only hours since she had seen him. That was irrational because, if he was not there, then he was not breaking her heart with gallant attempts to offer her marriage or thoroughly ungallant offers of quite another kind.

The meal dragged to a close without any sign of the returning carriage. Lady Moreland rang for Garnett and dismissed the services of the staff once luncheon had been cleared and the cold collation set out for supper.

'Maria, you and I must go and write letters. We have received so many with good wishes for the season I declare I am quite behind with my correspondence. Miss Ellery, I hope you and Mrs White will make free of the music room if you would like to play the pianoforte. Or there is a large selection of journals in the Blue Drawing Room. I gather you will be visiting the staff below stairs later?'

'Yes, ma'am. Thank you, we will be well entertained, I am sure.'

Dorcas went upstairs to play with Daisy, releasing Annie to join the other staff, and Tess curled up in the window seat overlooking the drive and waited.

My heart demands it, he said last night. What

did that mean? If he loved her, then he would have said so, surely? *Please do not love me*, she pleaded, leaning close to the window so that her breath fogged the cold glass and she had to rub at it with her hand in case it obscured the first glimpse of the returning carriage. It would be unbearable to leave him if he loved her, but she must. If he had been the younger son and willing to live out of society, a country squire as Matthew aspired to be, then perhaps it would be possible.

But Alexander Tempest, Viscount Weybourn, was not an obscure country squire and never would be.

'Miss Ellery.'

Tess woke with a start to find Dorcas leaning over her. She had fallen asleep on the window seat, her forehead against the cold glass, which was probably why she had a headache. That and the dreams. Alex naked in her arms, Alex in ermine-trimmed robes and an earl's coronet being dragged into the House of Lords while all the peers turned their back on her. Mother Superior explaining patiently, while Noel and Ophelia chased each other around her desk, why Tess must be thankful for even a menial position in a respectable household.

'I have been having such muddling dreams. What time is it?'

'Past three.' Dorcas jiggled Daisy in her arms and the baby chuckled up at her. 'I can hear fiddle music from below stairs.'

'He isn't back yet, is he?' Of course not, she would know if Alex was in the house.

'No.' Dorcas did not have to ask who *he* was, it seemed. Was she so very transparent? Tess could only hope Lady Moreland could not discern that Tess was head over heels in love with her eldest son.

The party downstairs was in full flow when she and Dorcas went down the back stairs, carrying the baskets of presents. As they entered the kitchen the Moreland staff fell silent at the sight of guests in their domain.

'A Merry Christmas, everyone. Please excuse the intrusion, but Mrs White and I have gifts for Lord Weybourn's staff.'

'Of course, Miss Ellery.' Garnett, almost unrecognisable out of livery and with a smile on his face, ushered them through to a second room. 'They said that they were expecting his lordship, so we have made the servants' hall available to them until after he has been down.'

'His lordship appears to have been detained.' Tess put a slight question into the statement, but the butler was too skilled to be taken in by a fishing expedition.

'So it would appear, Miss Ellery. One trusts he will not be much longer as the light is fading fast.'

Tess was greeted with beaming smiles and a chorus of Christmas greetings. MacDonald played a flourish on his fiddle, then put it down. They all gazed at her expectantly.

'I'm afraid Lord Weybourn had to go out today, unexpectedly.' *Unexpected for me, at least.* 'I know you will all be wanting to join the other staff here for your Christmas celebrations together, but I thought I ought to bring your gifts down in case his lordship is further delayed.' She put her two baskets on the table and Dorcas added another beside them. 'We'll leave you to your festivities, and a very happy Christmas to you all.'

'Won't you stay Mrs…Miss Ellery?' Annie said. 'Hand the presents out, seeing as his lordship can't?'

'But they are from him and it isn't my place—'

'Reckon it is, Miss Ellery,' MacDonald said. 'You're the lady of the house in London after all.'

'But I was only acting as housekeeper while Mrs Semple was unwell…' she began. How could they imagine for a moment that she thought of herself as anything else? Dreams, yes, but no one could be blamed for their dreams.

'That's not what I mean, ma'am.' MacDonald pulled out a chair while she gaped at him. 'Here, Miss Ellery, why don't you sit by the fire?'

'I… Thank you, MacDonald.' To even protest at his words would draw attention to them. 'Lord Weybourn chose all the gifts,' she added as she lifted the first from the basket.

'All by himself, Miss Ellery?' someone called.

'*Mostly* by himself.' She found she could join in the laughter and, gradually, as the presents were handed out and greeted with exclamations of surprise and pleasure, she relaxed. But there was a sadness in it, too. These were her people in so many ways, and she was going to miss them, miss their warmth and kindness, their loyalty and humour.

Annie looked as though she had grown two inches, she was so much the confident nursery maid, and the other staff seemed more knitted together, almost a family.

I helped with that, Tess thought and swallowed a tear as MacDonald began humming an air from the new sheet music and Phipps picked up the tune on his flute.

'Miss Ellery.' What had come first—the prickle of awareness at the nape of her neck or the sound of Alex's voice?

'Lord Weybourn.' She was on her feet, turning, finding a smile that was merely polite and not a betrayal of what was in her heart. 'I hope you do not mind, but we did not know when you would return.'

Alex looked...strange. Then she realised he was radiating tension, although there was a smile on his lips for his cheerful staff. 'I apologise, everyone. I should have been here to wish you the very best for the season, but I had an unavoidable visit to make.'

He wanted to leave, she could tell, although she doubted anyone else did as they clustered around, thanking him for their gifts, pressing him to take a slice of plum pudding, a sugared almond. Annie wanted to tell him about Ophelia, Noel emerged from the safety of his basket to wind himself around his boots and all the time he smiled and laughed and teased while his long body seemed rigid with the desire to be gone.

Tess began to watch the clock. Five minutes, ten. Finally, after quarter of an hour Alex said, 'Miss Ellery, I am sorry to drag you away from this delightful party, but I am afraid you are needed upstairs.'

'Of course. Thank you, everyone, the pudding was delicious. Have a wonderful evening.' She smiled and laughed at their rejoinders and rescued Noel from under Alex's boots. She promised to take Ophelia for a walk the next day and followed Alex out, through a maze of corridors and up the back stairs to the hall.

'Thank you for distributing the gifts.' He sounded stilted, probably with annoyance.

'I am sorry if I presumed, but—'

'Presumed? Don't be so foolish, Tess.' It was definitely a snap and not in the slightest bit reassuring.

'Where are we going?' she asked after a moment. Apparently he had not marched her upstairs to reprove her for usurping his place with the staff in that little ceremony, but now they were in the draughty hall Alex seemed frozen in place.

'We have guests I would like you to meet.' He took her arm and made for the front salon. The grip was verging on the uncomfortable; his face was set. Tess almost tripped over her feet keeping up with him. At the door Alex stopped abruptly, looked down at her, then stooped and kissed her hard and fast. 'Forgive me, Tess.'

He opened the door and swept her in while she was still gasping and flustered from the kiss.

The occupants of the room were grouped around the hearth. Lady Moreland sat on one sofa flanked by an elderly man and a middle-aged one. Two ladies sat on the opposite sofa with a young lady of about Tess's age between them. Lord Moreland stood in the centre, his back to the fire. He looked as though he had been interrupted in mid-speech. The others all turned at the sound of the door closing and the two other men rose to their feet.

No one smiled, although their eyes seemed fixed on her.

Then Lady Moreland held out her hand. 'Miss Ellery, do come in.'

Alex's hand released its grip and moved to cup her elbow, guiding her across the deep pile of the carpet towards the fireplace. It felt like walking through sand in a dream. Perhaps this was a dream.

Then the nearest woman moved abruptly. Tess looked directly at her and the floor seemed to shift beneath her feet. 'Mama!'

Chapter Twenty-Three

'I do not faint.' Tess heard her own voice, weak but indignant, and managed to open her eyes.

'You had a shock, my dear, that is all.' Lady Moreland's face, thin, concerned, swam into focus above her.

'I need to sit up.'

'Is that wise?' Another female voice, unfamiliar.

'Yes. I want Alex…I mean, where is Lord Weybourn?'

'I am here, Tess.' His mother moved aside and Alex appeared in her place. 'Let me put a cushion behind you.'

She managed to sit up, her gaze fixed on his face. 'I thought I saw… I am seeing things. Ghosts.'

'No, not a ghost. You saw your aunt's eldest daughter. I think your cousin, Lady Wilmslow, must be about the age your mother was when she died. Apparently there is a strong resemblance.'

Oh. So I am not going mad, I am not seeing things. Oh, Mama, I wish it had been you. Then the implication of Alex's words penetrated her spinning thoughts. 'My aunt? My cousin? *Here?*'

'To meet you, yes.' Alex straightened up and stepped back.

There was a moment of hesitation, then the three ladies came forward, the youngest dropping to her knees beside Tess. 'I am your second cousin Charlotte. I am so pleased to meet you! I've been wanting to know all about my scandalous Cousin Jane and no one would tell me anything.' She sat back on her heels, blonde ringlets bouncing, and beamed at Tess. 'We're muddling you—are we a great surprise?'

'A…shock,' Tess confessed. She swung her feet down from the sofa and sat up. The room shifted queasily.

One of the older women came and perched by her feet, the other—the one who looked like Mama—stood with her hand on Charlotte's shoulder. 'My dear Teresa. Did Lord Weybourn not warn you?'

Tess shook her head, looked round for Alex. He was standing with his father, both of them withdrawn from the group around Tess. He was watching her intently. 'I do not know what to say. My aunt told me that the family wanted nothing to do with either of us.'

There was an uneasy silence. The three women all looked at the elderly man who was still on his feet. He stared at Tess from under beetling grey brows. Lord Moreland cleared his throat and the stranger shot him a fierce glare. 'Don't you presume to prompt me, Moreland. I'll make up my own mind. She looks like a lady, I'll say that, not a chit born in sin and raised by a Papist.'

Tess's confusion cleared, leaving her oddly calm and very, very angry. With everyone. She got to her feet, ignoring agitated sounds from her female cousins. 'Are you my grandfather, sir?'

'I am Sethcombe. This is your younger uncle, Lord Withrend.'

Tess straightened her back, lifted her chin and took a deep breath. *I will not break down. I will not scream at him.* 'My mother intended to make a legal marriage. If she was not in full possession of the facts, then you, my lord, must take responsibility for not advising her of them. As for my aunt, she was a good woman who followed her conscience and was true to her faith. I was raised as a gentlewoman and that is all I lay claim to. I most certainly have no wish to lay claim to a relationship with you, my lord.' She turned and dropped a slight curtsy to Lady Moreland. 'I apologise, my lady, for any embarrassment I may have caused. I had no idea who your neighbours were until after I entered this house.

'I will retire to my room now and I would be most grateful if you would allow me a carriage to take me to the nearest stagecoach halt in the morning.'

'Tess!' Alex strode across the room to stand between her and the door as she turned amidst an echoing silence. 'You cannot do that. Your family has come to meet you, to make their peace.'

'I see no sign of it. My cousins are most kind, for which I thank them. But my grandfather considers me a child of sin by one daughter, raised by another whom he cast out for following a faith of which he obviously disapproves deeply.' Her voice wavered and she brought it back under control with an effort that hurt her throat. 'My presence in this house must only be a strain on relations between neighbours. An embarrassment.' She sidestepped and reached the door before he spoke.

'You are not an embarrassment to me and you ever could be. I wish you to be my wife, Tess.'

She closed her fingers around the door handle, the moulded metal cutting into her palm.

'I thought you might care for me a little, Tess.'

How that must hurt his pride, to make a declaration in front of his parents, in front of their neighbours. 'I do care for you, Lord Weybourn.'

She said it steadily and without turning. 'I care too much to stay and bring scandal on your family. You have only just found them again. I would not have you lose them.'

Somehow she made it to her chamber and rang the bell. Dorcas arrived five minutes later, pink cheeked and cheerful.

'I am sorry to disturb you, Dorcas, but I am leaving in the morning. Please could you ask one of the footmen to bring my portmanteaux down so I can pack?'

'But don't you want me to come with you, Miss Ellery?'

'I can't afford to pay you, Dorcas. I am very sorry. I will write a note for Lady Moreland and I am sure she will do her best to find you a respectable place where you may keep Daisy with you.'

'We'll come, too,' Dorcas said stubbornly.

'I have no money—only enough to afford some cheap lodgings until I can find a position. It wouldn't be fair to Daisy.'

'You can't go off to London by yourself. Look what happened before. We'll come with you—we can go to the lodgings you had with Mrs Semple—and we will find something we can do.'

'Dorcas—'

'I won't leave you.' Dorcas sat down on the end of the bed. 'You saved us. I'll get the bags.'

Oh, bless her. She was too grateful for the support to argue anymore. 'Knock when you come back. I am locking the door.' Not that there seemed to be any need. Alex was hardly rushing after her. He had probably realised all too clearly what a mistake he had made in bringing her grand—in bringing Lord Sethcombe and his family here.

She began to move about the room, opening drawers, piling her few possessions on the bed. She hesitated over the gifts from the Tempest family, then put them in the pile to pack. It would be ungracious to discard them.

Patricia sat stiffly on the bedside cupboard, blue skirts smooth, painted eyes beady. 'Oh, Alex. Of all the things to give me. I will talk to her, try to pretend I am back in an innocent childhood—and all the time I'll see you, look into your eyes, want to run my fingers through your hair.' She trailed her hand over the shiny painted scalp. 'I'll want to hear your voice and there will only be silence.'

'Tess!' There was a sharp knock on the door panels. 'Dorcas is standing here with your luggage. What the devil do you think you are doing?'

She found herself at the door, her hands pressed against the panels, as close to him as she would ever be again. 'I am leaving, as I said I would. Alex, how could you do that? How could you cause such embarrassment for your parents? You told me your father and Lord Sethcombe were not on good terms, and this can only make it far worse.'

'I thought it best to surprise you so you could not refuse to see them.' He sounded tense, but patient. 'He is an old man, Tess, and we are asking him to admit he blundered badly with two of his daughters and let blind prejudice estrange him from his granddaughter.'

'I am not asking him anything.'

'You will not forgive him, then? Not even for—'

Silence. 'For what?' Tess prompted. But it seemed Alex had gone. *For what—or for whom?*

It was the longest Christmas evening that Alex could remember. The Sethcombe ladies, distressed at losing Tess almost as soon as they had found her, were driven home by Lord Withrend. Lord Sethcombe stayed, apparently a fixture in the best chair in the study, drinking brandy with Lord Moreland, the two men exchanging occasional observations on matters that had no bearing on the problem whatsoever, so far as Alex could tell from his silent vigil by the window, hoping against hope that Tess would relent and come down.

At seven Annie presented herself, bobbed a curtsy that was one inch from insolent and announced that where Miss Ellery, Mrs White and Daisy went, she went and she hoped his lordship would take that as her notice because she didn't care whether he gave her a reference or not, she wasn't staying, not no how. At which point she burst into tears and fled the room.

'Excellent staff management, Weybourn,' his father observed.

'Annie's loyal,' Alex snapped. 'I'll not fault anyone for that.'

'That matters to you, does it not, Weybourn?' Lord Sethcombe said.

'Yes.' He shut his lips tight on the observation that if the older man had been loyal to his daughters this would not have happened.

'Do you love my granddaughter?'

'Of course I love your granddaughter!' Alex slammed the brandy glass down on the table beside him, sending liquid splashing across the polished surface. 'Do you think I'd have dragged my ailing father out on a bitter winter's day to try to make peace with you if I didn't? Tess made me see the importance of family, the importance of forgiveness, but she didn't teach me well enough to forgive you for this, I fear.'

'You've a temper on you, Weybourn.' Sethcombe observed. 'Didn't expect that. They told me you were a languid, elegant, care-for-nothing fellow. You gave me a shock, I'll not deny it. I'm not an easy man to shift in my opinions.'

Lord Moreland snorted. 'You may say that again, Sethcombe.'

The marquess glowered at him. 'Your son wants to marry my granddaughter. I've no objection to that—'

'With respect, sir, you have nothing to say in the matter. Miss Ellery is of age. As you don't recognise her your approval is irrelevant,' Alex said, hanging on to the tail of his temper.

'But you want me to acknowledge her. Will that be enough to see her received?'

'It will go a long way. The problem may lie in getting Tess to acknowledge *you*.'

The glare swung round in an attempt to wither him. Alex glared back. *Tess. I'm going the wrong way about this, locking horns with this old devil. I love you. I think you love me. Can I convince you that is all that matters?*

He got to his feet and both older men jumped as though they had been off in a world of their own. They probably had, he realised. Thinking about old battles, old hurts. To hell with the past; he'd been entangled in it for too long. He had a future to build with Tess if he could only make her believe in it.

She had locked her door and he was not going

to stand out there begging to come in. Nor would he act the lord and master by fetching a key and letting himself in. Tess's life had been short on romance. Well, he might not be able to do it in armour, but, by God, he was going to try something romantic for once.

Outside the moonlight was bright on the frosted grass, the shadows darkly dramatic where the topiary yews marched along the edge of the wide lawns. The trelliswork along the south front was bare, but the stems of the ornamental vines were thick and strong and he found no more difficulty climbing them than he had as a boy escaping from his tutor.

There was light in Tess's window, but when Alex reached it the room was empty. 'Tess!' He knocked on the panes, aware, suddenly, of the slippery soles of his evening shoes on the icy stems, the cold cramping his fingers. She was gone. 'You fool, you waited too long.' He let his head fall forward and banged it against the glass. *Idiot. She's run, gone off across the fields in this deadly weather.*

The despair was as bitter as the wind. Could he find her again? Dorcas and Annie would be with her, and little Daisy. They'd be careful for the baby, that was his only comfort. *Search parties—and the staff full of punch and mince pies. How long?* He slammed his fist against the window one last time and shifted to start the climb down.

His head was just below the level of the sill when the window swung open. 'Alex! What are you doing? Come in, for goodness' sake, or you'll fall.' Tess was leaning out, hands outstretched.

His hands opened with the instinctive urge to seize hold of her—safe and warm and *there*. *'Alex!'*

Their fingers met, gripped, then he let go with his right hand and climbed up to face her. 'You are falling out of that gown, Miss Ellery.'

'Infuriating man.' Both tears and laughter trembled in her voice. 'You would be falling out if you were female and were leaning out of a window in an evening gown with an idiotic viscount dangling from your hands over rock-hard paving.'

'I thought you had run away.' He gripped the window frame and hauled himself through, then almost fell out again as Tess threw herself into his arms.

'I'm sorry.' Her face was buried in his neck-cloth and the warmth of her body seeped into his cold skin like a caress. Alex held tight and prayed. 'You brought Grandfather here and it cannot have been easy and Lord Moreland went, too, even though he is so ill. And I'd wanted you to make up with your family, forgive your father—and I can't even forgive my own grand-father.'

'He's a curmudgeonly devil, but he's coming round. He knows he is in the wrong and he wants you to forgive him, but he's an old man and a proud one. I think you may have to meet him halfway, Tess.' He laid his numbed cheek against her hair and breathed in the scent of Tess, of woman. *My woman.*

'I had just gone out of the door on my way downstairs to see if he was still there when I heard the knock on my window,' she mumbled into his shirtfront as she began to burrow her nose between the buttons. 'Brrr, your chest is cold. What on earth were you doing?'

'I thought it might be romantic,' Alex said, attempting to resist the urge to pick her up bodily, toss her on to the bed and demonstrate that not all parts of his anatomy were frozen.

'To almost kill yourself?' Tess leaned back in his arms and glared at him. 'Of all the—'

He kissed her. Her mouth was hot and opened on a gasp of surprise, then she was kissing him back, stroking her tongue over his, sighing as she pressed close into his arms. She was here, she was his and he was home.

Alex broke the kiss when her knees were threatening to give way. Tess sagged into his arms and rubbed her cheek against his chest, the friction of the waistcoat edge a welcome irritation reminding her that this was real and not a dream.

'I know you wanted a knight in armour, a Sir Galahad, and all you had was a prosaic soul trying to do this by logic and negotiation. You needed sweeping off your feet.' His breath was warm in her hair as he nuzzled into it, pulling her close.

'I don't want a knight. I want my viscount—just as long as marrying me does not ruin you.'

'Truly, Tess?' Alex stepped back, let her go, his gaze fixed on her face. 'I love you. I want to marry you, raise children with you. It might still be difficult—I can't pretend it won't, even with our families' support. I won't be ruined, far from it, but there will be talk, and you might not be received at court.'

'I don't care. I only want you, only need you.' Once she had dreamed of seeing the Prince Regent. Once she had dreamed of a gallant knight. Now she had a family and a man she loved to build their own with.

'You showed me the way home,' Alex said. 'You gave me my father back.' A faint rumour of sound drifted in through the window with the cold breeze. The staff were singing carols. 'You gave me Christmas back.'

Tess held out her hand, tugged him towards the door. 'Let's go and tell them. How soon can we get married?'

'A month.'

'That long? Alex, I want to be yours the moment you can get a special licence.'

'And I want the biggest possible wedding.' He stopped at the head of the stairs and caught her in his arms, his smile a caress that made her dizzy with desire for him. 'A society wedding, an announcement that I love you, that our families love you and we are proud of you. I want you to have the pleasure of buying a trousseau and I want the pleasure of buying you jewels.'

'There's still my grandfather.'

'Just kiss his cheek, let him forgive himself.' Alex took her hand and led her downstairs, into the small dining room where Maria was filling a plate for Tess's grandfather and the rest of the family were carrying on what sounded like a desperately polite conversation.

'Teresa.' Her grandfather stood up. 'I cannot undo the past.'

'I know.' She found it easy to release her grip on Alex's hand, to go around the table and to stand on tiptoe to kiss the old man's cheek. 'But we can start afresh, can't we? I love Alex. We are going to be married. I want you to know your great-grandchildren.'

The cheek her lips were pressed to was wet and his voice was gruff as he said, 'I wish your grandmother was alive today.'

'So do I.' Tess put up one hand and wiped the tears off his cheeks. 'Alex will fetch me some supper and we'll talk about her.'

Maria was in tears, Lady Moreland fluttered a lace handkerchief, Matthew was slapping Alex on the back and Lord Moreland, seated at the head of the table, struck his knife against his wine glass.

'A toast to the future Lady Weybourn, my new daughter.'

Epilogue

'Your attention, please!' Alex stood in the door of the servants' hall, Tess by his side. Faces turned; the laughter and chatter died away. 'I have the honour to introduce you to my betrothed. You all know her and many of you made her feel safe and welcome in a strange city. You will all understand why I cannot live without her—'

Whatever else he intended to say was lost in the hubbub. Dorcas, predictably, was in tears. Annie, her newfound dignity forgotten, was dancing up and down, the Half Moon Street staff were clapping, Garnett, his face split by a huge grin, was leading his people in a rousing chorus of cheers.

The noise showed no sign of abating. Alex eased back through the door, taking Tess with him. 'Father's told Garnett to open the champagne. Goodness knows if anyone is going to be sober by tomorrow.'

They reached the ground-floor landing of the backstairs, but Alex kept climbing. 'Where are we going?'

'To bed.' He stopped at the next turn. 'Unless you wish me to retire to my own bedchamber until the wedding night?'

'Alex, you are scandalous.' And a terrible temptation.

'I am in love.' He shrugged, the movement of those strong muscles sending a delicious *frisson* through her. 'There's nothing to be done about it but make love to me, or banish me.' In the dim light he looked almost convincingly downcast. 'Besides, I wanted to unwrap my Christmas present.'

'Which Christmas present? Oh!'

He swept her up, shouldered open the door and strode down the passageway to her room. 'The one in my arms. The one the Fates sent me.' He set her on the bed and went back to lock the door.

'You have already unwrapped it.' Tess sat up, the better to look at him as he crossed the room shedding clothing as he did so. Coat, exquisite waistcoat, neckcloth landed where he threw them. He dragged his shirt over his head, wreaking havoc with his hair, and kicked off his shoes.

'What are you laughing at?' Alex demanded, his hands on the fastening of his evening breeches.

'You. The elegant, exquisite Lord Weybourn, careless of his beautiful waistcoat, his perfect hair.'

He smiled. 'If you only want me because of my tailoring, I am afraid you are going to be disappointed.'

'I cannot tell you how deliciously exciting it is to see that perfection in disorder because of me.' She watched him, blatantly admiring as he pulled off trousers and stockings in a few urgent movements.

'You, Miss Ellery, are developing into a hussy. What would Mother Superior say?'

'She would faint away, I hope. Alex, I do love your shoulders.'

'Only my shoulders?' He knelt on the bed behind her and began to work on the tiny fastenings of her gown.

'That was the first thing I found attractive about you, even when you were being infuriating and not letting me get a word in edgeways and making me miss my boat.' She reached back and caressed as much of them as she could.

'Not my fine profile?' Alex was working on her corset strings now, his breath hot on her nape.

'I wanted to box your ears. Besides, at least

two of your friends have more exquisite profiles than you do. I thought that y*ou* looked like a particularly wicked, rather dangerous, mythological creature.'

'A what?' In a flurry of skirts she was on her back, clad only in chemise and stockings.

'Mythological.' He was rolling her stockings down, pausing to lick and nibble at the most sensitive skin, the location of which he seemed to know by instinct.

'I am most definitely not mythological.' A nip. 'I do not have the hindquarters of a goat.' A nibble. 'Nor do I have horns.' A long, wet, wicked swipe of his tongue up the length of her bare right leg from ankle to mid-thigh. 'I am, however, having the most pagan ideas about what to do with you now you are unwrapped.'

He slid up her body and propped himself on his elbows to look down into her face. 'But first I just want to make love to you like this, so I can look at your face, drown in your eyes, kiss those lips.'

Without conscious thought she had parted her legs to cradle him where he fitted, where he belonged, against the core of her, his long, hard body pressed to her softness, his heart beating against hers.

'Yes, Alex.' Tess arched against him and he

entered her in one long thrust, then stopped, his forehead resting against hers.

'I'm home,' he murmured, his breath warm on her lips.

'So am I. At last. With you.' She kissed him, pulled down his head and clung to his lips as he moved within her, with her, pulling her into the whirlpool, the whirlwind. The storm crashed around them, tossed her into wave after wave of sensation and then drew her up into one perfect moment. *'Alex.'*

A minute, an hour, a year later she opened her eyes and found him watching her with his soul in his eyes. Her vision blurred. 'Welcome home, my love.'

He smiled and laid his head on her breast, and Tess felt his lips move against her skin. 'That is wherever you are, my love. Always.'

* * * * *

If you enjoyed this book, look for Grant's story
HIS CHRISTMAS COUNTESS
Out in December 2015

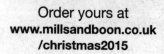

19